PRIMROSE HILL

Helen Falconer

Hel Fa

ff

faber and faber

First published in Great Britain in 1999
by Faber and Faber Limited
3 Queen Square London WC1N 3AU

Typeset by Faber and Faber Ltd
Printed in England by Clays Ltd, St Ives plc

A CIP record for this book is available from the British Library

ISBN 0–571–19613–6

2 4 6 8 10 9 7 5 3 1

To Jack

Primrose Hill

One

Me and the crowd were hanging on Primrose Hill, playing music, smoking a bit of draw, watching the brilliant sun go down, made blazing colours by the polluted air. And we were having this heavy discussion about how terrible it all was, global warming and that, but I was laughing because we were *basking* in it, man, day after day, all July, sunning ourselves on the burning hill – tropical London! I was feeling good, when Danny ran out of the beautiful sky and threw himself gasping on the ground beside me.

'I'm going to *kill* that fucker.'

I didn't need to ask. All the good feeling went out of the evening, like a separate sun suddenly going down.

'He's fucking done it again, Si.'

'Shit . . .'

'With a baseball bat.'

'*What?*'

'She had to call an ambulance.'

'Jesus, Danny,' I said, feeling sick, sitting up. 'What're you going to do?'

'I'm going to kill him.' And he clutched at his face, his expression of rage, like he'd rip it right off, like a mask.

I stayed silent. Someone was changing the tape. The crowd were spread out on the darkening grass. All around rose the sweet smell of draw, getting stronger as the tropical night closed in, and in the distance a drunk on a bench started up – 'Pah! Pah! Pah!' – like something weird in the rain forest after darkness falls. Our mate Luke came by with a serious spliff: 'You want a toke on this?' I did. I held it out to Danny, but he shook his head, like: not in the mood. I thought he should have some, though – come down a little, find a bit of space. 'One toke, Dan.'

Danny's mum fucked up bad when she was a kid – pregnant at fourteen, left home at sixteen, got herself a flat on a Kilburn estate, let the local dealer move in. He pinned her down and stuck the needle in her while she was screaming, 'No, no, no!' Or so she told Danny, but she was lying, right? What was she going to tell him? She'd thought it was this really cool idea? It was killing her; her whole life was fucked up by it. Even worse, this guy used to beat her up; he was psycho numero uno. One time Danny tried living with her, but it didn't work out because of this evil fucker. Danny brained him with a lump of wood. He was only twelve then, but this boyfriend wasn't up to much. Danny always called him Shortarse. He was man enough to beat up Danny's mum, though – that's for sure.

After a toke or two, Danny said, calmer, handing the spliff back to Luke, who wandered on, 'No, really, I'm going to do him, Si. Before he does her.'

'Yeah, I know, you're right,' I said. 'The guy's a complete arsehole.'

He pinched at the long black hair that hid his eyes, twisted it hard, and said, intense, 'No, listen, Si, I'm going to *kill* him, man. I mean *seriously* kill him, man – I'm serious.'

It gradually came to me Danny was being for real – like Tarantino, dribble of blood from the mouth, corpses to be got rid of, boots of cars, and that. First thing came into my head was, Danny didn't have a car. I stared at him, mouth open. 'Shit, Danny, you can't do that,' I said at last, like he'd claimed then and there he was going to stand up and spread his arms and fly right off the hill, floating fast away across London, a free black speck in the orange air.

'Why the fuck not? Why not?'

He was a big bastard, Danny, but he wasn't the macho type. He didn't hang out with those arseholes in Ralph Lauren shirts and YSL jeans and too-short hair who stand in all-white groups on the corners of buildings, comparing designer labels and waiting for someone to mug. He hung with *me* – with the crowd on the hill, the peace and love types, all growing our hair. We cared about the planet, played sixties stuff, wore friendship bands around our wrists – it was our summer of love, for fuck's sake. It was good: we were doing the hippy thing. I said, 'Get *real*, Danny.'

He turned on his back and pulled this old baseball cap he always wore down over his dark eyes, down to his big nose, and put his hands behind his head, like: end of story.

'You'll get *done*, man. What if you end up inside?' Though I knew that wasn't the point.

He looked at me over his arm, knocking up the cap. 'I'd rather that than she died on me, man.'

'Why don't you go to the police?'

Danny, rolling his big dark head away, lit a cigarette, no comment.

He was right, of course. I was being pathetic. What was I thinking? One waste of space scaghead beating up another waste of space scaghead. Who'd care?

I started to watch the stars, swimming into view light years above us. That summer, that's what I'd really been getting into about the hill, being able to see through a billion billion miles of open space, all the way up to the stars. It wasn't like being in London at all – not down in London where you couldn't see shit, but up here, closer to the sky, like we'd been living down a manhole and climbed up and pushed off the cover. You could imagine you were right out of it, maybe on a mountain top somewhere, real air and a sky you could see. Down in the hot, sweaty, concrete valleys hunted the short-haired packs, with their knives and their YSL jeans, but up here we old pony-tailed long-hairs were well out of it. Even the 'Pah! Pah!' drunk was a harmless old fucker.

Danny said suddenly, urgently, 'You know that Hitler guy, right?'

[5]

'Ri . . . ight,' I said.

He shook his big head impatiently. 'No, fucking look, man – if I'd met him before he started all that crap, I'd've *crucified* the bastard.'

Danny believed in doing the right thing. I got to tell you, years ago when the kids in school found out my dad was gay, you wouldn't believe the shit that went on. I couldn't keep one fucking book or decent pen from one day to the next. Every day I was having to jump in and punch someone out for the way the kid *looked* at me – I was acting like a hard man, but you had to get in first or else you were fucked. I'd known Danny right from primary school. We weren't like big mates then, but he knew I was in trouble and not only did he never look at me wrong, he started giving me back-up if things got rough. I didn't really know why at the time. It's just with Danny, a mate was a mate. You didn't even have to've done anything for him, he just knew you were his mate. It was lucky for me, though. He always was a big bastard. He kept me safe till things cooled down. After that we really were best mates, for good, for ever. If it hadn't've been for Aids, we'd've been blood brothers.

It was only about eleven, but the crowd was breaking up – going round Chetan's to play computer games, but I didn't fancy it. 'See ya, see ya,' people were calling; dark bodies peeling away from the dark hillside. 'See ya later.' 'See ya, see ya, see ya later, Martin. See ya later, Al, see ya,' we said. They were an all right crowd.

Danny turned to me in the dark; the little red circle of his cigarette swept my way. 'Do you want to stay at my place, man? My grandad's gone to bring her back from casualty.'

I could've done without seeing the mess someone could make of someone else with a baseball bat. 'Sure it's OK?'

'Yeah, yeah,' said Danny. 'Yeah, it's OK.' He sounded kind of lost, not like him at all.

When we stood up the air drifted cool under my shirt,

damp from the night grass. Below our feet the London lights lapped softly round the base of Primrose Hill, and stretched like moonlit water to the horizon of our sight. We were nearly the last to go, walking slowly down the long steep hill until the stars we'd seen so clearly from the top faded into the orange reflected light and the voice of the traffic rose to greet us – we'd descended into the sewer again, and the city's dirty sky settled over us, a close-fitting lid. The trapped-in air down here between the tall houses and the high-rise blocks was hot and wet, unmoved by the breeze on the hill. It had that strange metallic taste. The sweat broke out on me.

I called my mum from a callbox on the way. She sounded all right. She was eight months' pregnant, and I had to be around for her in case anything happened. Like, she was planning to have that baby at *home*. I was scared she'd try doing it all by herself and fuck up somehow. The only thing freaked me more than the idea of being there at the birth was not being there. She was so careless and slapdash about things, and that waster had deserted her. Us. Her. His child. (Fucking around about whether he wanted the baby or not until it was too late for her to have an abortion and then 'It all got too hard for me, man' and he left for the gutter he'd crawled out of in the first place.) The box was like a sauna. The waistband of my jeans was wet. I stood there waiting for the money to run out while she bitched on about how my nan'd been round bitching again. 'She says homebirth is self-ish! Coming from *her*!' Listening to her talk, in the orange light of a street lamp I fingered the cards stuck all over the inside of the box – like, French maid into correction, busty blonde, 40, 20, 40, gives golden showers (what? for fuck's sake) – and then this kid I'd never seen before in my life jumps up out of the dark into the orange light, leaping up against the glass like an animal in the zoo, and starts hammering on it: 'Oi, *you*, I seen that, you perve!' I nearly jumped out of my fucking skin.

My mum said, 'What's that?'

'Nothing. Some kid. Look, I'll see you in the morning, OK?'

After I came off the phone the kid was still hammering, my heart still hammering too, from the adrenalin rush. I was opening the door into the hot dark jungle air thinking, Fuck, here we go, and getting ready for it, when Danny stormed back from round the corner where he'd gone for a slash in the dark and grabbed the kid round the neck. I looked round quickly in the hot shadows for the big guys, but there was only one, sitting on a wall half-hidden by dark greenery, and he was scratching behind his ear and pretending not to notice.

'Oi,' screeched this kid, kicking and elbowing. 'Get off of me! What've I done to you?'

'I know you,' said Danny suddenly.

'Oi! Get off! Leo!'

(Other guy still looking casually away.)

'I know you,' said Danny to this kid, with more conviction this time, really threateningly. 'You hit my mate with a brick.'

'He did what? It was him bricked Viv?' This was something happened to a Bengali guy we knew. The Asian kids got constant grief from the YSL crowd. If you walked down the street with them, you got 'Oi, Paki-lover!' all the fucking time, really pissed me off. It happened when I was with Danny sometimes – his nan was Italian, and his mum told him in secret his dad was Italian too, a good mate of her dad's, married with a lot of hair (irrefuckingsistible, yeah). Anyway, some stupid fucker seeing Danny'd go, Ooooh look, dark skin, black hair, brown eyes – er, *can't* be English – er, Paki, innit? Black bastard! Oi, you! Paki-lover!

'I'll fucking *kill* you,' said Danny. He was gripping him so tight round the neck, the kid's eyes were nearly popping out. Then he held out the kid towards me with his knee up his arse and shouted, 'It's *you* he was calling a fucking pervert – hit him *now* if you like.' The kid was thrashing about like a scared cat. His shirt was out and soft stomach bare.

'It's all right,' I said, looking at the kid's plump white stomach.

[8]

'Hit him, man,' insisted Danny. 'It's the only way he'll learn not to go round being such a fucking *arse*hole.'

'It's all right,' I said.

'*Hit* him.'

'It's all right.'

'For fuck's . . . now fuck off and stay *out* of it.' He shoved the kid into a hedge. The kid scrambled out, coughing and choking, and ran off. Danny went right up to the half-hidden one who was still sat there and said, sticking his face aggressively into his, '*Your* mate hit *my* mate with a fucking brick! Made his head bleed!'

The guy said, 'What – him? He's not my mate. Don't even like him,' and he got up and walked away, lighting a fag.

When Danny came back he was still really wound up, but he lit a cigarette himself and started laughing. 'You know,' he said, 'after that kid landed that brick on him, Viv ran into an off-licence because it was the nearest thing and the off-licence guy said, I'm not serving you anything unless you've got ID. And his head was *bleeding*, man! And he doesn't even drink, for fuck's sake!' Danny thought that was well funny. He nearly choked on the fag. He stayed hyped up about it almost till we got to his grandparents' council place, a concrete maisonette, part of a block set sideways on to Adelaide Road.

Danny's mum was home from the hospital, sitting in the kitchen having a fag and talking to Danny's grandad in a quiet, unhappy voice. When I heard her in there I hung about in the hall, but Danny barged on in and I had to follow him. She stood up and turned round to us, and I couldn't help flinching away, but she didn't see me do it – she'd eyes only for Danny, who was amazing, he didn't gasp or cry, not even his eyes filled with tears, he only held out his arms in the most loving way to hold her.

'Oh, don't hug me, Danny darling,' she said, touching him gently on the arm. 'I'm that sore.' She looked fucking awful. She always looked shite anyway because of the scag – skinny as fuck and a bald spot on top. But now her mouth was all swollen up like a smashed plum, and her broken nose thickly bandaged and her eyes embedded in purple-brown dough-nuts of flesh with red splits in them, so you could see where he'd hit her with the bat across the face – once, twice – across her mouth, then again across the bridge of her nose. Under her thin white blouse, her ribs were strapped. I felt ill, like really ready to throw, and wished I hadn't come.

'Don't worry, Mum,' said Danny, very calm. 'I'll take care of him.'

'Oh, now,' she said, trying to smile, though her lip was all mashed up and thick. 'I'm all right. Don't you go getting yourself into trouble now, do you hear? It'd break my heart.'

'Don't worry, Mum,' said Danny.

'There's a good boy,' she said. 'You go to bed now, or watch telly or something. I'm just sitting here talking to Dad.'

Danny's grandad nodded at me. I was concentrating on looking as if everything was normal, nothing shocking. He wasn't an old man, just oldish, with heavy grey-black hair. But tonight he looked rough, wearing stained trousers and an old green top with fag holes in – he looked sad and old. His daughter did his head in. He never understood her. She told Danny why she'd pissed off from home so soon was, he never let her go anywhere, not after she got pregnant. She wouldn't tell him who the father was and he gave her a hard time about that. It was a joke, him not letting her out of the house. His hairy mate'd got her pregnant in the bathroom upstairs. 'All right, Si,' he said. 'Have you had something to eat, OK?'

'Some chips,' I said. It wasn't true, but I didn't want to get in the way, and I wanted out of the kitchen in any case. Me and Danny went into the front room. I thought he'd go into the killing thing again, but instead he said nothing, just searched around for the remote control. I didn't blame him for not being able to speak. I helped him look, but he found it before me, down the back of the couch, switched on the telly without a single word and fell into the armchair, his big feet in trainers cluttering the floor, his baseball hat pulled down over his heavy dark eyes, remote control stretched out before him. I lay down on the sofa and pulled a cushion under my head.

He'd barely begun flicking around when someone started banging, much too loudly, on the front door. Nobody moved in the house. Me and Danny waited, frozen, staring through the television. In the kitchen there was nothing but silence. Bang, fucking bang, bang. Danny's grandad came out of the kitchen and stood in the hall.

'Who's that? What do you want?'

'Who the fuck do you *think* it is, Jim, you old cunt?' yelled Shortarse. He sounded frighteningly loud, almost in the house, because he was yelling through the letterbox. 'Where the fuck is she? Josie – come on out here, you mad bitch!'

'She's not here!' Jim screamed back at him in fear and anger. 'She's in the fucking hospital where you fucking put her, you junkie fucker! Now fuck off before I call the fucking police!'

All went quiet outside. Several minutes passed. Still we stared into mid-air. I'd goose pimples all down my arms. Danny's grandad went back inside the kitchen. We could hear him and Danny's mum murmuring together. Slowly I let my muscles go, and found I was dying badly for a pee. I stood up. 'Gotta have a piss, man,' I said. Danny just sighed, a long shaky sound, and took out a fag.

Then a brick smashed through the window, straight between the curtains, and bounced on the floor at Danny's feet. Danny sat rigid, his eyes fixed on it, holding up an unstruck match. His grandad roared and came running in to see what the damage was, pushing me aside, and Josie was screaming her head off and went scrambling upstairs in a mad rush to hide herself. Another brick came through, and dented the wall.

'That's *it*,' said Danny, jumping up and throwing the fag away, unlit. 'That's fucking it.' He dashed past me into the kitchen and came running back down the hall with a carving knife in his fist, like a serious nutter – he went so quick he had the front door open, howling 'Die you bastard!' before me and Jim went after him. When I reached him on the crunching tarmac they were going in circles, Shortarse hanging on to Danny's stabbing arm with one hand and with his other trying to reach in and slash Danny's face with a switch knife. Danny was yelling abuse and pulling his head back out of the way of the whizzing blade.

'Get *off* of him!' I was dragging the fucker off when that junkie bastard went to cut me instead, and nearly did too, I couldn't believe it. Then Jim got punching and because Danny's mum's boyfriend was a skinny little bastard, he took fright and ran off a few yards. We wrapped ourselves round Danny's neck, but he was fighting us like mad to get free.

Shortarse got cocky then, and started waving his dirty fat switchblade at us. 'See this, son?' he was shouting at Danny. 'This knife's got your name on it, it has! When you're asleep I'll be coming through your window and whack! you're dead, you're a dead man, Danny, you're dead, all right?'

'I'll kill you first, you fucker!' screamed Danny.

'The police are on their way!' shouted Jim. It was a lie, but Shortarse started walking away, pulling up the collar of his manky suede jacket and smoothing down his hair and looking back over his shoulder every few steps and threatening Danny that he was *dead*, right?

When he'd disappeared into the streets, we took Danny back inside. His nan was awake, crouching barefoot at the top of the stairs in a short pink nightie showing her soft lumpy legs. She looked really upset, her voice was shaking. 'Has he gone, Jim?' she asked.

'Yeah, yeah,' he said. 'Everything's OK.'

'Josie's in a terrible state,' she said. We could hear Danny's mum in the background upstairs, still screaming and crying.

'Tell her everything's OK now, Gabby, he's gone. I'll put the kettle on.'

Gabriella came down to get Josie's tea for her. 'It can't go on like this, dear,' she said, like she was making polite conversation in front of the children. She was a really small woman. When she sat on a chair her yellowing toes dangled above the ground like a little kid's. She was always nice to me. She didn't need some arsehole putting through her windows in the dead of night. As she held the mug of tea in both hands her wrists were going, and the tea flooded in spurts over the sides of the mug. 'Poor Josie won't stop crying.'

'Everything will be all right,' said Danny's grandad. 'I'll stick something over the window and fix it tomorrow.' He began levering a cork noticeboard down off the kitchen wall with a breadknife. But he said to himself while he was doing it, 'I don't get it. How could she do this to us?'

Gabriella looked at Danny, who was sat at the table with his big fists still clenched on the plastic top. His grandad'd taken the knife off of him and put it quietly back in the drawer. 'Did he have a go at you, Danny love?'

'Sort of,' said Danny, indifferent. He was lucky to be alive, but he didn't give a toss.

'Oh, Danny . . .' She started wiping the dripping cup dry with the corner of her nightie.

'Don't worry about it, Nan,' said Danny. 'I'm bigger than him, aren't I?'

'He is that,' said Jim.

'I'm sorry you had to see that, Si,' said Gabriella.

'Don't worry about it, Gabriella,' I said, though I was still in shock. 'It's no big deal. He just ran off.'

'Praise god for that,' said Gabriella. 'I'll take Josie her tea, then.'

Danny let his mum stay up in his room that night, because she was too afraid to come downstairs at all. Jim offered me money for a cab, but I couldn't leave Danny to sleep down there alone. The noticeboard was nailed over the broken glass, but still the warm draught came gently through, drifting the orange curtains and rustling the stuff pinned to the cork, the bits and pieces of their lives: paper messages and shopping lists and photographs of Danny as a baby being held by his mother, who was younger then than he was now, and some crap painting Danny'd done years ago in primary school. On the pulled-down sofa bed beside Danny I lay fully clothed even to my shoes and covered myself heavily from head to foot in a winter duvet. I felt totally naked and exposed.

Danny spoke in the dark, and I twitched, saying, 'What? What?'

'I said, *now* do you see what I mean.'

'Absofuckinglutely,' I said, with feeling.

'You seen the mess he made of my mum?'

Too right I had.

'You hear what he said to me?'

'He said he'd kill you, Danny.'

'I *have* to kill him first,' said Danny, meaning it.

'Yeah,' I said. I could see where Danny was coming from all right. I was so cold I was shivering, even though the duvet was much too much for that hot summer's night. I couldn't stop thinking obsessively about Shortarse's threat to come creeping through the window with his knife with Danny's name on it and stab Danny to death – and me, too, if I was there, I supposed. Every time the nylon curtains blew forwards in the draught or the stuff on the noticeboard flapped around, my blood ran cold.

Danny rolled towards me and leaned up on his elbow. 'I have to . . .' he broke off, listening.

The feet crunched soft and slow over the tarmac out front. Then there was silence. Now there was nothing. Then we could hear them moving around heavily, creeping about.

'Here we go again,' whispered Danny. 'I'm getting the knife.'

I felt sick and my heart was going dangerously fast. 'Get one for me, too,' I said. I wasn't going in bare-handed this time.

While he was in the kitchen I crept along the hall on my hands and knees and soundlessly opened the letterbox. A fierce white light blasted in, blinding me, and I yelled out. Danny was right behind me, he came tearing down the hall in his T-shirt and boxer shorts, carving knife in hand, chucked me the breadknife, and ripped open the door shouting, 'I'll slice your balls off, you fucking bastard!' then froze.

The two policemen looked as scared as we did. Danny was hanging there in mid-air with his knife raised above his shoulder, black and white horror freeze-framed in the powerful torchlight; I was on my hands and knees, squinting up at them, brandishing my breadknife. Some really long seconds passed us by.

'Fuck it,' said Danny, at last, irritably.

The spottier, skinnier cop said, nervously winking, 'Now then, lads, why don't we try shutting the door and let's just start this one over again?'

Josie wouldn't come downstairs, not even for the police. They didn't really mind, they didn't want to stop – they kept looking at their watches as they spoke, like they'd rather be telling pedestrians the time. One scaghead terrorizing another scaghead? Just another day to them. They'd only come round because someone'd complained about the noise. They weren't that bad. They didn't hassle Danny about the carving knife – they called him 'son' and advised him not to take the law into his own hands. But they didn't take him under their wing, and when they left they left a loneliness: an emptiness without answers and without action.

Two

I thought I'd play guitar to chill me out, like usually works for me. But in the end I just held it, my arms around its smooth familiar shape, and pressed my face against the wood.

Walking back home through the early morning shadows, everywhere practically empty of moving cars, I'd been fucking jumpy. I'd felt a moving target in that junkie's world – *his* world, these uninhabitable streets, roaming in solitary state among the arsehole gangs, slouching along with his hands in his pockets – and who'd the guts to hunt that fucker down?

When my mum got up at eight, I was still sat there on our concrete lawn, hot already to my touch, my guitar in my arms.

Through the french windows, I saw her come into the kitchen, wearing some sixties-retro hippy patchwork sort of thing, slowly forcing her way round the kitchen table because her stomach stuck out so far it kept getting jammed. She was on leave from her nursery job, she didn't need to get up in the morning, but she said she 'couldn't get out of the habit'. Habit? What habit? She was so fucking lazy I never knew her once get out of bed by eight when she was working – running around freaking about the time.

She made it to where the kettle was, then stood holding her stomach, vacant-faced, staring at the cupboards. I could tell she was feeling the baby kick, its feet getting tangled in her ribs and guts. I didn't like to say this to her, right, but if I'd felt something alive and with fucking legs wrestling around inside of me, it'd *totally* freak me out. Like – you know the scene in the film. But she stood there as though it was no big deal.

I played a chord on the guitar to get her attention, and she came to the french windows, opening them. 'Weren't you staying at Danny's?'

'Well, I did,' I said, putting down the guitar. 'I thought I'd walk home before it got too hot.' I didn't tell her about the knife thing. She was eight months' pregnant and I thought I couldn't be responsible for the shock making her have a mis-carriage and losing all the hope in our lives, on top of me not being able to help Danny with his shit.

'Make us a cup of tea, then,' she said, sitting down, flicking back her long red hair. 'I'm too hot already.' She'd the chair pushed back against the wall, to wedge her stomach between her and the table. Loose sweat rolled around her forehead. 'Can you believe it, up at eight again? How can I sleep if I can't have a joint the night before? Eight long months, not one puff.' She was lying about that. Andy used to say, Go on, have a puff, you'll feel better. And she would, two or three. We were well shot of him, really. 'That's why he left, you know,' she said dreamily, combing her long hair with her fingers, thinking the same thing in a different way. 'It takes two to party. I wonder where he is now, the dopehead?'

'In a gutter somewhere,' I said. I wanted it to come out slightly jokey, don't-carish. But it came out like I was wishing it, being bitter.

'Poor old Si,' she said. I didn't answer. She said, 'I got the scented candles for the bathroom. And some Mozart.'

She wasn't just planning to have the baby at home, she was having it hippy-style. She said when she had me in hospital it was clinical and 'unspiritual' – they put her legs in green stir-rups, which sounds pretty weird. My dad, who at least man-aged to show up for the birth (well done, Dad!), complained it confirmed him in his gayness like nothing else. So much so he ran off to Canada and never came back. It was fucking typical of my mum to get married to someone gay – not that I'm say-ing it's a problem or her fault or anything. At least he left her a basement flat off the Camden Road. And money and shit. Yes, at least she got something out of *him*. Would Andy leave my mum a flat? When he did his disappearing act, he didn't even leave a forwarding address. He didn't even have an address to leave. Fucking dosser – it bugged me so much that summer, how he could piss off like that, let us down without a second thought, and his own child, too. He came to the hospital, saw it on the screen, sucking its thumb just like a real baby. It was hard to get my head round that: how he could be there, share all that and still walk away from us in the end. I couldn't have done it, not after seeing my child alive on screen.

My mum was chilled though, as ever. She wanted to lie in the bath while she was in labour surrounded by scented candles floating on the surface of the water and listen to Mozart. Note, she had to buy Mozart specially for the occasion – in real life, she said she thought classical music was boring. (But she listened to David Bowie, for fuck's sake!) Anyway, why'd she think her tastes'd change just because she'd gone into labour? What it was, she told me, plants grew more if you played them Mozart. She said when she had me she'd an injection in the spine (?), made her like paralysed from the waist down and she couldn't feel a thing, so this time she wanted to get in touch with her feelings, to be in control, feel the baby, to like . . . The whole idea scared the shit out of me. What if the midwife didn't turn up? You read about men having to help at the birth, with bits of string. It didn't sound much of a laugh to me. She'd bought a low stool, to sit on between baths. My nan kept saying how babies born at home always died or went blind or something. She said to my mum, 'You'll never forgive yourself, Louise. You'll be looking after a poor handicapped child your whole life, god forgive you. Maybe it'd be better if it did die.' And my mum would scream and quote statistics from Holland. My nan was a bit mad, but sometimes I think my mum went a bit too far the other way.

When I brought her her tea, she grabbed my hand without giving me a chance to back off. 'Here, feel it kicking.' Before I

[18]

could pull away, a hard lump bubbled up under my hand like a dog thrusting its nose into my palm. Scary stuff: mysterious monster child, unseen, untouched; floating in there in a sac of water. Life unknown. Alien about to burst forth.

I walked back up to Primrose Hill hot mid-afternoon, while my mum was sleeping. By coincidence I ran into Viv on the way and stopped him to tell him about Danny having a go at that kid outside the phone box. Viv, tallish, cool, with shoulder-length black hair, nodded. He'd had two stitches in his forehead, which pissed him off because he was chasing a lot of girls. I told him about Danny throwing the kid into the hedge. 'You know, I never even met that kid,' said Viv. I thought maybe the scar'd give him a bit of a glamorous edge, not spoil his looks.

'Is it right the off-licence guy asked for your ID?' I asked.

'He called the ambulance in the end,' said Viv, raising his voice as a bus crawled roaring by. It was a seriously busy road. You could taste the ozone, like having a cheap metal spoon in your mouth. The heat was slowly stirred by all the cars, inching along, pumping out global warming.

We were stood still in the middle of the pavement, because he'd been walking the other way. Suddenly, shrill above the traffic noise, the familiar cry: 'Oi, wanker!' A white kid was racing down the pavement on a mountain bike, bugging passers-by by zig-zagging between them, like he was on skis and they were those posts you've got to ski around. Seeing Viv with me, he changed it to: 'Oi, Paki-lover!' He had a big grin on. He was feeling cocky, even though he was on his own – he was on his bike, after all, sweeping along too fast to catch. He felt safe on it, like people think they're alone in their cars. 'You're a fucking Paki-lover!'

I wasn't sure if he was the kid from last night. I'd only seen him in the orange light. I thought it might be the same one, but then they all look the same to me. Usually I would've just ignored him, but that felt harder to do today. For one, I was still wound up from the knife thing. And as well I'd just been telling Viv how Danny'd stuck up for him and I didn't want him to think I didn't care as much as Danny about that racist crap. And those things really piss me off anyway. I stuck my foot out just as he went past and kicked the back wheel of his bike really hard.

You should have seen him go. He tried to keep the bike under control, legs flapping like a pigeon's wings, and for a bad second I thought he was going to end up under a lorry, but instead he finished up in a swirling heap under a newsagent's window, the bike practically wrapped around his neck. He hit that wall with a hell of a bang. It made both me and Viv wince.

The kid didn't move right away, and me and Viv sort of looked at each other, like: what do we do now? Probably we should have walked off and left him, the little fucker, but it was kind of hard. Actually I felt a bit shaky with the shock of him nearly going into the road, and I thought, Supposing he's broken his neck or something? We went over cautiously and stared down at him. I picked the bike off of his chest. The kid'd painted its frame by hand, some techno logo – must've taken him a while. The crash'd mangled the front forks, and one of the wheels was bent in half. The paintwork was fucked. The reason the kid was keeping quiet was, he wasn't dead or bleeding or anything, he was trying not to cry.

'You all right?' asked Viv, bending down and touching the kid's arm, which was flung up over his face.

'Get off of me, you black cunt,' said the kid, throwing off Viv's hand. He'd difficulty getting the words out. He was a freckly pig-faced kid with ice-cream stains around his mouth. He wasn't the kid from the night before.

'He'll survive,' I said to Viv.

'They always do,' said Viv.

I was still holding the bike in front of me. The kid started sitting up, and I propped the bike against the newsagent's window beside him. He touched it tentatively with his finger, with squeamish horror, like it was this pet dog he'd found bleeding in the road, looking at it disbelievingly, how it was all fucked up. And he turned his head to scream abuse at us, but when he opened his mouth all that came out were floods of gut-wrenching childish wails, and the tears came pouring from his piggy eyes.

It was awkward, embarrassing, the whole thing. I thought maybe it'd be better just to get out of it. 'So, you want to come up the hill?' I asked Viv, taking him aside.

He hesitated. He hadn't been going to, he'd been off to see another mate about a possible part-time job. But in the end he decided to come. I think there was something about the situation. When we walked off the kid was still sitting there on the pavement, crying too hard to speak. I looked back before we turned the corner. An old woman with a carrier bag – the first person of all the people passing by to take any notice of what was going on – was bending over him. But he must've said something shitty to her, because she scuttled off quick. The kid dropped his head and covered his face with his hands.

Me and Viv didn't talk about it. We just walked to Primrose Hill. It was a real relief to get there, I can tell you. When we started climbing I felt like I was climbing out of the filth, leaving the bad violent part of me behind in the streets, up into the light, breathing open air again. Viv said, wiping his sleeve across his scarred forehead, 'Fuck me, it's hot.' When we got to the top not many of the crowd were there yet, just a few of the lazier ones drinking lemonade and eating chocolate Hobnobs and comparing the depths of their tans in a noncompetitive sort of a way. Viv went over and started talking to tape-deck Martin, an old mate of his from way back. They'd a band together once.

Myself I lay face down on the uncut grass, hot soil on my mouth, sun on my back. Martin wasn't playing his tapes; there was no music to block out my mind. I was kind of listening to the voices instead, but not hearing the words, just letting the sound of them wash over me, trying to chill out, thinking about things.

You know, I didn't want to end up like them, those fuckers with their hair cut short, roaming the streets looking for someone to beat the shit out of, hate and shit bursting out of their seams. Suppose I'd killed that kid? It could've happened. One minute you kick out at some nasty little racist, the next you've got a full-scale tragedy on your hands: kid squashed flat, blood everywhere, mothers weeping – fuck's sake, you can imagine it – teachers telling the papers what a bright promising future he had, like they always do when a kid bites the dust. (Never, 'Well, not to worry, he was no brain surgeon.')

But I wasn't a killer that time. Instead, that hot then boiling July afternoon on the top of Primrose Hill, I found myself a girl. At least, she called herself my girl. I don't know what I thought about it, really, whether she was or not. Anyway, it was more like she found me. I was just lying face down on the hill, getting sunstroke, thinking about things.

I didn't have a girl at the time. I'd been too busy chilling out, staying cool, just concentrating on having a good time. I wasn't looking for complications. It was a bad scene for getting it together, that year. You'd only to stand talking to someone, and your mates'd go, Did you *do* anything, then? Oh yeah, right there on the pavement, gave this benchful of winos a terrible shock. No, seriously, did you *try* anything, then? Absolutely. She let you? Jesus . . . was she *hot*? Great, give me her phone number! Her mates'd go, Did you let him *do* it, then? No shit! Do you *love* him, then? What about *him*? What did he say? Did he call you yet? What's his name anyway? (That's nice.)

Her toes were barely an inch from my face, and jammed between them was a Yale key. A long time ago she'd painted her toenails crimson red but now the colour was almost gone, just lingering in the cracks where nails met flesh. I turned my head on one side. She was sat right up against me, her feet together and brown knees apart, the too-big green T-shirt she was wearing tucked down between her legs. She was leant towards me, her forearms resting on her knees, elbows stuck out, up and sideways, like thin brown wings, her very dark brown hair – almost black – falling springy and curly out from behind her ears. In all the great airy space of Primrose Hill she was pressed right up against me, like we were in a rush-hour tube. She never did have much sense of personal body space, did Eleanor. She had pale green staring eyes.

She plucked the key out from between her toes by the leather thong it was tied to, and stuck the point of the key in her mouth, and then looped the thong around her neck. She had an odd face, like one of those hip twelve-year-old models everyone freaked out about. She looked like a special twelve-year-old, but she wasn't, she was quite a bit older. I didn't know her name, I'd just seen her hanging around on the hill. She came up sometimes with a bunch of girls who weren't really part of our crowd but liked to fool about nearby, stretching out and making a big deal of rolling their tops up and sunning their flattened stomachs and sharing suntan lotion between them like it was this big bonding thing, and giggling like babies if a guy actually talked to one of them, then slagging the girl to fuck. Real girlie girls – arseholes, really. None of them was around yet today. Only her.

'Hi,' she said, the key falling out of her mouth down into the neck of her baggy shirt.

I leant myself up on one elbow and said, 'Hi.' I picked a really small stick out of the dirt and combed the blazing grass until it broke.

'Do you fancy me?' she asked. 'Most guys do.'

I lay down flat again, like: OK, go away now.

If I'd known her then, I'd've known hints like that flew over Eleanor's head like birds. If you wanted her to hear you, you had to really shout. She lay down in the grass beside me. 'You've really nice hair and sexy eyes. Is something bothering you?'

[23]

I could've got up and walked away, but I didn't. That pig-faced kid was going round and round in my head; I was still wound up about everything. I said, without exactly meaning to, 'I nearly got knifed last night.'

She laughed. 'Yeah?' Like it was amusing. She sat up again and hugged her knees. She said, 'Go on, then, tell us.' She thought some everyday thing'd happened, that I'd got mugged at knife-point or something and was hyping it up to impress her, which must prove I fancied her. Man, I can't stand those kids who say they saved their whole family from a fire when all they did was dial 999 before they ran out of the house and stood waiting for the fire brigade to arrive while everyone else left in there nearly fucking dies.

I said, 'It's not important.'

She was smiling, patting her hair, which bobbed under her hand, turning her bare foot this way and that in the hot grass.

I said, frustrated by her taking the piss, 'This scag dealer bastard tried to kill my mate, all right?'

She looked startled at me, eyebrows raised, like: no shit. 'Why doesn't your friend do *him* in, then?'

'Yeah, right. Cool idea.' I took the snapped stick and tried out whether the two broken ends would fit neatly back together. I was still really into my summer of love, now I was back up Primrose Hill. Yet last night I'd seen what an obvious answer it must seem to Danny, how practical, how fucking easy, even, it would've been just to rub that fucker out entirely. 'He's his mum's boyfriend.'

'Seriously?'

'He beats her up.'

She sprang to her dirty little feet and ran off. I thought she was leaving me, but she just ran in a big fast circle, round the back of where Martin and Viv and Chetan and some others sat rolling their first spliff of the day. I watched her all the way. She was wearing pale denim cut-offs under her T-shirt, with threads that trailed behind her when she ran. Crashing back down beside me, even closer this time, her pale brown leg thrust hard and urgently against my own, she said, with childlike enthusiasm, 'No kidding, I'd *love* to murder someone.'

I started laughing, and that made her mad – she shot me a look like I'd gone to the top of her list.

'Try me,' she said, all pouty.

'Oh, right, go on, kill *him*.' I pointed at someone – anyone – Chetan, who was sitting nearest us, a few yards away, not facing in our direction, minding his own business, relaxed and happy, totally unaware he was on the critical list.

She was annoyed. 'Not *him* – Jesus! You'd have to have an excuse.'

I didn't answer, but after a while I looked in her face. She was grinning at me with sharp little teeth. I said hastily, 'Anyway, he'd end up spending fucking years inside.'

'Who would?'

'Danny, I mean,' I said.

'Oh, your mate.' And she picked some of the longer grass and wound it round her small brown fingers.

Some of the girls she hung with came up the hill then and sat down right near us. 'Hey, Eleanor,' they said. 'How's it going?' Then they went shrieking among themselves, because Eleanor was talking to a *boy*. They laid themselves flat on their backs, rolling up their tight body tops that little bit further than they were meant to go. They offered Eleanor a big bottle of Diet Coke, and she gave me a drink of it, bubbly and warm. They kept looking over at us, giggling. Eleanor started picking the remaining bits of crimson varnish off of her toenails. I rolled on my side, facing away from her, staring out over the city.

Chetan came up to me and sat down and offered me a toke. 'Good shit, man,' he said. 'Chills you out. Like, if I smoke this while I'm playing a beat'em-up, I'm so mellow, I just have to let the computer win. It's cool.' He brushed the hair off of his forehead, and smiled.

I kept getting these girls giggling in the background. I

wanted to tune them out. I made out to myself we were on an island and all Eleanor's friends were seals, flopping about, making mindless barking noises. The more I thought of it, the more it was like we were on an island, and all around us, as far as I could see, was the pale blue-purple polluted sea, and the sounds of the traffic were soft and submerged like a long-gone city was sunk beneath the waves.

Now, working her way slowly and complaining up the hill came a younger girl in glasses, who, getting within squealing distance, squealed, 'Hey, Eleanor!' I looked at Eleanor, who sighed and slowly closed her eyes. 'Eleanor! Eleanor!' Amazing: the kid was Eleanor's genuine clone. It must be weird to be pestered and followed around by a smaller, shriller you – like a photo of yourself at ten years old come horribly alive: a living reminder of a you you'd rather forget. 'Eleanor, Richard says hurry up!' Eleanor jumped to her feet. The grass-green T-shirt was so long that when she stood you could hardly see her cut-offs, only the hanging threads of them, fingering her legs. She jogged a little way down the hill, then stopped where several foot-worn paths met below us and waited. All her mates looked at her over their naked stomachs, then looked at me. Copying them, Eleanor's clone stared accusingly at me, her spectacles striped with light. Fuck! My first instinct was to take the spliff back off Chetan and let them all dream on. But I felt kind of bad about the idea of humiliating her. I looked again. She was still standing there, pretending to admire the hazy city. Fuck!

I ended up humiliating myself, of course – her sister shrieking as I heaved myself up, sweeping the dry grass off of me, 'Eeugh, look, Eleanor's got a *boyfriend*!' (Chetan laughed), and me knowing all the way down those girls were watching me and weighing me up. When I caught up with Eleanor, she looked for a moment so relieved I thought maybe I'd done the right thing. But then she switched on this fucking act of total cool, just to impress her arsehole audience. She skipped on down the hill ahead of me, grinning, with her chin in the air, hardly looking back. I should have left her to it but that pack of girls were sat watching my every move, and so I followed her, a sad fuck.

She only kept it up till we were far enough down the hill and then fell back beside me and announced, 'You're wrong, you know. Why should anyone go to prison if this guy gets murdered? He's a drug dealer, isn't he? Everyone kills drug dealers. It's, like, practically normal.' She could never get her mind off murder for very long.

'Normal?'

'Have you got the time?' I had – rather a flash divers' watch my mum gave me when Andy left, handy if your bath is forty foot deep. 'I've got to get back,' she said, and sat down on a bench at the bottom of the hill, and swung her feet up. 'Sit down.' I was fucked off at the way she'd managed to drag me down the hill. I stood with my thumbs in my pockets. It seemed kind of stupid not to sit down just because she wanted me to. I sat down. She tucked up her feet under her arse and pulled her grass-green T-shirt down to her ankles.

'Why do you have to be back?' I asked.

She looked at the filthy tips of her fingers. 'My uncle wants to see me,' she said.

'Your mum's boyfriend?'

She raised her eyebrows. 'Her *brother*.'

'Oh . . . right.'

Eleanor added, 'Of course, he's incredibly rich.'

'Yeah?'

'He owns a record company.'

'Nice. That's nice.' I leant back on the bench, hooking my arms behind, looking back up the hill. I was pretty disappointed by this kiddy fantasy crap, but funnily enough it took me back to some old private stuff of my own: I'd the record company boss thing too, once, about my dad. I was really into music and my guitar. It was my thing. I used to have these little dreams: rock star dreams. I didn't, like, tell anyone, though. It made me sad, her coming out with all that shit.

[27]

'I like your hair,' she said, pulling herself along the bench by her hands, closer to me, her toes digging into me. 'It's nice. I like blond hair.' She picked a piece of grass out of it. I shifted my head. 'You should tie it back,' she said. 'Well, I don't think it's long enough yet,' I said. It wasn't blond either – just bleached.

'No, wait.' She dug around in her pocket and pulled out a knotted green elastic band, with her own curly hairs twisted up in it. 'I bet it is long enough.' She made me turn the back of my head to her, and fixed my hair back in a pony-tail. Where her fingers touched my neck I wanted desperately to scratch, but didn't like to. Most of my hair fell out of the elastic band, but some of it stayed in. 'It looks great,' she said. 'You should keep it like that.' Her own hair, bruised-brown, bounced all over the place. 'You know all those girls up there?' she asked. 'They all fancy you.'

I laughed.

'No, really,' she said. 'They do. They think you're sexy. They think you look like the singer in a band because you're thin and you've got big eyes. They wish they'd got your eye-lashes.'

'For fuck's sake,' I said.

'Check the time,' she said.

It was half past five.

She bounced off the seat and stood facing me, arms slightly held away from her sides, poised. Not knowing what she wanted me to do, I just sat. 'It's not far. You don't have to come,' she said.

'I will if you want,' I said, unsure what she meant.

'You don't have to,' she said.

The clone streaked past us towards the gate, screaming, 'Eleanor, it's half past *five* . . .' and disappeared flying into the street. Eleanor glanced sharply behind her and then, as I started to stand, threw her arms around me and went to kiss me on the mouth. I staggered and caught her by the ribs to steady myself. She felt very slim and slippery under her shirt.

[28]

She pulled down hard on the back of my neck and thrust her tongue into my mouth. I wasn't expecting it; I didn't push her away. But she dropped off of me and ran. I could feel the warm skin of her like I'd touched her naked. I brought my palms up to my face and sniffed at them, getting the hot cotton smell of her shirt. Hearing voices, I turned, looking over my hands. Her mates were coming down the hill, a thin chattering spider of arms and legs. When they saw me looking back at them, they stopped talking and just kept glancing at me quickly on and off as they sauntered by, giggling and poking each other with their elbows.

I think she only did it for the show.

Three

Eleanor was mad – seriously mad. She was driven by a mighty force I didn't understand, like a little boat being blown along in a big wind. I shouldn't have got tied up with her at all, but I did.

She'd talk endlessly away about how beautiful she was (I'm going to be a model; talent scouts stop me – see, I've got their cards; I'm so beautiful; no one'll ever forget me), and then she'd tell you how she was going to die sometime soon, before she was twenty anyway, like twenty was unbearably old – like only sad fuckers lived to twenty-one. She was fifteen herself. Not long to live then, Eleanor.

Also, she came out with some seriously weird stuff. Like, the first day after I met her, she asked me right out did I want to have sex with her – just right out. I was . . . Jesus! I wasn't expecting that.

What happened was, she came up Primrose Hill in a plain white T-shirt, walking very purposefully, an ice-cold bottle of Perrier in her hand. Danny'd brought up his Walkman and we were lying on the tough overcooked grass wearing long shorts and listening quietly to some indie stuff, one earplug each. A few of the crowd were about, generally feeling too hot. The only guy with a drink was hey-man Luke, who was spread out reading the *NME*. He'd offered what he was drinking around, of course, but unfortunately it was this totally flat, *hot* lager. He was pretty hurt when we passed on it – Hey man, it's good to share, right? Not *that* fucking good, Luke. I'd taken my top off and draped it over my head. I felt odd, with a bad headache – brain fluids boiling again. Looking out over London was like looking out to salt sea. I was that thirsty, I was even thinking of taking Luke up on his offer: real park-bench stuff. And then she started up the hill from the distance, and as she got nearer I could see she was holding this bottle of water by the neck, and I was, as they say in the magazines, consumed by desire.

She didn't come right up to us, but when she drew near our circle, she stood a little way off and beckoned me with a funny secretive movement of her hand held down by her side. She knew I'd seen her. I wasn't sure whether to react right away. She beckoned again, urgently, jerkily. Danny, who was a true mate, pretended not to notice, staring off into the hot sea-blue haze, humming to the music in his left ear. She held up the Perrier and frowned. It was no good. 'Gotta have that water, man,' I said aloud for Danny's benefit, and took the earplug out of my ear.

'Why are you sitting *here*? It's so hot,' she demanded when I went up to her. I held out my hand for the bottle, but she walked away, saying, 'I'll show you a good place to sit.' I followed her, dog-like, under the trees and there, overshadowed by leaves, was a gentle dip in the ground filled with long dampish grass into which she plunged knee deep and lowered herself down carefully on to her arse as into a hot frothy bath.

'This is much better,' she said confidently. I sat down beside her and a tiny hectic spider rushed over my calf. 'Aren't your legs hairy?' she said. I nearly blushed. Then she handed me the bottle. Oh, blissful shock! It was freezing cold, wet and slidey with condensation. I gasped – it startled my hot hands – and wrenched the cap off and poured an icicle down my throat.

'Jesus, that's good, that is so good.' I actually groaned with pleasure. 'Am I glad to see you.' I was easily bribed.

She was so delighted by my pleasure, she squirmed about in the long grass and boasted, 'I had it in the freezer till just before I came out.'

'You're a wonderful person.' I'd drunk the iced water so fast my stomach was in a convulsed knot, but it was a good pain and I was enjoying it. I was a dried-up lawn being watered.

'Do you want to have sex with me?' she asked.

Oh, man! My stomach, already tight, nearly fucking imploded. I couldn't really believe I'd heard her right, and I just looked at her with my mouth open, aware my hair was sticking to my lip, and finally and feebly said, 'What?'

'Do you want to have sex with me?' she repeated. It was bizarre. She didn't look nervous or even particularly keen – she made it sound like it was no big deal. You should have seen her: she wasn't one of those big, fat, don't-care fourteen- or fifteen-year-old girls who wear grossly tight tops with huge freckled tits bulging out of them and talk dirty with their friends on the top of the bus in between leaning over the seats to make sexual passes at horrified cringing boys. She was different – she was . . . sort of delicate – beautiful, really – you know what I mean? But so young-looking.

A weird bunch of thoughts went through my head. The first was: OK then. Fine by me. But at the same time I was asking myself, Why did she say it like that, like she doesn't give a shit? Why's she just offering herself like fast food? She made more of a deal out of bringing me the Perrier. Is it a wind-up? Have her mates put her up to it? I thought, Is she planning to go off and boast about it to those airhead arseholes – aargh! And then I thought, in a burst of panic, Has she had a lot of sex before, and if so has she got Aids?

All this time she was waiting with a bored expression for me to answer, and I was staring at her with my mouth open and my hair still in my mouth. Finally she looked up at me, surprised, and said, 'Don't you want to?'

'I . . . it's just . . . Jesus, Eleanor, I don't know.' I was embarrassed for myself, how pathetic I sounded, like the cringing, trembling boys on the bus.

'Oh.' She frowned a little, then cheered up, squeezing her

knees in her arms. 'You can use a condom if you like. I don't mind.'

I felt badly caught out, her coming out with that. It was like what she'd heard me saying was: I'm not going to touch you because I don't know where you've been. But that wasn't what I meant her to hear. Yet I had had that thought. The bottle was still cold in my hands. I touched my face to it. Its iciness cut itself across my cheek.

'Oh, come on,' she said impatiently. 'Don't be silly.' She beat the grass with her small brown hands. 'You don't have to pretend. We can just get straight on with it. Shall I take my T-shirt off?' She went to lift it by the hem.

'No! Stop!' Jesus! Why stay under the trees? Why not out on the fucking grass, just in case anyone *didn't* see us?

With a double hand-flap of irritation, she dropped the top and said aggressively, 'What, then? What? What did I do now?'

'Eleanor . . .' I didn't know what to say to her – I pressed the bottle against my sun-boiled brain. 'Eleanor . . .' I kept rubbing the grass with my other hand like I was stroking fur, like the whole hill was this green agitated cat about to run off.

She startled me then by throwing her arms above her head but all she did was rip down two handfuls of leaves with a violent childish tug and cry tearfully, 'Oh, god, you don't *fancy* me!'

I thought, oh, yeah, really . . . her eyes are so green and pretty and her mouth so arched. 'Eleanor, please, everything's OK. It's not I don't fancy you. Everything's OK.'

'I just don't *get* it!'

I held the bottle out towards her. 'Really. It's OK.'

'You finish it.' And, closing her wet eyes, she sank with a despairing moan, clutching her leaves, back in the long grass till it came up to her chin.

I lay perfectly still under the hot rasping canopy of trees, letting the one spot of sunlight burn my right knee, letting an ant climb my ankle – not moving – trying to stay cool. Something bad was happening to me: I found myself getting angry out of nowhere. It started with, I was thinking over and over: Has she done it before? And without meaning to, I saw it: Eleanor little and naked, someone's arms holding her. And I thought, Whose? And I felt like I really wanted to know. And just like that, I started getting angry. Then I thought, Probably it's all complete fucking bullshit. It was definitely all bullshit. I closed my eyes, but I couldn't close the eyes inside my head. The scene of Eleanor hugged and stroked in arms attached to some great wodge of flesh played on and on.

'. . . a cruise,' said Eleanor. 'Si?'

I said, 'What?'

She made like exasperated. 'I'm going on a Mediterranean cruise.'

Oh, right – one minute quick sex on the hill and the next it was: I'm off on a cruise, don't you know (the Med, of course). And I wondered what I was doing, hanging round with her. 'That's great.' The modelling stuff was like that too, I suppose, like: When I grow up I'm going to be a beautiful princess (until I'm nineteen and a half, that is, and lay me down in my glass coffin).

'Richard wants me to crew on his stupid yacht.'

'It's his *own* yacht? Excellent.'

She added, sticking her chin in the air, 'But I don't want to.'

Well, who would, in their right mind? I sighed and sat up, and smeared an ant that was biting me all over my arm with a good slap.

'Don't do that!' exclaimed Eleanor angrily. 'How'd you like it if a fucking huge hand came down out of the sky and squashed you flat out of nowhere? You're a pig!'

I paused, hand in air. I mean, yeah, OK, peace, man, and I try not to kill insects usually, except wasps, but – *ants*? 'Excuse me? The girl who wants to murder the world?' It was a bit fucking much, coming from her.

'Oh, that,' said Eleanor. She looked up into the air. 'He wants to take me all round the Mediterranean, actually.'

[34]

'Issit.'

She yawned, her tongue quivering behind her teeth. 'It'll probably be boring. I really don't fancy it.'

'Well, you know, Eleanor,' I said. 'I think you're absolutely right.' I scraped the flattened corpse from off my arm. 'It sounds fucking awful.'

She looked at me sideways. 'No,' she said. 'He's horrible.'

'Of course he is. Rich uncles are always horrible. That's how it goes.' I couldn't get the damn insect off of my finger-tips. I was scrubbing them with a leaf. 'Pig ugly, too.'

'I'm going to go!'

'Of course you should go! – see the Taj Mahal and the pyramids and stuff. Go and see the volcanoes.'

She burst out wailing, a real baby.

Straight off, I felt really bad. I didn't think I'd been hardly taking the piss at all; I wasn't thinking; I'd been distracted by that ant, my mini-murder (I was trying to cover my tracks) – and now she sounded so sad. Her white T-shirt'd slipped from her shoulder, and her collar bone showed so fragile under the skin. Watching her weep, I wanted to stroke it, and hesitated, but did. She flung her thin brown arms around me and sobbed her heart out with genuine tears. I had to sit really awkwardly in the grass, pulled sideways by her arms around me. 'Everything will be all right,' I said hopefully, with my chin on her shoulder.

She wept. 'My mum says I'm a crazy bitch.'

I thought that was pretty perceptive of her mother. I said, 'Shit, did she really say that? That's bad.'

'Yes!' She sobbed some more, like for the sake of it, and then let go of me, and tore up some grass to wipe her face. 'She's such a bitch.' She'd a strand of grass stuck to the bridge of her nose. 'Really.' She took a quavering breath. 'God.'

I didn't dare set her off again, so I just lay down and watched her cautiously from a little way off, like wildlife.

'It's just I'll be so lonely,' she said, in a bored, angry voice. 'Nothing to do. Just sitting around all day. Nowhere to get away to. Bored out of my head.' Then she grabbed her curly hair and pulled it, crying out passionately, like I'd said anything different, or said anything at all, 'You don't know how lonely I get, it drives me *mad* – how can I stay *still* so long? I get things in my head . . .'

I stared at her, amazed. 'Take someone,' I suggested. 'If you're going to be bored, take along a friend.' Hell, someone like her must have a stack of imaginary ones in her attic.

'Oh, would you?' cried Eleanor. 'Would you really?' She was overjoyed. 'Would you mind coming too? You're really wonderful!' And she grabbed me round the neck again and actually shrieked, only this time instead of being in the depths of despair she was completely over the moon. Poor old Eleanor – she was forever right up and right down, like some kid on a swing being pushed too hard and too high by some bullying adult she was too scared to make stop.

I hadn't meant me at all. I'd only known her for a day. Not long enough to go floating across the deeps in a fantasy yacht. You end up drowning like that.

'He can't not let me bring you. He always does what I say.' She was really pleased with me, and delighted with herself. Without reason, a surge of pleasure washed over me too. It was like I was suddenly in her dream, a dream of the tropical abroad, and I could see, as through her eyes, the blue transparent sea and dolphins, millions of dolphins, charging sleekly through the waves with the sun on their backs.

'If your uncle is too boring, we'll just push him overboard,' I said – and into the dolphin-strewn ocean in my head there fell a big, foamy splash.

'Yes,' said Eleanor, grabbing my wrist, her eyes shining. 'Yes!' She laughed, acting like a little kid again, only a nice happy little kid this time. It was sweet to see her so happy.

'Si! Si!' Danny was calling, from a distance. He was too polite to follow us under the trees. I started to get up, but Eleanor grabbed me down.

'Is that your mate – the one you were talking about, whose

[36]

mum's boyfriend tried to kill him?' she asked, whispering.

'It's, like, he doesn't want to talk about it,' I said quickly.

'Si!'

'We're in here!' she shouted, hanging on to my sleeve.

'Si?'

'Tell him we're in here,' whispered Eleanor.

'Over here, Dan!' I shouted reluctantly.

After an uncertain pause Danny came shouldering slowly through the leaves, his head hunched down, carrying the Walkman. He sat down on the edge of the long grass.

'It's cooler in here, isn't it, Danny?' said Eleanor. 'Me and Si are going on a Mediterranean cruise.'

Confused, Danny averted his eyes. 'Er . . . are we going for this swim, then, or what?'

'A Mediterranean *cruise*,' insisted Eleanor, puzzled.

Danny looked at me appealingly. I think he assumed cruise was some sort of rude metaphor, and felt left out. 'Swim?' he asked tentatively.

'Me and Danny were going for a swim up Swiss Cottage,' I said to Eleanor.

'Oh, what a good idea!' she cried. 'And I've my swimsuit on already. Do you?' And she picked up and gave Danny the rest of the Perrier, sickly warm now from the air and our hands. He took it off her like it was a bomb.

The pool was packed with overheated kids whose mouthy voices echoed off the roof, slapping the water into each other's eyes. Me and Danny, who came out of the changing rooms first, dived a few times off the side, enjoying the hard hit of chlorine on our faces, when suddenly arching over us came Eleanor in a tiny bright blue bikini, flying like a flying fish, a lovely clean dive from which she didn't resurface until reaching the other side. After that me and Danny started divebombing instead, narrowly missing those brave little kids who struggle along fiercely out of their depth. Eleanor did a handstand, her pointed toes jutting just above the surface.

'Is she really your girlfriend, then?' asked Danny, standing on the wet tiles, watching. Her bikini was practically a fucking G-string only, the brilliant blue of a kingfisher's back. The top was pretty small too. Her tits were small, I guess.

'Maybe,' I said cautiously.

'No, but is she your girl?'

'Maybe.' Jesus!

'Well, *is* she?' He kept staring at her while he was asking me.

'I only just met her, for fuck's sake.'

'You . . . done anything, then?'

I winced inside, and did the macho betrayal. 'Maybe.'

'Maybe?'

I dived for cover, under the noisy water.

Under the water, suddenly I couldn't move upwards. Someone had locked themselves around my knees. I opened my stinging eyes and thrashed about – bubbles rising around me in the unbreathable world. For a few seconds I thought, Some little fucker from Swiss Cottage is trying to kill me – the bastard. But I was released, and flew upwards, breaking angrily into the air. Eleanor surfaced a second later, face streaming water, laughing. 'Got a fright?'

'Hi there,' I said. 'How you doing?'

'I'm sorry if I scared you,' she said, changing attitude, making out all anxious, testing a little power trip.

'What? Come on . . .' I sort of tried to jump on her, like it was all just fun and I could play too, sort of like I was this big pathetic puppy, but as my wet skin slid heavily over her wet skin, she rolled out from under me and swum away so fast in her bikini I would've looked stupid trying to follow her. I just dog-paddled about in the water for a while before swimming back to the side, little kids screaming like they were dying all around me.

Danny was sat with his feet pale in the water. I swung clumsily up beside him. 'She swims pretty fast,' he said, staring and staring after her. His eyes were bright red with chlorine, like the eyes you get when you take photographs with a flash. 'So, listen, is she . . .'

'Fuck's sake, man!'

He dropped his eyes from Eleanor, picked his nose and flicked it into the pool. Then he said, 'You know your mum's pregnant, right?'

'Ri . . . ight,' I said. And then suddenly I really did know it, hit by an adrenaline rush of panic and looking forward. I thought, Must ring.

'Well, so's mine. Four months, she found out in hospital.'

A kid leapt right over our heads, showering us. I didn't get what Danny meant at first. I was amazed, wiping the water off of my face. 'Jesus, great – that's a coincidence,' I said.

'Oh, yeah, really great,' he said.

I looked at him, blowing my nose on my fingers. 'What?'

The pool got really shrill all of a sudden, and he shouted over it, 'Those babies scream the place down.'

I didn't get it. 'What?' That's what babies do, right?

'Si – they *hurt!*' And he leapt from his sitting position into the water, disappearing down under it, his arms over his head.

I got then what he was saying – like: junkie baby and that. For fuck's sake, can you imagine that? A tiny soft growing baby, not safe and snug like it should be in the warm, but lonely and scared in the frightening dark with heroin seeping through its threadlike veins – not even born but already suffering; dreaming withdrawal dreams of . . . what? What does an unborn baby fear? Huge hairy spiders chasing it round the womb? Unable to get away. As he resurfaced, I cried, appalled, 'But she won't go back to him now? Not after what he just did?'

He held on to the bar at the side. 'She's going back to him.'

'No. No.'

'They said she was lucky she hadn't lost it, with the way he smashed her up. Lucky!' He laughed – not really laughed, I mean, just made the sound of someone laughing.

[39]

'Fucking hell,' I said.

The water, kicked by passing feet, surged into his open mouth and made him spit. 'She says the baby needs a dad!'

'It needs a *dad*?' Like one that'd already killed it nearly?

'He'll fucking kill her!' he said, in anguish.

'Shit . . .'

'Kill *him*,' said Eleanor.

I jumped a fucking mile. Eleanor was crouched down, smiling, behind me, slender and pale and nearly naked in her bright scrappy bikini, water running down her smooth stomach, her hair almost flat on her neck, eyelashes soaked and stuck together in points. Danny was speechless.

'Fuck's sake, Eleanor,' I said. 'This is a private conversation, right?' I didn't like Danny thinking I'd been gossiping about his private stuff.

Like I wasn't there, Eleanor leaned forward, leant right over the edge of the pool into Danny's face, her small hands gripping the edge, the bare white cheeks of her arse in the air and her knee against mine. 'What if he kills her? What if he kills the baby? How can you let him near her? How could you live with yourself?' She said intently, 'Listen to me. Trust me. Kill him. Trust me, Danny . . .'

Danny stared back into her face as she went on and on, just hanging there under her, without expression, his big pale body drifting behind him in the water. I hoped he was just politely waiting for her to finish. But in the end, when she straightened up and sat down beside me with her thin legs folded under her and started untangling her black sodden hair with her fingers, like nothing special'd happened, he looked up at me with a hypnotized sigh, clinging to the bar and paddling his feet beneath him, and said in a dreamy voice, 'She's right, you know. She's so fucking right.'

Eleanor smiled sideways at me and winked, like: sorted. I didn't know what to say. There was something so fucking wrong about Eleanor.

Four

Danny and Eleanor were into plotting murder. We still went up Primrose Hill most days, hung out, listened to music, chatted, did normal pleasant stuff, that was OK. As summer moved to August, the sun shone harder and more and more concentrated, roasting us human joints of meat – we browned and sizzled in our own fat, turning ourselves pale side up on the yellow grass. I took my guitar up sometimes, and played some stuff, and when I played stuff people thought they recognized, they sung and whistled tunelessly along. Every new day I thought, Well, today will be a great day – we'll just hang with the crowd, me with Danny, me with Eleanor. But by the end of the day it was always the same: Danny and Eleanor, cross-legged and face to face, plotting murder in quiet, urgent voices, while I lay around like a prat (getting 'You poor prat' looks off those arsehole girls – like, really, really embarrassing). As the days passed by and the pair of them still banged on and on about the top ten ways to stab, strangle, shoot or generally kidnap and dismember someone, I became more and more disbelieving and impatient.

At first they wanted to buy a gun off some dodgy guy that Danny sort of knew and shoot old Shortarse from a distance in the street.

'Don't be ridiculous,' I said. 'As though nobody'd notice.'

'By the time anyone'd realized it was us, we'd've disappeared,' said Eleanor.

'No one'd know it was us,' said Danny.

I said I couldn't help thinking the police being there when Danny wrenched open the door, knife in hand, shouting, 'I'll cut your balls off,' might make him a possible suspect.

'That's not proof,' said Danny.

'They'll find out somehow you bought a gun,' I said. 'And match up the bullets or something.'

'This guy I'd buy it off wouldn't say nothing,' said Danny, threateningly.

'Everybody says something,' I argued. 'All he has to do is be in a pub and tell a mate of his that he sold a gun to the son of the girlfriend of this guy who's just been murdered, and this mate tells the police, right?'

Danny looked down his big nose offensively. 'It's not like that in real life, man. You been watching too many police things on TV.' He was trying to flash off in front of Eleanor.

Then they thought maybe instead they'd sell him some extra-pure scag. Like, get someone to sell it to him for them, that is. Then he'd overdose and die.

'Foolproof,' I said.

'A really horrible death,' said Eleanor. 'Blood comes out their nose.' (What had she been watching?)

'Yeah,' I said. 'A dealer completely taken in by too pure scag. A dealer who doesn't know how to check his own supply. Like, doesn't know how to cut the stuff. He's a *dealer*, Danny! It's his living, for fuck's sake!'

Danny said, 'Eleanor thinks it's a great idea,' like I'd just been fucked over by an expert witness, rather than a kid with a big scary thing about death.

I made like: OK, you win. 'Jesus!'

However, in the end they changed their minds completely and decided to stab him in his own flat.

'Yeah, right, like he'd let *you* in,' I said, really pissed off by this time, all this waste of a good boiling summer with weirdo game-playing and general fucking-about. 'Like he'd go: Oh, hi there, Danny, come on in. He probably would and all, and stab you first.'

Eleanor was all fired up: 'I'll do it! I'll go in and stab him! He won't recognize me!' (Danny speechless with admiration.)

I suddenly realized the whole conversation was so seriously off the fucking wall, I started laughing.

Eleanor was really hurt. She yelled at me, 'Why are you laughing at me? You're horrible! I'm supposed to be your *girl*!' (Which was the first time she'd said that.) But before I could say anything one way or the other, she cheered up again – she'd had another amazingly brilliant idea. 'I'll dress up as a prostitute and go to his door and ask him for some drugs! Then Danny'll run in behind me when he's not looking and stab him!'

'Well, how'll you look like a prostitute?' asked Danny.

I looked at him curiously. I tell you what was sad: he was really keen to know.

Eleanor laughed, like she knew he did, and put her foot alongside his, a teasing touch, on the grass. I thought she was a bit of a bitch, the way she played up to Danny. The thing was, she'd say to me behind his back, very off-hand, 'Oh, he's nice, your friend Danny, but he's a bit weird and heavy.' She really came on to him sometimes, though. Enough to get him going. Poor old Dan – he was too fucking loyal to make a play for her, so he could never find out what she really wanted.

'I don't know,' she said. 'What d'you think I should wear, Danny?'

'I d'know,' he said, embarrassed.

'Oh, go on, I can't think . . .'

He burst out, blushing (for fuck's sake), 'Tight stuff, you know.'

'Tight?'

'With holes in!'

And Eleanor looked at me, grinning with little white teeth, taking the piss. It was quite funny. But he was my best mate. '*Holes?*'

He said desperately, 'Everything prostitutes wear has holes in!' He should've known – his mum'd been there, I think. Anyway, we all knew.

'Innit,' I said, trying to be helpful.

[43]

'I think,' said Eleanor, 'I think I'll wear a really short skirt, like right up to my bum, and a really tight top (I gotta red one) which comes right down to my tummy button, and tights – tights with *holes* in, all right, Danny? – and these really high shiny black heels . . .' She was looking from me to Danny, and from Danny to me, really closely, seeing whose tiny boy brain she was fucking with the most.

I said quickly, to snap her out of it, 'But Eleanor, you got to be *sick* to be a prostitute.'

'Are you saying I'm fat?' she asked, getting in a little high-voiced flap. Yeah, sure, Eleanor. And fat is the opposite of sick. What I meant was, she was too good-looking. She'd a weird thing about fat, though: she was always asking, Am I putting on weight? That, and was she wrinkly. She was afraid of looking old. She told me once, Girls of my age, we have to use a lot of moisturiser. (I'm going to kill myself before I'm twenty.)

'You just have to look sicker.' You should see them outside the King's Cross post office. You'd think they'd have to be a small bit good-looking, at least not strikingly ugly, for some-one to want to *do* it to them, even for as little as a tenner. But they're not, poor fuckers. They stand about in black skirts and freezing legs looking really pissed off, and they're not just ugly, they look like they've the flu. If you stand and watch, you see men going up to them, kind of excited.

'I have the right marks,' said Eleanor, looking with raised eyebrows at me out of the dark corners of her eyes.

'What the fuck do you mean?' exclaimed Danny. He actually went pale. He thought she meant track marks.

With a little show-offy gesture she pulled up the long sleeves of her white shirt. She'd been wearing long-sleeved shirts for several days now. From her wrists to the inside of her elbows were two long ladders of slashes, now crusted over with dark brown. It was a really horrible sight, particularly the way she'd a little immodest smile on her face, like she'd done something oh, so clever, waiting for us to be

[44]

impressed. My stomach turned over heavily, a park-bench drunk disturbed.

'Oh, god,' said Danny, at first relieved but then disgusted instead. 'You look just like my *mum*. And all her fucking friends. Too fucking right you look the part. Why do women go around cutting up their fucking arms? It's so fucking girlie it makes me sick.'

'Well, fuck you,' said Eleanor, immediately tearful, pulling down her sleeves in two sharp jerks. 'I can't help it if you don't understand.' She'd been proud, but now she was really insulted. It was like she'd read us some very personal poem she'd written, and we'd laughed. She sprang up and jumped away down the hill, jumping and sobbing. But all the same she didn't want to leave us – while still in sight, she threw herself on the ground and hid her head dramatically in her thin wounded arms.

'Oh, well done,' I said to Danny. 'Mr Tact.'

'She fucking deserved it, man,' said Danny, his voice shaking. 'I thought she meant, you know, but it was just that girlie crap. I can't stand that shit.' And he spun round on his arse and sat hugging his knees with his back to me. I thought it a bit weird, him acting like that, when I thought he really liked her.

Me being so soft, I went up to her and sat down. 'What did you do it for?' I asked. 'It really looks horrible, Eleanor.'

'Life is horrible,' she sobbed. 'You don't understand.'

I sat there tying my shoelace, and untying it again. She was quite right. I didn't understand at all. I knew what Danny meant, about arm-slashing being a girlie thing. I'd never come across a boy who did it. A couple of the girls who'd been in my class were really into it. They compared arms. I thought it was pretty fucking disgusting. I was really, really surprised that Eleanor was into it – I hadn't realized she was that sort of person. It must hurt to cut yourself like that. Quite brave, really, to push a knife into your own skin. If life was so horrible, why make it worse?

'Show it me,' I said; I thought by looking at her slashes maybe I could understand her pain. Mournfully and uncertainly, she rolled up her sleeves. There were lots of cuts but they were only small, no stitches or anything, but they looked shit. She started scratching in between them, carefully. They must've really itched her. 'Jesus, Eleanor,' I said. 'Why?'

'It makes me feel better,' she answered, sighing. She'd stopped crying, but her face and hands were still covered with tears. 'Sort of like pressure builds up in me, and it lets it out. Like steam bursts out of my arms.' Suddenly I could see it, little sharp bursts of hot white air spurting out of her arms under the point of the knife. 'I feel such pressure,' she said sadly.

I thought how spoilt she was compared to Danny, when she'd none of his trouble. She lived with both her parents, she always had money on her. What was her fucking problem? A burst of impatience made me silent. I wanted to say what I was thinking. I tied up my lace again in an undoable knot.

'You have to help us, Si,' she said, rolling down her sleeves, wrapping up her scars, tucking them away and just like that treating them as old forgotten things. She nodded her head, frowning, up the hill to where Danny still sat, his back to us and arms around his knees, brooding blankly. 'I've been really thinking, and you have to help us, y'know? I mean, Danny's mum's boyfriend's mad, right? Suppose he kills us? I don't think just me and Danny can do it, just us two on our own; I don't know, really. I've been thinking about it a lot.'

'Don't do it, then,' I said.

'Oh, but we must,' she said. 'I've got to help him.' Sometimes I thought she did really fancy Danny, she was so fucking keen to help him out. 'I've got to do this,' she cried out, in desperation. 'You just don't *get* it.'

'Do it, then,' I said, angrily. 'If you *have* to do it.'

'You don't care if I die!'

'Of course I care!' I hate it when they make you say you care, then go, but if you *really* cared, you'd – flush your head down the bog, whatever – wouldn't you do that for me? 'I'd care if you jumped in front of a fucking train. But I don't think you should jump in front of a train, right? Jesus!'

'Jump in front of a train? That's a stupid, cruel thing to say! You just don't care!' She rolled over with her back to me.

Who did she think I didn't care about? Danny – my best mate? Her? The state of the whole fucking world? What're you supposed to do? Sit around like Danny and Eleanor endlessly planning to get your own back? Anyone can do that, but it's a load of shite when you got no power. It was games they were playing, no better than saying you're going to be a model or sail the world on rich men's yachts. We don't get to do these things; only when we were kids in our heads. And yet I knew she felt she was serious, that in a big part of her she really was upset, not just trying to wind me up. I lay down beside her and put my arm over her, half-holding her. At first she elbowed me away, but then in the gap that left between us she rolled back towards me and slung her own arms around me. Under her long shirt sleeves around my neck I felt suddenly conscious of all those stupid shallow scratchy scars, and immediately I went all withdrawn and cool inside, like she was right and I really didn't care for her that much at all. It filled me with fear and disgust.

'You have to come and see Richard,' she whispered in my ear.

'Who?' I asked suspiciously, wondering what game she was switching into now.

'Richard, my uncle. He says you can come, but he wants to see you,' she said.

'Come where?'

Sitting up, she poked my chest lightly. 'Come on this cruise, of course. It's soon. In September.'

So in one flip of Eleanor's coin we span from murder and madness to the Mediterranean; sprang from the unknown blackness of the grave and the familiar sickness of the soul into the bright blue liquid of a foreign sea. My mind filled suddenly like a sink with that warm, salty water; her dreams felt so heavy they were pulling me down: her stones around my drowning neck.

'Fucking hell, Eleanor,' I said. 'Leave it out.'

'So you'll come and see darling Richard, then? He's so cute.' You see, she couldn't even remember from the last time she was on about this cruise how terribly lonely she was going to be with him.

'Leave it out.'

'Why don't you come and see him now? You better come now – we're going really soon.'

'Now?'

'Sure.' She looked at my watch. 'If we go now, he'll be at my house. I promised I'd be back anyway.'

Of course I didn't want to go; didn't want to hear why he wasn't there this time but would be the next; didn't want to get politely trapped in the endlessly disappointing history of her harmless kiddie lies.

'I got to go – walk me, Si. Come back with me. I don't want to go by myself.'

And so I said, 'Wait – just let me tell Danny we're going.' Climbing back up to him, I said, 'I'm just off for a bit; I'll be back later.'

He didn't look at me. 'Going with her?' he asked, still shaken up and angry.

'Well, and I need to phone my mum,' I said. That was true. She could have the baby any time now. It was due in a couple of weeks. I needed to keep in touch. I phoned her every few hours when I wasn't there.

'You should ditch her, Si,' he said.

'What – Eleanor? I thought you liked her?'

'Bad news, man.'

'Well, you can't just ditch a friend for being stupid,' I said.

With hostile exasperation he snapped, 'Don't chat shit, Si. She's not your friend. She's your *girlfriend*. Of course you can ditch her.'

[48]

In terms of etiquette, of course, he was right. I opened my mouth but found nothing to say, so left him sitting there, dark on the hot hill.

What was I expecting? Some small flat, down a few steps or up a few floors; somewhere like where all of us lived: spaces crammed with families and other furniture.

She took me down one of those roads just round the back of Chalk Farm tube, roads of tall grey brick, thin houses with rhododendrons and railings and balconies and french windows. And she stopped in front of one of them, and she said, 'This is it.'

I stood on the pavement and squinted up at it, because the sun was bouncing back blindingly off of the long windows.

I said, 'Here?'

She said, 'Didn't I say? It's not just my uncle's rich, my mum is too. They own the same company. He's her brother, yeah? My dad's just this session drummer she met through the business – total waster, honestly – *big* mistake. Richard says the hormones got to her.' She pushed up the hair at the front of her face and cried with a skip, 'Richard's better than him. Richer and handsomer and nicer and everything. He's so lovely. Me and my mum *love* Richard.'

Outside the house was parked an incredibly flash green Jag with dark green seats of which you could smell the leather right through the locked doors.

'You have to be nice to him,' said Eleanor, stroking her hand along the shiny car. 'Friendly.'

Speechless, I watched her climb the four or five hot stone steps, thin dirty weeds in the cracks, up to the brass-knockered front door. Then suddenly she raced back down, gripped my elbow hard and started giggling hysterically.

'What now?' I asked. And I waited for her to say, it was all a wind-up. Or maybe more likely make out she'd forgotten nobody was home and she didn't have the key. 'What?'

'I have to tell you,' she said with difficulty. 'He thinks

you're a girl.' And she burst into more frantic giggling, eyeing me, and covering her mouth with her hand to stop the saliva spitting out. It was hard to tell whether she found the situation funny or scary. I just got a bad feeling about it. I wrenched my elbow out of her hand.

'You told someone I was a *girl*?' I was some *semi*-imaginary friend?

She gasped and choked. 'No, no, it's him, I just said you were a friend and I can tell he thinks you're a girl because it just wouldn't enter his head I know any boys, that's all. Serve him right. He's going to be a *bit* surprised.' And she ran back up the steps with her lips pressed tightly together. She was trying to stop giggling, but the laughter inside her kept bursting her pink lips apart and making little bubbles.

Just as she was about to put her key into the lock, a man opened the door, rather plump – pale in a London way, or at least like Londoners used to be pale before we became this tropical city on the edge of Essex deserts. His face was wide around the eyes, with smooth soft cheeks like sliced white bread and hair heavy dark brown to black like Eleanor's, cut a little long and curling at the edges. I don't know how old exactly – fortyish? If he was in a suit he would've looked like the guy you imagine when someone says, 'He looked like an accountant.' I never met an accountant – I don't know those people. I see types on the tube who might be accountants, but are they? How would I know? Probably the people I think look like accountants are actually pet-shop owners or something. Anyway, instead of a suit he was dressed in a T-shirt and jeans and trainers, but you could see from a mile off it was designer stuff (not YSL and Ralph Lauren, but an older, richer man's version), which was for him like wearing a suit while pretending to be cool. After opening the door he just stood there, saying nothing, as if he wasn't sure what we wanted, as if we might be Jehovah's Witnesses or something and start trying to convert him. His eyes were pale green, long black eyelashes, like hers.

Eleanor'd stopped giggling. She smiled up at him and said, 'Hi, Richard, darling.'

'Well, hello,' he said. He didn't say anything else – just stood there. He didn't look at me but went on staring patiently at Eleanor, like he was waiting for her to explain herself.

Eleanor said, buttoning her sleeve, 'This is my friend Si – the one I'm bringing on the yacht?'

He kind of glanced at me. 'Your mother's out,' he said to Eleanor. 'I thought you'd be by yourself.'

'I know, but I thought you'd want to meet him,' said Eleanor, smiling again.

'You don't usually bring anyone round,' he said.

'Yes, but – I thought you'd want to *meet* him,' she said, a little anxiously.

I said to Eleanor, 'You know, I really should go.'

Then he did look at me, but not really at *me* – only to check me out, not to make contact. He looked at my body and arms and legs as well as my face. While he was doing it, he took out a pair of dark-rimmed glasses and put them on. 'You said your friend was a girl,' he said. They were cool glasses, in a sort of anti-cool way.

'He's a *friend*,' said Eleanor.

'I think I'll go, Eleanor, OK?' I said.

'Or have you had a sex change?' he asked me. I'd say that's a pretty weird first question to ask anyone. I pretend-laughed. I could have killed Eleanor. 'Have you?' he asked.

'No.'

He raised his eyebrows above the dark-rimmed glasses at Eleanor. 'Well, *that's* a pity.' I believed he was making a joke. 'He's pretty enough for a girl.'

Eleanor hopped about like a kid. 'He can come on the cruise?'

He said coldly, 'You ask so much, Ellie.'

'Yes?'

'Whatever. Yes. Do you like the Mediterranean, Si?'

[51]

Standing there melting my soles on the pavement outside this I'm-a-rich-bastard house, I went to myself: There's a yacht? There *is* a yacht? This is for real? When I thought I was just getting to endlessly cruise the weird inside of Eleanor's head, I really was being invited to sail across some ancient sea? I hadn't realized, till this extraordinary moment, I'd even wanted it to be true. Yet if you'd looked inside my heart when Richard asked me if I liked . . . you'd've seen a whole football stadium of fans rise as one, fists in the air, screaming, 'Yes! Yes! Yes!'

I smiled woodenly. 'Yeah,' I said.

'That's settled, then,' he answered politely.

Eleanor had her arms wrapped around him and her cheek pressed very hard against his chest. 'Darling, darling, Richard!'

He staggered in the embrace of her affection and looked at his watch over her head. He wasn't that tall, just average. 'Six o'clock.' He asked me, 'Would you like to come in and have a beer?'

So it really was him – the crushing bore with the yacht and the record company. I thought, That's what a guy who owns a record company looks like – kind of cool, but not that cool. Medium cool. I'd sort of imagined, when Eleanor first dreamed him up, something with longer hair. I didn't say no to the beer.

We followed him through the green-carpeted hall into a kitchen, blindingly white and smooth but not as clean as you'd think a kitchen in that sort of house'd be – even I noticed it, and I live with my mum. It was a big house. It was a fucking huge house. The sort of house where to get from room to room you actually *walked*.

He took a couple of flashy beers out of the tall fridge and opened them with a bottle opener that was lying on the kitchen table. 'There you go,' he said, handing one to me.

'Cheers,' I said. He didn't offer Eleanor one. He poured his own into a glass, after wiping the glass round with a tea towel.

'So,' he said, sitting down on one of the kitchen chairs, pushing carefully away a plate with the steaming green remains of a lettuce leaf on it, and curling salami, and mayonnaise trampled by a pair of colourful flies. 'What have you been doing with your life, then, Si?' He leant back in the chair, crossing his legs. His eyes looked bigger and closer, because of the glasses. Eleanor stayed standing, leaning her back against the draining board. She couldn't take her eyes off of him.

'Well . . . school and stuff,' I said.

'That's it? Nothing else?'

I said, because I had to, 'I play guitar. I'd a band last year.' I had done, but the others got bored. I didn't get bored. I was really into it. It was what I wanted to do.

He just smiled a thin smile, lowering his eyes, said nothing. Immediately, I was really fucked off with myself. What did I expect him to say? 'At last, what I've been looking for all these years – a teenage boy who plays guitar and wants to be in a band!'

'I'll show you a couple of pictures,' he said. Lifting his buttock like he was going to fart, he took a wallet out of his back pocket and pulled out a couple of photographs. 'Me and Eleanor.' He was sitting with Eleanor on his lap – Eleanor was a lot younger, maybe nine or ten, looking exactly like her sister, in a little red bikini and a massive smile. Richard was slimmer and his hair longer, very curly. They were perched on a pile of rope on the deck of this really cool yacht, all white and plastic-looking, absolutely beautiful, white sails, and a little cabin right behind him. 'That's my baby,' he said.

'I can see why,' I said, standing next to him with the beer in my hand.

'We're in harbour here. Do you remember, Ellie?' Eleanor looked in the picture like she really loved being there, with him, on the yacht. But now, older, she just glanced at him expressionlessly over her shoulder as she pulled a big bottle of coke out of the fridge.

'Love it,' said Richard, closing his pale green eyes. Looking down on his face, I could see how long his black lashes were, lying behind the glass on pale full cheeks. 'The sun, the warm wind rushing up against you, diving overboard into the sea like a bath, dolphins following you about everywhere.' He opened his eyes and smiled up at me. 'Would you like to swim with the dolphins?'

My stomach leapt like a dolphin. (Yes! Yes! Yes!) 'It'd be good, yeah,' I said.

Eleanor was mooching about, taking mouthfuls of coke straight from the neck of this big bottle, deciding not to pay any attention.

Richard said to her, uncrossing his legs, 'So, Ellie, if you're bringing a friend, I think I will too.'

She stopped mooching and glared at him sulkily. 'What?'

'Your sister, I thought,' he said.

That got her attention all right. She asked, like she really couldn't believe her ears, 'What, Debbie?'

Looking down, pushing out his lips, he delicately pulled the seam of his designer jeans away from his rounded inner thigh. 'Eleanor, if you have another sister, tell me *now*.'

She was really staring at him, open-mouthed, like he'd given her a huge shock. 'Debbie?'

'What's the matter?'

'You can't bring *her*!'

He murmured, smiling but without looking at her, self-consciously twisting the strap of his watch, 'Why on earth not?'

She went to say something, glanced hesitatingly at me, then dashed over and whispered coyly in his ear like she was kissing it, cupping her hand around his ear and her mouth, touching and slightly lifting his dark hair.

He caught her, laughed, winked at me over her head, mouthed her curls. 'Ellie, Ellie,' he said, 'you really should try to get on with Debs. She's a sweet kid.'

Pulling away from him angrily, she cried, '*I'm* your baby!'

'But, Ellie . . .'

'*No!*' In her fury she actually stood stamping her foot, her face heaving like the sea.

'Ellie, darling . . .' stretching out his soft white hand.

She screamed at the top of her voice, 'Leave me *alone!*' and ran out of the room. I heard her feet up the stairs and a door slam shut. I was left in the kitchen, alone with him.

Richard sighed, and turned the damp beer glass in his hand, thinking to himself.

'Well, I better go,' I said.

He grinned up at me, remembering me, taking his glasses off, wiping the dark curling hair out of his eyes. 'Poor old Ellie, she has to be my only little girl,' he said. I said nothing, moving my weight to my other foot. He stood up, restlessly scratching his shoulder, and walked around the kitchen, looking at me, putting down his glass on the draining board, picking it up and putting it down again, drying his fingers on the tea towel.

'I'll be off, then,' I said.

'She's always been like that, you know,' he said, propping himself impulsively against the sink, nibbling at the edge of his nail, looking at me, up and down, long eyelashes rising and falling. 'Ever since she was ever so small. Mad, really. She always gets her way. Poor little Debs: she'll have to wait for me.' He lifted his eyebrows as he nibbled away. 'Has she got you wrapped round her little finger, then, like she's got me? Do you give in? I do. But tell me, do you think it's good for her? How did she manage to get so strong while we're . . . while I am on my *knees* to her?'

'Can I use the phone quickly?' I asked.

He pointed towards the hall, without taking his eyes off of me.

In the soft green-carpeted hall I stood listening to the phone. A voice picked it up, but it wasn't my mum. I thought I'd the wrong number and went to put it down, but she said, 'Is that Si? Thank goodness you rang.'

[55]

I stayed silent: I couldn't think.

'Are you still there?'

'Who's that?'

'It's the midwife – isn't it *great*?'

A sick panic came over me. I nearly broke the phone in my hand. I sat down on the pale green carpet. I needed to be at home, but I wanted to stay here, safe and distant on the floor of a strange house.

'I'm on my way,' I said at last.

'Oh, no,' said the unknown voice. 'You can meet us there. Do you know the hospital?'

Hospital? I thought. What's that? What's wrong? What happened to the famous home birth? The scented candles? The Mozart? The fucking bath? There must be something wrong with the baby. Maybe they couldn't hear its heart or something. Maybe it'd stopped breathing. Maybe it's being born blind. 'What?'

'Everything's going to be just fine. Do you want to meet us at the hospital? Please don't worry.'

'I'm not worried,' I said. 'I'm going to the hospital now.'

'Hang on a minute,' she said. 'You should speak to your mum. Hang on a sec.'

She left the phone. From a mile or so off the sounds of home drained faintly straight into my ear – her telling my mum I was on the line, and my mum telling her to 'Fuck off' . . . What? What? As I stood like a prat with the phone to my head, a key turned on the far side of the door and this woman stepped into the house with a sigh, twisting at the waist to close the door, tall and narrow in brown high heels, and long brown-black curling hair down to her arse like a model's, over her tight brown dress against which her nipples and hip bones elegantly pressed. She smiled round at me with wide green eyes.

'Hello,' she said, then saw beyond me and said again, straightening, in a softer voice, '*Hello*.'

My mum came on the phone. She was out of breath. 'Hi

there, Si,' she said. 'You all right?'

'You all right?' I asked, looking at the woman. She was unhooking a small crocodile-skin-type long-strapped bag from her shoulder. She let it swing from her hand almost to the ground. I said, 'What was all that about?'

'Nothing. Of course I'm all right – are you all right?'

'I'm all right.'

'So *glad* you're all right,' said the woman, strolling past, dropping the shining bag on to the table by the phone. I trailed her with my eyes. Richard was standing in the kitchen doorway. She kissed his mouth quite hard, and squeezed his hand.

'I'm going up the hospital,' said my mum to me, down the line.

'Right.'

'I came back early to catch you,' said the woman.

'And here I am,' said Richard, watching me through her curls.

'It's not I don't want a home birth,' said my mum. 'But you just don't realize, like, without injections and things . . . oh, fuck, here we go *again*.' And she put the phone down on me, just like that.

I sat on the floor with the phone still warm in my hand, as if, though silent, it still connected me umbilically to my home through the long coils of dead, unbreathing wire.

'Are you all right?' asked Eleanor, standing at the top of the stairs.

'My mum's having the baby,' I said.

'Good god!' exclaimed the woman, turning to Richard, laughing again. 'What a surprise!'

'Mum,' said Eleanor, peering at her over the bannister on tiptoe. 'Don't laugh. His mum's having a baby . . . Richard!'

'What, sweetie?' asked Richard, stepping forwards and looking up.

'His mum's having a baby.' Like she was expecting him to do something about it.

[57]

'I've got to get to the hospital,' I said, then thought I was coming over ridiculously melodramatic, like I might then shout, Out of my way! Or, Is there a doctor in the house? I got to my feet, realized I was still holding the phone and put it down.

'I'll drive you,' said Richard suddenly. Eleanor's mother made a face, flattening her long-fingered hand on his chest.

'Oh, thank you!' said Eleanor, running down the stairs.

'No, really, I can walk – it's not far,' I said. I wasn't being funny: it wasn't far at all – probably only twenty minutes' fast walk.

Eleanor's mother smiled at me again.

'I'll drive you,' said Richard, his voice sounding louder without him actually raising it at all.

'Thanks,' I said.

The woman swivelled noisily away on her high shoes into the kitchen.

'I'll come,' said Eleanor, eagerly.

'No,' Richard said. 'You won't.'

'Oh . . .'

Her mother interrupted, without looking back, 'Don't bother him, Eleanor. He'll soon be back.'

Of course the flash dark green Jag parked outside Eleanor's house was his – who else's? I'd thought I could smell the leather through the closed windows, but I couldn't believe it when he opened the door: it was overpowering, man, that smell of hot green leather. If ever I smell leather now, I think of him, and I think of being with him in that flashy car; I remember the sinking of my seat; I remember the way the engine started somewhere in the distance; I remember the gold ring on his pale hand as he laid it gently on the wheel. I remember, as we waited to pull out on to the main road, him with his soft pale cheeks and slightly podgy mouth and Eleanor's eyes half-looking across at me and saying, 'Ellie's too young for a sexual relationship, Si – I hope you know that.' And I remember the way he laughed, in a 'friendly' way, like people do when they want to be able to act surprised if you get annoyed.

I thought, Fuck you: so that's why you wanted to drive me, and wouldn't let Eleanor come. And I thought you were trying to do me a favour. 'Right,' I said. As of that moment, I was too worried about my mum to waste my time discussing Eleanor. Suddenly I didn't even care that much about the cruise – in fact I felt faintly sick of the whole set up.

'I won't come if you don't want,' I said.

'Oh, god, nobody's saying that,' he said. We swung beautifully into the main road, but he was going slowly, and he kept looking across at me in between driving. 'I'm glad she has a nice friend,' he said. He emphasized 'friend', like to imply as long as that's all it was. I didn't say anything. 'Look,' he said. 'There's no need to be annoyed. I didn't mean to insult you. She's quite a funny girl sometimes, Ellie, that's all. She lives in a bit of a fantasy world. Sometimes I think she says things she doesn't mean. Sometimes I worry she gives the wrong idea. That's all I mean.'

I chilled out a bit, then. After all, the man was right. What about that day on the hill, when she asked me if I wanted to have sex? Maybe he knew she sprung things like that on people. Maybe he was just trying to protect her from herself.

'Well, she's never given me the wrong idea,' I said.

'Anyway, she's only fifteen,' he said. 'She's under-age.' And he gave a shadow of a laugh, like he was pleased to remember that. He turned the car into the hospital. 'You know why she's wearing long sleeves these days?' Pulling the car over and letting the engine run, he leaned on the wheel and looked at me to see if I knew. I turned away, embarrassed. 'So you see,' he said. He waited. I said nothing. 'But after all, she's a sweet little bunny,' he said. 'I wouldn't want her coming to any harm. Now you run along and see your poor old mum.' He reached across me to open my door, and turned his face so close to mine I thought for a moment he was trying to kiss me. Eleanor must've got her sense of personal body space from him. 'Well, see you on holiday, then,' he said. His mouth was still so close to mine – nearly, his lips on mine – that however far back I pressed my head into the leather seat, I could smell the smell of violet flowers – his fucking breath freshener, mixed in with the green leather.

Five

I'd never wanted to be there, but my mum said it'd be this amazing experience. I never wanted to be there, but who else was around to do it? There was no father in waiting to say hello to this still invisible child after it'd elbowed and clawed its way into the light, forcing itself headfirst through the living doorway of my yelling mum.

Amazing experience! Like fuck.

It wasn't much like the plan my mum'd come up with. In that, Mozart played softly in the background, the scented steam rose from the soothing bath, my mum got in touch with he great mystical production of life, etc. My nan, won over (even made slightly tearful) by the great universal process, stopped making bitchy remarks and made instead cups of herbal tea. A couple of friendly, homely, home-birth-loving midwives would be sitting around chatting, and I – I thought at least I might be able to hold hands, mop brows, do the business, be like this essential supportive person in the team.

I just felt so lonely. Nobody was there. There was this midwife coming in and out, but she was mostly always going out. My nan wasn't there because my mum was too embarrassed to admit she'd chucked in the towel and run into hospital at the first sign of unbearable agony, leaving a trail of overturned birthing stools and unlit candles in her wake. The worst thing was, after all that, she was still waiting for the anaesthetist to give her a paralysing injection two hours after I got there. He was a busy man, apparently.

So here we were, in pain, in hospital. The walls were papered with little rose buds, yellow, to give it that 'you could be in your bedroom at home' feel, but I can't say they fooled me. Stainless steel machines, gathered around the bed like anxious family members, beeping indiscretely, gave the real game away. At constant intervals my mum clapped a ridiculous rubber mask over her face and became an image from the Second World War. Gas and air didn't seem to do much for her pain-wise, but her eyes glazed over more and more, like she was smoking a really big powerful spliff, and from time to time I thought she was no longer really there, until another contraction jerked her ruthlessly back to life, her red hair flying forward.

Then she would scream at the midwife, if she happened to've dropped by, 'Where's the fucking *anaesthetist*? If I wanted to die, I'd have stayed at home!'

And the midwife said, ironically, 'You're doing well, Louise, you're doing well.'

And I was alone, perched on the edge of my chair with my hands between my knees like a child not allowed to touch expensive things, watching in silent shock what seemed to me a fight to the death between my foul-mouthed mother and the frantic, struggling being inside her, thrashing around, so desperate to break out, like a caught bird trying like crazy to free itself from human hands. It was like she hardly cared I was there. In the two hours after I got there, all she'd said to me, in a one-off lull between the storms, was (through her teeth, in a less than friendly way): 'This reminds me of having you.' That and, 'Don't *touch* me,' when the midwife, trying to give me something useful to do, gave me a flannel to wipe her face. Apart from that, just the endless swearing, not even at me, just at the midwife and the flowery wall.

The midwife spoke to me, 'Are you all right there?'

'Fine.' I was trapped by the plot and had to sit it out to the end. I couldn't even look away – I was glued to my seat.

'Why don't you go get something to eat?' she asked abruptly, on her next flying visit. 'The canteen's downstairs. I'll wait here till you get back.'

[62]

I looked at her suspiciously. I thought maybe something was about to happen. I wasn't planning to miss the climax of the action, not after all this. I didn't want the kid arriving naked and without luggage on our doorstep with nobody home.

'Go on,' said my mum. 'It's all right.' It made me jump to hear her voice and see her looking at me. But as quickly as she'd come back to me, she was gone again, plunging into the front line.

I was starving. I wandered into the canteen, a refugee from the war, my legs floppy and my shoulders stiff. The food was a load of shite, dodgy mince pies and chilled sandwiches in plastic boxes, cold and soggy with condensation. I bought a Kitkat and a strawberry yoghurt and sat down at one of the canteen tables where the yellow Formica curled up slightly on one corner and someone'd written 'I'll be back' five times on the surface with a green felt pen. I peeled the top off the yoghurt and looked up – and guess who I saw, walking in, with his fucking nerve.

Fucking Andy. 'Father' to the kid just about to burst out; amazing vanishing boyfriend; useless wanker extraordinaire. Seeing me, he smiled, waved, started to come over, knocking past old people drinking tea. He was a tall and clumsy man. I was astonished; I couldn't fucking believe it; I didn't know what to think. All my hate of him for deserting us came flooding in as powerfully as when it was brand new, yet at the same time I felt this huge sense of relief – thank Christ, someone to help out. Then again, there was another voice in the back of my head going: Oh, yeah, Si, you go through the whole thing, pregnancy and labour and everything, and he just turns up at the last minute, and I bet she's going to be so *pleased* to see him, and it's not going to be important you being there any more because this lazy fucker has swanned in at the last fucking moment and stolen your chair.

'Hi,' he said, 'hi –' from a few yards away, coming closer. I stood up to walk away from him but ended up not moving.

[63]

'Don't get up,' he said, reaching me. 'Finish what you were eating.' His brown hair had grown to just below his shoulders. As always, he was badly shaved. Slowly I sat down, and for want of anything better to do started eating my yoghurt. He pulled up a chair, leant his elbows on the table, broke a bit off my Kitkat and ate it. Unbelievable, man. 'So,' he said. 'How is she?' Unfuckingbelievable.

'Oh, she's having a great time,' I said.

'Right, right,' he said, ambiguously, staring down at the table. You could see he really wanted to believe me, that would've made it so easy for him, but it was too obvious I was taking the piss. He twiddled a bit of his hair and then sucked the tip – an irritating old habit of his – and hunched up his sloping shoulders. 'I figured out the due date,' he said. 'Thought it'd be about now, so I came round and you were gone and next door told me you'd gone up the hospital already. Pretty good timing, right?' he said, smiling, shy but proud, up at me from under his long hair. He was really ever so pleased with himself. I looked at him coldly and his smile fell. He bit at his hair. 'So, how's it going? Taking a break? Poor old Si, it must be tough on you, yeah?'

I stared at him. I really, really wanted to punch him out, so badly that I froze, couldn't speak or move, because if I did, that's exactly what I'd've done. I thought, How *dare* he come in here after all this time and accuse *me*, just taking a five-minute break after hours of non-stop freakout, of being no better than him, of finding it easier to keep out of the way. Well, he could fuck off for a start. I pushed back my chair abruptly, grabbed what he'd left of my Kitkat, and headed for the lifts.

'Si! Si!' He was padding along beside me in his soft shoes. 'Wait up. Where are we going? Do you think she'll want to see me? I thought I better come along, offer a bit of support, you know, don't want be a complete bastard, you know. What d'you think? Will she mind? How's she doing?'

I couldn't shake him off. I stood steaming, staring at the lift doors, willing the lift to hurry. It came, but he got in with me. Whatever aftershave he used, it had a familiar smell to me, bringing back memories of standing in the bathroom with him at home. I could have cried. I'd thought he was a nice guy once – well nice.

'Look,' he said. 'I know I haven't been around, and that's bad . . . look, Si, I don't blame you for being pissed off – I want to be supportive, you know, do my bit. Look, I'm sorry – do you want me to go away?'

I felt like my head was going to blow off with rage. How the fuck could I say whether he should stay or go? He was pathetic, trying to make me take the responsibility for what he did. He couldn't even make his own decisions. I stormed out of the lift as soon as the doors started to open and marched down the corridor without looking back. He followed behind me: 'Wait! Si! Wait a minute!'

The door to my mum's room was open. I could hear the midwife telling her how great she was doing. Louise didn't look up when I came in – she was in the middle of a contraction, sweating and grunting like a pig, clutching her shins under the sheet, her long red hair soggy with sweat. It was clear the incredibly busy anaesthetist hadn't managed to slot her into his crowded schedule for that week (maybe lunch next month . . .?). But when it faded away, she looked up tearfully at me, and then her eyes went past me and she was really shocked – not pleased, just completely taken aback to see him. Andy shuffled over towards the bed, like a child who thinks it might be in a bit of trouble, but only a bit, nothing serious. 'Hi, there,' he said. 'Thought I better show up.'

My mother was speechless, shaking her head.

'Thought you might like a bit of support, you know,' he said.

She stopped being speechless. 'What the *fuck* are you doing here? How dare you! How fucking *dare* you! You left me to get on with it all by myself, *your* baby, *your* baby, and then you have the fucking cheek to turn up here and offer

[65]

your fucking *support*. This is all your fucking *fault*!'

'Now, Louise,' said the midwife, intrigued. No doubt these were the best bits. 'Don't get tense.'

Andy shot a quick embarrassed look at me and the midwife. 'Well, I'm here now, honey.'

'Here now?' screeched Louise, getting louder and louder. 'Here *now*? *Honey*? You're a waster and a wanker and you said you wanted this baby until it was too fucking late to do anything about it, and then you fucked off and left us and you're here *now*?'

Andy couldn't believe it. He blushed on all his visible skin. This wasn't my dopehead mum like he'd known before, who'd say, 'Oh, that's OK, give us a drag, I'm so laid back and cool nothing ever bothers me' to every fucking crappy trick he'd ever pulled.

'Oh, god, Louise . . . look . . . I'm really, really sorry . . .'

'Sorry? *Sorry!*' Then she leaned back and pulled her knees up and put her head down and started to breathe fast.

'Jesus Christ, man,' he said across the bed to me, staring down at her as she pressed the rubber mask over her face. 'Am I making this worse? Perhaps I better go.'

'Yeah,' I said, holding my pain secretly inside: glad to see the back of him; angry to be left alone again, and so soon.

'Maybe that would be best,' said the midwife, disappointed.

My mum, coming down off the contraction, ripped away the mask and snarled, 'Oh, no, you fucking don't; don't you fucking dare sneak off again; you're going nowhere.' To the midwife she said, 'Get him a chair.'

'Oh, right,' said Andy, humble, smug at being so indispensable, deeply alarmed at having to stay around for once in his life. 'Right.'

The midwife brought over another chair and set it nearer the foot of the bed, but Andy sat down in my chair, by my mother's head, and took her hand. 'I'm sorry, Louise,' he said. 'Really I am. I didn't realize.'

Another contraction started, but she didn't snatch her hand away, as she had from me, but kept hold of his hand, which made me feel bad and displaced, until I saw him go white and afterwards feel his long fingers cautiously up and down for fractures. As the next contraction started and she reached for the gas and air again, he kept his hands to himself and wildly asked me, 'She been like this for long? This can't be right – why aren't they giving her something?'

'The anaesthetist was supposed to come,' I said. 'But it looks like he's not.'

Leaning over the back of the chair, flapping his hands, he hailed the midwife like a passing cab. 'Hey! Nurse! This is crazy! She's suffering! *Do* something!'

'She's doing very well,' said the midwife, ignoring him, cruising past. 'Aren't you, Louise? Not exactly the home birth we planned, hmm? But you're doing very well.'

'Fuck that,' said my mum. She took one more mighty gulp of gas and air and fell back glazed and incoherent.

'Jesus Christ,' said Andy. 'This isn't right. She should be on something that *works*.' Louise grabbed his hand again, which he'd foolishly left lying about on the bed, and an involuntary groan escaped him. I nearly smiled. Her fingers breaking his, he cried in panic, 'Louise, honey, tell me what to *do*!'

Looking suddenly frightened, she rolled her eyes towards him as her knees were slowly dragged back up towards her chest under the sheet like on a separate string, and answered in a whisper, 'Andy . . . help me . . .'

One thing he knew about all right – drugs. He made the midwife quit arseing around waiting for the anaesthetist to come back off of his holidays and instead give my mum a jab of pethidine. After that things went along better for a while but weird, because Louise started freaking out about white rats scuffling under the bed. Andy handled it OK. He didn't tell her it was all in her head, he just told her they weren't rats but friendly little mice, and she believed him – wanted to feed them invisible cheese even. To me, he said, 'What a trip, man.

Powerful stuff. Oh, yeah.' The midwife gave him a dirty look.

I began to feel OK about him being there – it was like old days again – having this lazy incompetent man around, all of us, all three of us together. I nearly forgave him for taking over my chair, because in the end he was sharing in the shit.

The trip didn't last for ever. My mum started shrieking; the midwife was yelling at her to push, and wait, and push. The sheets were off. Andy, looking like he was going to faint, was chanting, 'Fucking hell, fucking hell.' I couldn't watch, I couldn't leave – I was crouched in a ball in the hospital chair, covering my eyes and ears; I thought all hell had broken loose: birth of the innocent unknown heralded by screaming demons and buckets of blood.

And my mum was going, 'Andy . . . Andy, come on – you can look now . . . Si, are you there? You all right? Si? come on, Andy, you can look now . . . Andy . . . *Andy*!'

Cautiously, my head turned half-away, I looked. The midwife'd drawn the sheet back over Louise's knees, but huge blood stains were splashed on it, and there was wet blood on the floor, like murder'd been committed. Crashed face down on my corpse-pale mother's chest lay this tiny frog-like thing, silent, delicate ribs rising and falling, coated all over in blood and gunge. I lowered my feet to the floor.

'Si, come and look,' said my mum. 'Isn't she beautiful?'

It was a girl. Standing, I bent my face towards her. The baby with its head on one side stared straight back at me, its blue eyes wide open, in total shock.

'Touch her,' ordered my mother.

Reluctantly I touched the little girl's purplish skin, slimy with mucus, just with the tip of my finger. Andy, his elbows on the edge of the bed, was head down, still shaking uncontrollably, clutching his hair and panting. 'Hi, Sophie,' I said, to the baby. Sophie was what me and my mum'd decided to call her if she was a girl. I was the first person ever in the world to call her by her name. It was like I was the first man on the moon.

At that, Andy finally opened his eyes. 'Sophie? What?' He stared, open-mouthed. 'Jesus Christ. Is she supposed to be that colour?'

Louise looked at him, hard.

'No, purple's a great colour,' he said. He touched the baby's nose, very gently. 'Hello, frog face.'

'She's your daughter. Her name's Sophie,' said Louise.

'Yeah?' asked Andy. He added, suddenly proud, 'My daughter.'

'My sister,' I said quickly.

'Your sister, my daughter,' he repeated.

It really was a fact, then: this gunky handful was my sister Sophie. Out of the agony and aggression, blasted out in a shower of my mother's blood, a new life had exploded into our world.

'I suppose we ought to tell people,' said Andy. He was so pleased with himself, he started acting like it *was* his baby.

Louise said, 'Si, go phone your nan, will you?'

Andy looked gloomy. I don't think my nan was who he'd had in mind. I think he wanted someone who would congratulate him, not loudly commiserate with the baby for having him for a father. But he gave me a reluctant handful of ten pences – startlingly efficient.

It was sneaky of Louise, sticking me in it. My nan was really insulted the whole thing had happened without her. Furiously: 'She's *had* the baby? Why didn't anyone *tell* me?' Suspiciously: 'Why are you calling from a callbox? Where are you?' Hysterically: 'The *hospital*? Is it dead? I *knew* this would happen!' Smugly: 'There, then, I knew she wouldn't last two minutes with that hippy home birth rubbish. And you can tell her I said so. No wonder she didn't dare ring.' Eventually: 'Well, is it a boy or a girl? What does it weigh?' Disbelievingly: 'What's the point of phoning me if you don't know how much she *weighs*?' Parting shot: 'She's not still thinking of calling her Sophie, is she?'

Putting down the phone I felt exhausted – I wanted to talk

to someone who'd think having babies was a good idea. It was about eleven o'clock. I phoned Eleanor's number. Richard answered the phone. He was very pleased it was a little girl. He shouted, 'Eleanor! Eleanor! It's a girl!' When Eleanor came on the phone she sounded faintly depressed, almost but not quite as if she'd been crying.

'My mum's had the baby,' I said. 'It's a girl.'

'That's nice,' said Eleanor, without paying much attention. I felt quite annoyed with her for not being excited.

'Well, see you, then,' I said, letting the annoyance show.

'No, wait,' she said, 'have you spoken to Danny?'

'I'm going to ring him now,' I said. 'Find someone who's a bit pleased.'

'Don't tell him about the baby,' she said.

'What?'

'Don't tell him about the baby,' she repeated.

Oh, thanks. First she's not interested, then she wants it to be our secret. 'What do you mean, don't tell him? What's it to do with you? Of course I'm going to tell him.'

She dropped her voice. 'No, listen, Si, I rang him to tell him about your mum, but he told me first he just found out his mum was in hospital this morning and she lost the baby.'

'Shit, that's sad,' I said. 'That's bad luck.'

'Well, it wasn't bad luck,' said Eleanor, crying.

The hairs stood up on my arms. 'What do you mean?'

'She moved back in with that sick fucking boyfriend of hers yesterday and he kicked her in the stomach until it happened.' I was silent. Eleanor added, 'Danny says the hospital said she was more pregnant than they thought – about six months. It was a little girl.'

A girl, a baby girl – born on the same day as my sister, beaten unconscious from her mother's womb; born like my sister in a welter of blood, flushed out in pain, but pointless, to no purpose, no future, ended before she was started, already dead, already murdered. Poor little baby.

'I have to ring him,' I said.

'They can save them at six months,' said Eleanor. 'But only if they're born *alive*.'

'I have to ring him,' I said. 'I'll call him now.'

'But you have to help him, Si,' she said, urgently. 'You can't leave him to do all this by himself.'

'Eleanor,' I said, like: shut the fuck up. 'He's my best friend. I'll do anything I can to help him.' Putting down the phone, I stood with my forehead leaning against the wall. I had to ring Danny, but I didn't much want to. I looked at the phone. I had to ring him. I *did* want to. Then I thought, He won't be in – took a deep breath and picked up the phone and dialled.

Danny answered the phone.

For a moment I didn't speak.

'Who the fuck *is* that?' he said.

'I just spoke to Eleanor,' I said at last.

'Oh. It's you. Right.'

'I'm really sorry to hear about your mum, Danny. It's shit.'

'Right.'

'Surely she'll press charges this time?'

Suddenly more animated, Danny snapped into the phone, 'What, and risk getting her fucking scag supply cut off?'

'I know but . . .'

Then he went indifferent on me again, removed, almost polite, as if I were someone he hardly knew. 'Look, Si, I don't really want to talk about this.'

I suppose I should have respected his private space or whatever, but what he said really hurt. 'Oh, fine, you talk to Eleanor but you can't talk to me, right?' I said bitterly. 'What's the fucking point?' I felt like slamming the phone down, but hung on to see if he would say anything.

'Well,' said Danny, 'that's the trouble – what is the point talking to you about it? All you do is say how shit it is. Well, I already know how shit it is. At least Eleanor wants to help sort it out. She understands what has to be done. There's some point in talking to her. It gets me somewhere.'

[71]

I was gutted. He was my best friend from when we were kids, and he was in the biggest trouble of his troubled life, and he thought I'd let him down, he didn't even want to talk to me. A screwed up weirdo like Eleanor with scars all up her arms was doing more for him than I was.

'Anyway,' he said, 'gotta go.'

'No, wait – wait,' I said. 'Look, I'm sorry, I know I've been . . . look, I'll help, OK?'

'Help how?' asked Danny suspiciously.

'Anyway you want.'

'You know what I want to do,' he said, lowering his voice. His grandparents must've been around.

'I know, I know.'

He dropped his voice even further. 'We'll talk later, OK.'

'Yeah.'

We hesitated on the phone. 'OK, gotta go now,' he said again. Then: 'Si?'

'Yeah?'

'Thanks.'

He left me pumping with adrenalin, charged with dramatic images of death and blood strangely overlaid upon the images of birth and blood that had filled my mind before calling Eleanor and then him. I wasn't sure what I had just signed up to, but I knew I had to help him. My heart was racing. I really needed to talk to someone, but I couldn't talk to Louise about it – she'd've totally freaked out. Then for some reason I thought it'd be OK to talk to Andy about it, now he seemed to be back in our lives. He'd be a bit more detached; he might even see the best thing to do. I could picture him listening to the story, sucking on his hair, nodding. Later that evening maybe.

I wandered back down to the labour room. My mum was sat up in bed breastfeeding Sophie. Andy didn't seem to be there. 'How did Mum take it?' asked Louise, smiling down at the baby.

'Fine, fine – where's Andy?' I asked.

'Oh, he's gone,' said Louise, indifferently.

'Oh.' I watched the baby suck. It was having a good time. 'So, when's he coming back?'

She looked up suddenly, directly at me. 'Si . . . you know he only came to be here while she was born, you know. I mean, I'm sure he'll be in touch, but . . .'

I went abruptly back out into the corridor and leant against the wall. So, the fucker hadn't come back for me – us – at all, just to see his fucking baby born. To take my place at the bedside. To be a pretend dad to a baby he didn't care enough about to stick around five minutes. He'd left us to get on with it by ourselves again. Fucking great. Fucking great. What had I been thinking of, planning to talk to him about anything? Who cared about him? There are some right fuckers in this world, I thought, and we can't let them get away with it. What had there been to discuss with that waster Andy? Danny needed my help, and he was going to get it. All my anger went shooting towards Danny's mum's boyfriend like a huge fucking bolt of light, illuminating him in my mind like the devil in a dark room. Andy leaving when he did had pretty much sealed that fucker's fate. And set me on the path towards my own.

Six

I let myself into the dark flat around midnight. It was a relief to be there, alone, with the sweet familiar smell of dust instead of the hospital's stench of orange juice. I was that shattered I should've gone straight to bed, but instead I went into my mum's street-lit room and checked out the cot I'd fixed up a week ago, giving it a shake, seeing if it was still solid. It was an old one someone'd given us, a bit on the shaky side, so I'd whacked in an extra couple of nails to give it a bit of backbone. It was OK. Then I lay down on my mum's bed and shut my eyes and thought what it was going to be like, having a living baby in the cot, because when I was hammering in the nails and Sophie was still unborn, still dead to me, I remembered it felt weird, like I was setting up a sort of shrine, banging together an empty bed for a ghost.

And I couldn't stop thinking how if a cot'd been got ready for Danny's little sister, it would've waited unfilled for ever and ever, because she'd been rushed from pre-life to death, from one eternity to another, from dark to the dark without ever passing through the light. The ghost had been born a ghost. Like Danny said, the man had to die.

In the morning we brought our own living child home, and the cot was filled.

She slept on her back, eyes closed and open fingers resting neatly on the sheet, unable to move. Her head was pointed, a genuine alien. When she was awake, she couldn't look at you, couldn't smile. She was so weak you'd to hold her head up for her. She was fucking hungry, though. She clung to my mum day in, day out: a weak greedy leech. She was scarily single-minded. She didn't give a fuck about us – the only thing she cared about was getting fed. Like I said to big Al, when some of the Primrose Hill crowd came round for a look, 'A bit like you, Al.'

My nan, sitting in the kitchen, with her bulky stomach propped up against the table like a bag of shopping she was holding on her knees, knitted pink baby clothes – because girl babies wear pink, of course. But in reality she wasn't trying to be helpful – she was taking the piss. She knitted day-glo pink and dog-sick pink and punky purple pink and everything except ordinary bog-standard baby pink. My mum wept, because it was all so horrible. My nan said, 'It's what I dressed *you* in, Louise, and I didn't hear you complaining then.' She said bitterly, 'I suppose you want to put her in dungarees – haven't you learnt *any*thing from that home-birth fiasco?' My mum ran screaming from the room, and my nan knitted smugly on, some unrecognizable object in orange-pink splat-tered-vomit-effect. She said to me, 'I hope that poor dear baby doesn't take after its father.'

'Too right,' I said, but because I was agreeing with her she thought I was being sarcastic and turned nasty with an inar-ticulate snarl. But I wasn't being sarcastic at all. My mum'd made me swear on various family graves (rose bushes, actu-ally) not to tell about Andy turning up at the hospital and fucking right off again. But that was one thing I wouldn't've minded hearing my nan bitch on about at all.

Several Primrose Hill types came round: Luke, Chetan and big Al, all a bit glazy-eyed because they'd been wetting the baby's head in vodka; Viv with a thin gold necklace; Martin got sweet and made a tape of nursery rhymes (himself singing them, unfortunately); but I didn't call Danny, because I didn't know what to say about the baby.

Eleanor turned up almost straight away. She was still in her long-sleeved shirt, but she was in a great mood, sunny as hell. She swooped on Sophie: 'Isn't she the *sweetest*? Si phoned me from the hospital as soon as she was born.'

'Really?' said my mum, looking at me, like: really!

'Let's go see your room,' said Eleanor to me, linking her arm all friendly in mine, pressing her black-brown curls to my shoulder. She'd short red leggings on and strappy red sandals with a heel, and the backs of her calves were dark brown almost like she was wearing stockings.

In my room she bounced her arse off the bed and read out the music posters, and hadn't heard of half the bands, and messed with the guitar and checked out my CDs and computer games, throwing them on to the bed one after the other, after just reading the titles. I'd a really embarrassing duvet on the bed, Superman, from when I was about ten and into saving the world. She didn't slag it off. She was chattering away about how hot it was outside, and how sweet babies were. She stuck her head out of the window, squinting against the sun, and said, 'Your whole garden is in pots. What's that funny thing, like – plastic?'

I leant out of the window beside her. 'What?'

She said, 'You know, plastic fruit.'

'Oh, right.'

'Right what?'

'We got a lemon tree. That's what it is.' It stood in the middle of our concrete lawn, looking an artificial thing among the overflowing pots of real green my mum kept watering.

'*Real* lemons?' she said, reaching out her hand to it, but she couldn't reach it. 'Can we make lemonade?'

'In a few more years,' I said. 'When things are, like, *really* tropical.' I liked the lemon tree, though. I wanted an orange tree as well. It was going to get hotter, wasn't it? Everyone knew that. In a couple of years we'd be sitting around in our concrete garden, eating the sweet fruit off of our trees like we were foreigners abroad. I'd never been abroad – I was just waiting for abroad to come to me.

'So.' She sat back down on the bed, leaning back against the wall, pushing aside with one hand the mess she'd made. She kicked off one sandal and crossed her ankles just above

[76]

the floor. Squares of sunlight fell across her lap. 'OK, what'd he say to you, then?'

'What?'

'Him! Richard!'

It was funny, for a moment I thought she was talking about Andy. 'Oh, nothing,' I said, slightly down.

'Well, he must've wanted you to himself for a reason,' she said.

I shrugged. It was awkward, what he'd said about her being too young for sex. I didn't want to really think about it, or to piss her off, or embarrass her.

'Come on,' she said, banging the wall just lightly with the flat backs of her outstretched hands. 'Come *on*, Si. Did he slag me off?'

'No!' I said. But he had, a bit.

'Did he tell you he didn't want you on the cruise?'

'No.'

She didn't go 'Oh, good' or anything to that. She looked not pleased but kind of thoughtful, even anxious, like she was trying to work out what it all meant – feeling her way along a string in the dark. She sighed. Then she gave a little bounce. 'Do you like him?'

I said, cautiously, 'He's all right.'

'Well, did you *like* him?'

I said, 'Do *you* like him?'

'Oh . . .' She jumped up impatiently, swatting her hands about, turning to the window, leaning her elbows on the window-frame, looking out, scratching the back of her calf with the buckle of the one sandal she was still wearing. 'He's all right.' Then she said, 'He's nice, sometimes. Sometimes he's *really* nice.' She looked at me over her white-shirted shoulder. 'He cares a lot about me, actually.' (Like I'd implied he didn't.)

'He seems OK,' I said.

She ran over to me and grabbed me urgently by my top. 'So, what did he *say*, Si? Did he say I was nice?'

[77]

Jesus! 'Of course he did.' (Didn't he?) 'I can't remember, Eleanor – a lot's happened since then.'

'It was only yesterday,' she protested, pulling my T-shirt, pulling me about. 'How much can happen in one day to make you forget? You must remember, Si – what did he *say*?'

I couldn't believe she was so fucking obsessed with that guy she'd forgotten what'd happened to me since I last saw the man. I blurted out, 'He said you're too young for sex!' It was embarrassing, right, but I only told her because she wanted to know.

She let go of my shirt. She looked screwed-up annoyed and really shocked. She stood with her arms folded and turned half her back to me with her head lowered. Then she went and threw herself, arms crossed against her chest, face down on the bed. I heard a CD cover crack under her, like a stick in a wood. I didn't know what to do because I thought I'd really embarrassed her. The idea of people discussing whether or not she should have sex when she wasn't there was pretty disgusting. I said, 'Look, it's not like we were discussing it, right – it was *him*, and I said nothing, nothing at all. I thought it was really crap, him talking about it. But I suppose he just wants to make sure you're all right, that's all. He does care about you. You know what people are like.'

Slowly, slowly, like she was forgiving me, slowly she turned over towards me on the faded Superman duvet, and all the buttons of her shirt were undone. I couldn't see anything, only the smooth brown skin of her stomach and tight hole of her belly-button and the smooth pale skin slightly damp with the heat between her tits, but her buttons were all undone, all the way down, and she didn't have a bra on. Her hip sunk into the duvet as she turned. 'Do *you* think I'm too young to have sex?' she asked, in a lazy, furry voice, like she was falling asleep. Her hair was in her eyes, but she didn't shake it out. And with her one bare foot she toed off her other shoe, and it lay there, the shoe, on the bed, the red straps falling loose.

The red leggings she wore only came down just under her knees. One of the legs had rolled up slightly by itself, so you could see the hollow at the base of her knee.

'Well, *do* you?' she snapped, springing open her eyes.

It made me jump – like, for a moment I'd forgotten I was there, it all seemed so distant and odd and sleepy and far-away; I forgot I was there, a part of this weird scene, a part of what was going on. I thought I was just an observer.

'*Do* you?'

'I don't . . . know.' My voice was far-off, like I'd spoken too quietly or was going deaf. There were plenty of girls her age and younger who did it – had proper boyfriends and cried when they split up. Old enough? Jesus, there were twelve-year-olds who liked to mess about, would let weak-minded fascinated boys look down their bras and in their pants for two, three quid. But Eleanor . . . I think she was talking about the real thing, neither love nor messing about, but the real thing, sex like in the magazines, where girls lay back and opened their legs and men . . . observed.

The sun coming through the square panes of glass lay over her like a handful of cream napkins dropped over her body. She shook the shirt off one shoulder and it fell towards the bed, and I could see her breast. It was so small and so pale, I wanted to cover it with my hand. I thought she was beauti-ful, Eleanor. She was beautiful – beautiful with her beautiful face and beautiful curls and beautiful eyes; and I thought she was gorgeous, and cute, and sweet. But even that summer, when I young, I could see how young she was. She didn't have the breasts of the fat, fun girls, swingy and squishy and squeezable tits. She was only a kid after all, with such small breasts.

'You do fancy me, Si,' she said. 'You do, you know.'

I knelt down by the bed, and I kissed her and stroked her hair. She smiled, and buttoned up her shirt. 'Not here, Si,' she said.

'No,' I said. 'Not here.'

I was in the kitchen making tea. The french windows were open: sun and the polluting hum of Camden cars hung round us. My nan was knitting, saying, 'Put enough tea in the pot for once.' I was feeling OK.

The kettle boiled. Someone was tapping on the glass panel of the front door. I squeezed past the new (old) pram to get to the door. It was like that all over our flat now – once there'd been room for us to move around, but after three days the alien in the cot'd seized so much of the available space that the rest of us were living out our humble lives squashed up against the walls.

It was Danny. He came into the sun-filled peace of our house like a blast of dark cold air.

'We need to talk,' he said, stopping in the hall. He looked into the empty pram. 'We need to talk *now*.'

'I know,' I said.

He said angrily to me, 'Why didn't you tell me your mum had the baby? Like everyone else keeps telling me. It's like I'm dead, or something. Aren't I your mate? Eleanor's been round. Luke's been round. Viv. Fucking everyone. What's the fucking matter with you? Aren't I your mate?'

'All right,' I said. 'All right. I didn't *ask* them round.'

'Why didn't you tell me?'

'You know why I didn't, Danny – you know why not.'

'Like, *why*?'

'Like . . . you know why.'

'When you rang me . . . You could have said – I'm not a fucking kid . . .' He kept letting out his breath like he was exhausted. Then he said, 'Born on the same day? They could have been twins. Little twin sisters.'

I said, 'It was sort of . . .'

'Everyone else knew. You made me look a moron. Why didn't you *tell* me? I'm your fucking mate.'

He felt like shit, and I didn't know how to make him feel better. 'Danny, I really . . .'

'Yeah, well, anyway, I just came round to say congratulations and all that,' he said, hurriedly.

'Is that Danny come to see the baby?' called my nan.

'Do you want to see her?'

'We need to talk,' he said, loudly, as if he'd only just come in the door. I think he really was nearly out of his mind.

I took him into the garden. As we passed through the kitchen, my nan said, 'Come to see the baby, Danny?' Danny kept shivering in short rattling bursts. A cat was collapsed in our path. We stepped over it and went to stand at the back of the garden, red flowers and green stuff heaving out of barrels, falling, drying, on the concrete around us. Danny lit a fag in a hurry, scattering matches by opening the box upside-down.

'Go on,' I said.

'We have to do it right away,' he said, lighting the fag, head down.

'Why?' I asked, sounding cool.

'I shouldn't have left it so long,' he said. 'If I'd done it before, she wouldn't be dead.' He meant his sister. He put his hands to his face, the cigarette poking through his fingers, and gasped. I couldn't say anything, not without getting in the way. He took down his hands, calm. 'Anyway, we have to do it before my mum gets out of hospital,' he said, taking a drag. 'Before she does something stupid like go back to him and get herself fucking killed. Anyway, I wouldn't want her around when we kill him. She'll get upset. I don't want her knowing anyway. We have to do it before she gets out. That gives us a couple of days at the most.'

'Surely they won't let her out so soon?' All I could think, really calmly, was, I have to make myself some time here. I thought, This is too soon. I wanted him to give me some time.

'She'll discharge herself as soon as she can walk – she always does,' said Danny, despairing of her. 'Crippled, bashed up, in bits and still bleeding – straight back to him, I tell you, Si –'

I remembered how she'd looked in Danny's house. I

[81]

remembered the dead baby, washed out of her on a river of blood. And I felt again the blinding anger I'd felt, standing alone in the hospital corridor – felt it again. My stomach tightened up. I was filled with the intensity of his rage almost as much as he was, because the intensity of his rage was partly mine: it was my fate after all. I'd sworn it in the hospital. I was going to help my best friend save his mother and avenge his dead sister. Surely some people don't deserve to live? That's what I said to myself, standing in the garden with the red flowers moulting over my trainers.

'In the next couple of days, then,' I said.

'Tomorrow night,' said Danny. Then he added, 'Or tonight.'

'Tomorrow,' I said quickly, suddenly shocked by how it sounded when brought forward into real time. 'We have to be prepared.'

He laughed, just a hard noise in his throat. 'Oh, I'm prepared,' he said. 'I've been prepared for a *long* fucking time. I just wish I'd done it before, that's all.'

'We don't want to get caught.'

'Yeah, right,' he said.

'Danny, we don't.'

'No, right.'

I knew then he didn't really care about that bit of it, and I came over all cold. It's a pretty scary business, planning a murder with someone who doesn't care what happens to them next. My advice would be to anyone: don't do it.

'We need a plan,' I said. 'We can't do this without a plan.'

He made an impatient gesture. 'Sure.'

'We need to sit down and work it out.'

'OK, OK.'

'Come on, Danny . . .'

'OK, OK – we'll get Eleanor, and we'll do it.'

'Eleanor?' Her name knocked me back. Maybe I'd thought with me in, Eleanor'd be out – like she'd been just a substitute for me in Danny's game, and there was no need for her now I'd come running on to the cheer of the crowd. No, it wasn't only that: after she'd unbuttoned her shirt on the faded Superman duvet of my childhood, I'd taken her and stored her in a completely separate part of my head – a secret part, a dream part, a place where I stood and stared and thought about it; like when I was a little kid watching the polar bears swim, bubbling under water through the thick underground glass at Chessington Zoo, and, OK, they were real, but not in *my* world they weren't. In my world they were just amazing things to be observed. With Eleanor, it was like I'd forgotten her existence – not forgotten *her*, just forgotten her existence.

'Eleanor – still?' I said.

He looked taken aback, amazed by my innocence in the art of murder, and threw his fag end aside into the red flowers. 'She has to go to the door and knock,' he said. 'He doesn't know her, don't you see? I've it all worked out, right. She has to go to the door and knock.'

'Oh, yes. I see,' I said. 'I see. I see.'

My mum stood at the french windows in her dressing gown, calling, holding out the baby. She went, 'Come and look at her, Danny! She's beautiful! Really lovely!'

He stood with his arms by his sides, staring at the squashed, contented child, dreaming a little dream of the red wet womb. 'What's her name?'

'Sophie.' She looked past him at me, a bit pissed off. 'You are the dopiest git.'

'No, he said,' lied Danny. 'I forgot.' He stood looking down at her. 'Sophie. Yeah, I remember. She's a girl. She's cute. Like a little doll.' He said, 'Si, come for a walk?'

'Yeah.' I wanted to get him out of there, anyway.

'It's no good, Louise, trying to get them interested. Boys,' said my nan, not pulling in her chair as we squeezed past. 'They think all babies look the same. Mind you,' she said, looking up from her knitting, recognizing a good wind-up when she saw one, 'it's not much better when they grow up into men, is it, Louise? They all run when they see a baby.'

'It was ages before I realized my dad couldn't possibly've

[83]

been old enough to die in the war,' Louise said to me and Danny.

'He died in the war?' asked Danny, politely.

'I *never* said that!' snapped my nan, rattling her needles like an ambushed porcupine.

I was wrong about Danny. He really had it all thought out.

'What we need to do, right, is you and me, right, hide round by the bins and Eleanor knocks on the door, right, and asks for some gear, right, and he opens the door wide, then she steps aside, like she's looking for her money or something, right, and you and me rush in and jump him, and you hold him down, Si, and I'll . . .'

As a plan there was no faulting it. What I mean is, in a way it was so bad it made me feel more secure – like, this is *never* going to happen, right. But it was terrifying, these thinly spread so-called plans.

'You hold him down and I'll . . .'

'Kill him,' said Eleanor. 'Kill him.' She wriggled about on the hot dry grass, tugging at her sleeves and scratching in her curls.

We'd gone to her rich-bastard's house (Danny gob-smacked) but she hadn't been there. Only her smaller holo-gram'd opened the door – Debbie, complaining, 'You're Eleanor's *boyfriend*,' and screwing up her nose so her glasses rose and fell. Out of sight, a woman shouted, 'If you see her, tell her to come *home*!'

We found Eleanor up on the hill, poised above London, sideways on to the crowd, chin on hands, moody about some-thing she wouldn't say. All the way walking up to her I was watching her, sussing it out, thinking about kissing her hair as she lay on my bed and said, 'Not here.' 'Not here,' I'd said as well. And so, if not here, where? And when, Eleanor – when? You wouldn't believe how much I'd this sudden urge to tell Danny about it. But I couldn't do that – talking it over like a fisherman, like: her tits were *how* big? *This* big (indicating with both hands – a definite lie). Not about her, anyway. I thought she'd say something, or look something, to me about it, help me out, but she was moody and far away from us and I was left without a sign. However, she cheered up right away at the prospect of imminent murder. One thing that got her going, all right: death.

'I can hold him down, too. Can I have a knife? I can have one in a bag, with the money.'

'Supposing he doesn't open the door? Supposing he puts it on a chain or something?'

'No,' said Danny. 'He'll see her and he'll think she's safe.'

'What do you mean, safe?' asked Eleanor, pissed off.

'Like, you're just . . . a girl,' said Danny. He looked at her tanned delicate legs. She was wearing her cut-offs. 'You're a girl.' He kept looking at her legs.

'He'll soon find out what this girl's like,' said Eleanor, smiling at him, pulling up chunks of dying grass. 'I'm going to stab him too.'

Danny said anxiously, 'No, you can't. You're just there to get him to open the door. *I'm* the murderer.' Right out loud on Primrose Hill – right out: *I'm* the murderer.

I looked round anxiously at the crowd, but nobody looked up, asked 'murderer?' or anything. It was like we weren't in the same space as them any more, like we were invisible, inaudible – could shout out 'murder' and not be heard – wave dripping knives and not be seen. They were all there, as ever, listening to music and drinking cans of lager, chilling out with spliffs in hand. They were all around, lolling on our high island above the warm polluted city sea, but we were no longer with them. It was us who'd disappeared. We sat apart, not talking as we once'd done about poetry and stuff, but talking about bitterness and evil, and now planning to live it. Not lying on our backs in the sun, but sitting hunched up and heads down, like we were the only humans washed up on this island of peaceful, happy animals.

'*I'm* the murderer,' cried Danny.

[85]

I thought to myself, Yeah, and I'm the murderer's accomplice. Then it came to me in a blinding, cowardly flash of inspiration: I can lie to the court. Say I didn't know Danny meant to kill him. I'm young. It'll be all right. Then I thought, We won't get caught. Who cares about a dealer's death, late at night on a rough estate? What does his life mean to anyone, anyway? Who cares if he lives or dies? Apart from Danny's mum and the people he deals to, and they'd be better off without him even if they don't know it. We were making the right choice for them. I pulled off my top in the heat. The boiling city at the foot of our hill sent columns of shimmering steam into the sky. The sun was burning a hole into the top of my head, like it was being directed through a magnifying glass. I draped my top over my head and tried to listen to the mad, mad conversation Danny and Eleanor were having.

Eleanor said, in the spirit of one-up-manship, 'Well, I'm going to be a murderer, too, soon. Me and Si are going to push my uncle Richard off his boat in the middle of the Mediterranean, aren't we, Si? The sharks'll eat him. You'll see.'

It was pissing me off, the way I was always condemned to a secondary role in all these elaborate crimes of passion.

Danny got annoyed with her: 'Look, this isn't a fucking game, Eleanor. We're doing this tomorrow night, right. We have to talk about it. It's not a game. It's going to happen.'

I said, 'It's going to happen.' I said it aloud, experimenting with the sound of the words, tossing them around, feeling their weight. 'It's going to happen.' But it didn't sound very convincing, not while we were sitting on the top of the hill in the sun, not with that nice hippy crowd hanging about, even if they were on a different planet. 'It's going to happen,' I said again. And I thought, Is it true? Is it going to happen? Like a child asking if they were going to die. Yes, dear, you are – in formal terms, it's the truth. But in your heart of hearts you know it's a lie.

'We need to take a look at the place,' I said. 'I mean, where are the bins and things? It'll be difficult in the dark, if we have to look. We have to have a *plan*. We can't just rush up there and jump right in.' It was weird, the way I'd started clinging to 'plans' as a way of putting things off, stopping us rushing in. 'We can't do it without a *plan*' – I set each plan down as an obstacle between us and there. Yet each plan, completed, had to take us one step further; I was building the road into the future myself.

'OK,' said Danny. 'You're right. Let's go and look right now.'

'Now?'

'Good a time as any.' However much I tried to make it unreal, Danny still managed to make it realer by the minute. He leapt my obstacles like he didn't even see them.

He lived in Kilburn, the boyfriend, in a grotty estate of low-rise redbrick maisonettes where the grass between the tarmac strips was more broken glass than grass – so much so, the grass reflected the sun. Even as we got there some five-year-old was encouraging a blond, slightly older boy to smash a bottle against a concrete bin. The other boy got his cheek cut by a flying piece of glass and ran off crying and bleeding. I didn't like the place. It was classic wrong territory stuff. We shouldn't've been there. There were too many older kids hanging around various corners who looked bored and pissed off and aggressively white (like, not just white – we were white – but white and *meaning* it). One of them stepped in front of Danny. Instantly I realized what I hadn't thought of when I suggested coming – that even though his mum lived there, Danny hadn't been to the estate often enough for anyone to recognize him, and especially not enough to have territorial rights, so it looked like we were in deep shit. The kid grabbed the baseball cap off of Danny's head. I have to tell you, Danny goes ape-shit if someone nicks his precious fucking cap, and there were (quick count) eleven of them and three of us, including Eleanor, who would no doubt run for it. So then I knew, with fatalistic sadness, we were all going to die, quite innocently, before doing a thing.

[87]

'Where you goin'?' said the kid (he wasn't asking – just challenging). He was a lot shorter than Danny, pale, plump and pimpled like a defrosted turkey leg. He was the short, ugly, spotty-faced one, the one they send in first, the one with the shrill, irritating voice so you're really tempted to land him one, so all the rest can pile in. Danny made a grab for his cap. The kid waved it around and spat on the ground, real spit – nasty loose creamy phlegm. 'Where you goin'?'

'Fuck you,' said Danny. And the whole crowd of bored spotty kids drew themselves up as one. 'I'm goin' to see . . .' and he named his mum's boyfriend by his real name. And they all faded away like smoke. They knew that name, all right. He must of been quite someone on that estate, to make a gang of teenage kids afraid.

'That showed 'em,' said Danny, well pleased, picking up his cap from where the little kid'd hurriedly fucked it on to the ground. And for a good long moment I, too, was glad to be alive. But then I thought about it and panicked.

'What the fuck d'you do that for?'

'What?'

'Tell them his name? Now the police'll be able to find out we were looking for him – what's it going to look like if he turns up dead?'

'Oh, that lot won't say *nothing*,' said Danny. 'Get real.'

'*When* he turns up dead,' said Eleanor, too loudly.

'Fucking shut up! No, *you* get real – what've they got to do all day except hang about and talk about who's doing what in this shite place?'

'They won't talk to the police. They know I'll be back for them if they do,' said Danny, and in my racing mind, wet with adrenalin, I saw in vivid colour an estate littered with teenage bodies in designer jeans, bleeding from their upper halves like liquid pours from broken bottles, Danny and me standing over them, machine guns loosely dangling . . . just more unswept broken rubbish . . . Fucking hell, what a picture! How lovely, how liberating, how *free* it would feel, just to kill them all . . . How fucking crazy was I now? In my head, getting like the rest, getting like the arseholes in YSL jeans.

'Oh, yeah – how the fuck're they going to know that?'

'Anyway, they don't know who we are. Nobody knows we're going to've anything to do with it, right? Calm down, man. It's OK. Really, it's OK.'

'Shit, Danny, who's that?'

'What, what?' hissed Eleanor, staring round.

He'd come out of nowhere and I knew from the way Danny stood so still that I was right and it was him. Even Eleanor was speechless. We were trapped in the open, half-way across the glass-filled, crunchy, glittering grass beneath a shaky solitary swing. I'd been holding the upright of the swing with one hand, and my grip tightened, and the weak metal creaked. Eleanor was sat on the swing, her toes pointed forward, head frozen on one side. There we were in full view, and there was he, swinging his way across the tar-mac between the redbrick flats, head down, right shoulder to us as we stood staring. Why hadn't we expected to find him here, on his home territory? It wasn't as if he went out to work. Our unthought-out carelessness frightened me almost as much as this small thin man's presence. We should've just driven on to the estate with a loud hailer like we were running for election.

'Just look at him,' whispered Danny. 'The bastard.'

There wasn't much of him to look at – short and thin, unwashed hair, his hands in the pockets of his dirty jacket, walking rapidly, looking at the ground – probably trying to avoid the dog shit, which was everywhere. He never looked up, never saw us standing there in the open, in broad daylight – never even saw us, because he was so fucking busy trying not to step in the shit. And he was gone.

'Let's go,' said Danny. We hadn't looked at where me and him were going to hide, or studied our plans. I figured we could do that tomorrow night. We got back out on Abbey Road, and walked on rapidly without waiting for a bus.

'That was *him*?' asked Eleanor. 'That guy?'

'Yeah, he's it,' I said.

She thought about it. She said after a while, 'He's short, isn't he?'

I wondered how she'd pictured him before. She'd never even seen the man she longed to kill. I imagined she was disturbed by how small and actually fragile-looking he was. Probably the man in her head had been a big, ugly, killable sort of guy. Things'd started to come real for her now. Danny'd gone charging on ahead. I walked beside her, watching her expression. She was still wearing long sleeves, over her thin slashed arms.

'What, d'you feel bad – him being short? Does it make you feel bad about doing him in?'

She said, 'No, I'm thinking it's lucky, him being small. It'll make it easier for us to hold him down, won't it?'

I really didn't get her, you know; I got her less and less. She seemed so far away from my world. I was kind of into her, but I didn't really know if I wanted to follow her, not to the place she was in: her strange, distant place. I thought maybe something was seriously wrong in her head.

Suddenly she cried, 'I told you – you wouldn't listen!'

'Did what?'

She said fiercely, like I was being deliberately thick, 'I *said* we should kill him before he killed the baby. And now she's *dead*!' She said, her eyes gone mad like a cat's as she walked along, 'I know *all* about what he's like.'

I moved away, staring at her, sort of scared by her, I don't know why: it felt as if she knew things she couldn't know – a psychic making terrible predictions. She came after me relentlessly, taking my arm in both hers and hugging it tight against her like a parcel of something she was carrying home.

'I was right about him, wasn't I?' she asked, looking intently up into my face. 'You should've listened, shouldn't you, Si?'

And it was true, of course – she was right. But I'd thought she was just a bored, spoilt kind of kid who liked to stir things up, get something going, get involved in something weird for the hell of it.

'Well, then,' she said, hanging on me heavily, as if she could read my mind.

Danny headed straight for the hill, but he didn't climb it. He sat down on a bench under some trees at the foot of the hill and waited for us to catch up.

'Let's go up,' I said.

'Next time I climb the hill,' said Danny, looking up to the top, 'he'll be dead, right. We'll have a celebration. A big fucking celebration party. I don't want to climb back up till then. It's only one day, right?' He was unnaturally flushed, in patches, and breathing hard.

'Are you all right?' I asked. Danny'd had asthma as a little kid, but not for years. But he was breathing badly.

'Fine,' he said. 'Fine.' He closed his eyes and took deep breaths through his nose and pressed his hands down on his knees to keep them from shaking. Up till now I'd just thought about how scared I was by the whole thing – now I thought, Jesus, Danny is shit-scared too. Only Eleanor seemed cool, and I thought maybe she was going mad.

'We don't have to do this,' I said.

His dark-lashed eyes shot open and he said angrily, 'Well, *you* pull out if you like, mate.'

'Fuck's sake, Danny – I just thought you looked ill, all right?' I said. 'Nothing changes.'

'Yeah, right,' he said, closing his eyes again, softly. 'Nothing changes.'

'We have to meet,' said Eleanor. 'Early on.'

Danny, with his eyes shut, said, 'No. How much time do we need? It can't be that fucking hard. How long's it going to take? We're not going to be at it all fucking night, I suppose. Just kill him and go, that's all.'

'Kill'n'go,' said Eleanor, humming a little tune. 'Kill'n'go.'

She conducted herself with both forefingers, not moving her hands.

Danny said, 'We'll be back long before anyone wakes up. You know, like, if it comes to it, we just want to've been asleep all night, right? Not that anyone's going to ask.'

'And the next day?' I said.

He looked at me, like trying to figure out what I meant by that. 'What? Next day will be next day, innit? One more fucking day in our boring lives. Just he'll be dead, and that'll be that, and we can just get on with it.'

'Right,' I said.

'The world will be a better place,' he said, like he'd thought about it and this was his answer.

'Oh, yeah, sure,' said Eleanor.

'What?' asked Danny.

'Yeah, sure,' she said, with a different meaning. 'I'll meet you here. When'll I meet you?'

'Two,' said Danny. He stood up and examined his pockets. 'Come round tomorrow, Si. Stay over, right?'

To my surprise he walked off without saying anything else, looking into the palm of his hand like he'd found some change. Just walked off – how could that be it? Were there to be no more plans? Were we standing on the edge without a fence? I wanted to call him back, like: Hey! Oi! You! I've not finished speaking to you! Like I was a teacher and he one of those independent, strong-minded, doomed-to-failure kids who just walk out of classrooms when they've had enough. Hey – you! Gone.

'Si,' said Eleanor. 'Si!'

Anyway, it was late. I had to be getting back. The sky was going past dusk to night-time orange.

'Come up the hill,' said Eleanor.

'It's getting late,' I said. It wasn't that late. I wanted to be by myself, think about this weird fucking mess we'd got ourselves into, track back the journey in my head from where we started – that hot lovely night with all the crowd

there on Primrose Hill when nothing was real, I knew now –
to here. I wanted to be by myself, I needed to figure out how
the film'd left the screen and come into the fucking cinema.

'Come up the hill,' said Eleanor.

'OK,' I said.

People were stoned when we arrived. Big Al'd been rolling a
lot of spliffs. The air was sweet. Their smiles were sweet, lit by
orange flames. Tape-deck Martin welcomed us: 'Hi! Here!
Want a drag?' Viv said, 'Go on, have a toke.' They were all
feeling both lazy and silly – heavy bodies with very light
heads.

I thought it was just what I needed to stop my brain going
round, the same thought trekking round and round like a
goldfish in a bowl, acting surprised every third second (not a
very interesting thought, by the way, it just sort of went, 'Oh
. . . shit . . . '). The draw slowed it down to every four seconds.
Eleanor had some, choked and got the giggles. She was a real
kid sometimes.

'Come over here,' she said.

'Oh . . .'

'Come under the trees.'

I checked around. They wouldn't have noticed if I'd run
around shouting, 'Look at me – I'm going under the trees.'

I could hardly see her. She said, 'Sit down. Sit down.' It
was cooler and darker and damper, under the trees.

'I thought Danny seemed pretty fucking nervous,' I said.

She said, 'Yeah.'

'Not surprising.'

'Oh,' she said, 'it'll be all right.'

'You think?'

'After tomorrow night, it'll be all right.'

'What?'

'After tomorrow night.'

I was sat, more like squatting, fingering the invisible grass.
'I don't think it's really going to happen – do you?' I really

[93]

wanted to know how she was thinking about it, gamewise – or not.

She thought I was being funny. 'What? You are *weird*, Si. You say the weirdest things. Come here.'

I shuffled vaguely on my doubled-up knees, going nowhere. 'You really think?'

'When are you ever going to stop talking?' she said. 'It's *done* now. When are you ever going to stop talking, and give me a hug?'

I stood up and looked out from between the trees. It'd come pretty dark. I could see orange cigarette ends jogging about, trailing off down the hill. The draw must've run out. I think they were off to someone's house – a party to which I was certainly invited. But I didn't follow them. I stood looking out from between the trees like a lonely neighbour behind a curtain. 'They're all going,' I said.

'Oh, come and sit down,' she said, like she was calling me away from the window. 'What's the matter with you?'

I nearly laughed. 'What's the matter with me – are you serious?'

'Come and sit down.'

So I did. A shallow lukewarm breeze was blowing, and the tops of the trees started moving in it with a sound like tissue paper tearing.

'That's better,' she said. 'You're all tensed up.'

'Maybe we should call it a night,' I said, settling my back against an uncomfortable trunk.

'I know a good way to relax,' she said. She rolled over the grass and early dead leaves towards me and put her arms around my waist, so her head was face down in my lap. Then she brought round her hands and started undoing my flies. I didn't move. It was a dream thing. Every bit of me was just the sensation of where she was, the press of her stomach against my knees, the weight of her slashed forearms on my thighs, the struggle of her fingers with each stiff button. My prick stood up and cried for air. I leant my head back into the tree and put my hand gently on top of her head, and it was like I was pushing her down on me. 'Eleanor . . .' I said. 'Oh, Eleanor . . .'

She twisted her face to one side, and because her skin was pale, I could see her grinning like a child's monster grins under the bed. 'I give great head,' she said, forcing her little fingers through the opening, looking up at me from bottom-less eyes. 'What I do is, I cover my teeth with my lips and make my mouth soft and tight.'

I knelt upright, spilling her off my lap.

She knelt up too, on the rustling ground. She was ruffled, offended, hands on hips. 'What, you think I'm going to *bite* it? I just told you . . .'

'No! Look . . .'

'Everyone goes for blow jobs. Don't you like me? . . . I asked you on holiday . . . Don't you *like* me? Just close your eyes and . . . fuck's sake, let's get this over with!'

'Oh, Eleanor . . .'

'Let me suck you off.'

Oh, god, why not? I *wanted* to. She was offering it me on a plate, wasn't she? What was I, some sad fuck soft in the prick as well as in the head?

But oh, her lips, drawn down over those little white teeth – you should've seen her, like she'd become an old woman with no teeth; I never told you how cute her mouth was to me, her childish mouth with its pointed arch – I'd so much wanted to kiss it all along, and now she talked about it like it was some hole, and her lips only there as pink flaps of flesh to cover the razor edges of her teeth and make her mouth, her kissable mouth, into this smooth dark *hole*: this grim, soft, toothless tunnel down to her gut.

She said impatiently, dismissive, flopping down on her back, 'Oh, well, you can do it to *me* if you prefer.'

'Eleanor . . .'

'Fuck me, Si – for fuck's sake get *on* with it!' She leant up on her elbow, getting furious now. Before I'd time to even move, she bounced up on to her knees again. 'Why are you fucking about? What's *with* you? I'm so sick of you!' With each accusing cry her voice jumped up. She grabbed her little-girl curls and tugged at them like she would rip them right out of their soft sockets. Then, leaping on to her feet and running round in a tight angry circle like a tormented dog on a leash, she screamed hysterically, *'Why won't you fuck me?'*

I didn't know what I was seeing. I knelt there, doing up my flies, feeling frightened and sad. She just kept running, round and round in this tiny circle, inside the trees. I stood up and grabbed her and lifted her up, and for a few seconds her feet in trainers but no socks kept running aimlessly like a dog does, lying on his side in his sleep. I put her down. She looked around, scared. 'There's someone watching us,' she said, clinging to me. 'Someone big. Someone bad.'

'There's no one here, Eleanor – just us,' I said, my arms around her.

She kept looking over my arms, left and right, staring at dark nothings.

'There's someone watching us,' she said. 'He's got an axe.'

I knew no one was there. But, holding her shaking body, I, too, could feel the madman's terrifying presence, like I was picking it up from her: bad vibes.

'Stop it, Eleanor.'

The trees shushed us. She held me tight enough to leave fingerprints. 'He's moving towards us . . .'

'It's the trees, Eleanor – it's the *trees* . . .'

She trembled in my arms – I felt her blood going rushing round. She pressed her head into my neck, sighing, vibrating like the trees themselves. Was there bad shit in that joint? But no – I'd smoked the same one – it was just grass. I wondered if she'd taken something weird without me knowing about it, and now it was wearing off. 'You all right, Eleanor? You want to go home now?'

'You come with me,' she said, mouthing wet against my cooling skin. 'You gotta come with me, Si.'

Down the black hill we walked hand in hand towards the city's sparkling orange sea, like drowned kids wandering down a beach in hell.

Crossing Adelaide Road towards her house, I asked, 'Will your parents be worried?' It just struck me it might be a bit late for someone in that sort of house.

'No, they don't mind,' she said. She was walking a bit funny, between stiff and floppy, like cardboard. She added, 'They're not there, anyway. They've gone away.'

'You by yourself?' We'd stopped on the opposite side of the road from her house. The lights were all on.

She said, like slightly puzzled, 'Yes,' but added, rubbing her forehead, 'no. Richard's staying.'

'To look after you?'

'Just staying. He always does when he's in London.'

'Maybe he'll be worried,' I said.

'Well,' she said, like: maybe so, don't give a fuck.

She'd her key in her pocket, and crossed the quiet road. I stood and watched, leaning back slightly into a hedge. I just wanted to see she was OK. Like the first time I'd been to her house, the door opened before she'd got her key in the lock. He stood there in the bright hall, looking out, a quick left-right, too blinded by light to see me standing opposite in the dark, drawing her towards him with one hand on her shoulder. Because the road was so quiet, I heard him say, 'Jesus, I've been worried. Where've you been? I nearly called the police.'

'Sorry,' she said.

'I waited and waited . . . it's such a relief to see you . . . Oh, god, Eleanor . . .' And in desperation he pulled her more urgently into the hall, letting go the door. It didn't swing shut. As she stumbled towards him he folded her into his arms, closing his eyes; sticking out his foot, kicking shut the door.

I thought, I didn't see anything. It was nothing. It was OK. I ran all the way down Chalk Farm Road towards Camden

Town. Some tall guy tried to stop me to mug me on the way, but I was in too much of a hurry. By the time I got home I'd made myself sick with running.

Seven

I wouldn't let him in.

He stood in the basement area in the raging hot August morning, going, 'Oh, come *on*, Si.'

'What do *you* care?' I said.

'I do. I do care. I got up really fucking early to get here,' he said. It was eleven o'clock. The crack of Andy's dawn. He held out a small exhausted-looking rabbit, with £2.99 stuck to its ear. 'A present,' he said.

'For me?'

He looked worried. Did I really expect and want him to give me a crappy old cheapo toy rabbit? Would I be upset if he said, 'No, it's not for you, it's for *my* child'? Was I joking? Would I be offended if he took me seriously and said, 'Yes, it's for you, dear Si, I've been thinking of you . . . really missed you'? Had he come to the wrong house? Was there a way out? Listen hard, and you could hear the rusty wheels in his head turning, like, maybe a full quarter-turn before they seized up.

'I . . .' He absent-mindedly tightened his long-fingered grip on the rabbit, which in protest squeaked so loud it startled him into apologizing – to the rabbit, that is: 'Shit, I'm really sorry, man,' he said, looking it anxiously in the face. Fuck's sake! He'd apologize to a rabbit, but not to me.

I said, 'What the fuck are you doing?'

'Well, is Louise – you know, your mum – is she in?'

'She's asleep. She's been up all night.' (It was a lie. She was dossing about in bed reading crap magazines.) 'She's totally exhausted.'

He shuffled about, faking wrinkly concern. 'I, like, thought

I could give her some support.' For fuck's sake! Not again!

Behind me in the kitchen my nan shouted out, 'Who *is* it? Jehovahs? Don't talk to them – slam the fucking door!'

Andy looked sick. The rabbit, feeling the pressure, let out a long, shrill, panic-stricken shriek.

'Maybe I better . . .' he said, putting one foot delicately behind the other.

'Oh, go on, come in, then.' I flung the door open so wide it crashed off the wall. He had to follow me.

My nan went, hands squarely on hips, like, 'Oh, so it's the great five-minute father.'

Andy said, 'Oh, hi, Gloria – fancy seeing you here.' Bad move, mate.

'Fancy seeing *me* here?' she repeated, bug-eyed, like: totally fucking astonished. '*Me?* Fancy seeing *you* here! I don't leave it four whole fucking days before I find out what my own daughter looks like!'

Andy, sulking, perched the rabbit on the table in the centre of her volcanic knitting. 'Kind of saw her before you did, man.'

'Don't be ridiculous,' said my nan, like she'd smelt shit.

'Did so. Birth, man – real or what?' He was getting distracted by the pile of puke-pink baby wear, gazing at it dazzled, tucking his sweat-wet hair behind one ear.

'You did *what*?' She was still really pissed off with Louise for not having phoned her for the birth.

'Yeah, kind of sorry not to see you there, actually, Gloria. Thought you were waiting by the phone for the call.' He peered again, hesitantly, at the knitted pile. 'Man, is this what . . . Jesus!'

My nan yelled, raising her bright pink chin, 'Louise!'

Andy picked up the rabbit and, looking straight at me, squeezed a small triumphant squeak. It was quite funny, really.

'*Louise!*' They were so fucking childish. What did it matter who was where when? People're so fucking territorial all the time. (Andy taking *my* chair at Louise's side.) Beating each other up just for crossing into their street.

As for me, you know, good old Si – let's see, what did I have on that day? Oh, yeah – just tangled up in some weird murder plot. My mum swanned around in her dressing gown, baby in arms, raising her fluffy red eyebrows at me while Andy and Gloria bitched – she raised her eyebrows at me and winked, like we were the only adults in the room. Couldn't she see me standing here? Look at me – unable to get the image of a dead baby out of my head, or Danny's mum with her baseball-bat-sized bruises, unable to get the image of a dead little girl . . . of a mad living girl, walking down to an orange sea . . . walking into the light . . . and him . . . don't even think about it. Yeah, I wanted to scream at them to shut the fuck up all right.

When Andy decided to show his support by taking Sophie for a walk, I went with him to make sure he didn't forget what he was doing and leave her in the park or something ('It all got too heavy for me, man'). I needed to get out of the place, anyway.

His long hair draping forward into the pram, hunched over as he pushed because the handle was too low for him, he kept poking the sleeping baby gently with his finger, pulling the sheet back, touching her naked face, prodding, making split-second dents in her upturned cheek. 'It's so amazing, man,' he said. 'So incredibly weird, so, like, *intense*.'

'We better get back,' I said, after hours of this crap.

'We hardly got out,' he said. 'Come on – it's only been ten minutes – we can get a cup of tea somewhere. She's asleep, isn't she? This is really cool.'

'We better get back,' I said. 'If you wake her up, she'll scream.' The truth is, which is pretty sick – I couldn't really handle him touching Sophie. I knew it was only Andy, but in my head I kept going, What does he want, touching her like that? Poor old Andy – if he'd guessed, he'd've been really shocked. 'But I'm her *dad*! How could I hurt her?' Yeah, right.

How ever could you? He never could. I know he couldn't. He knew he couldn't. How can you know? What was he up to, Richard, pulling Eleanor in the door like that? What did I see? Nothing, I guess. It was OK.

I'd said I'd be round at Danny's by seven, and I was. He was lying on his back in the lower bunk listening to some sixties stuff – Small Faces, I think, what we were all into then. After all, until Danny came up with his great fucking idea of death, this summer had been our summer of love. Yeah, and on Primrose Hill, the hill Danny wouldn't climb until he'd done his thing, our summer of love was still going on without us – I'd almost forgotten that, until I heard him playing that music. It was weird, sad, hearing it. He was lying there with his eyes shut, thinking.

I said, 'All right, Danny?'

'All right, yeah.'

'Everything OK?'

'Yep.'

I sat down on the floor on his old Dennis the Menace bean-bag (same age as my Superman duvet), got my arse comfortable and listened to the album right through. Near me, against the wall, was a stack of old *Beano*s. He used to keep every copy, and even though he hadn't bought them for years, he never got round to chucking them out. I sat leafing through, for a laugh. Everything used to be Dennis the Menace with Danny, back when he was a little kid: T-shirts, socks, pencil case – it was his thing. He'd a baseball cap back then, too, with Gnasher on it. He only stopped wearing it and got the one he'd now because his head got too big. He still had the old Gnasher one in the top of a cupboard somewhere. Back when he was a little kid, when Danny grew up, he wanted to write cartoon strips for the *Beano*. He'd an idea for a strip called Norman the Nutter. He used to spend all his time in school practising drawing cartoons: Norman the Nutter beats up his best mate; Norman the Nutter has sex with his neighbour's dog – that sort of thing. He was sure the *Beano*'d go for it. I used to think they were hilarious.

'Hey, Danny,' I said. 'Remember Norman the Nutter?'

He opened his eyes towards me, then shot up on one elbow. 'Be careful with those, man,' he said. 'They're, like, collectors' items, you know.' They were filthy, with all sweets and dirt and stuff, from having been read way too many times. Collectors' items, my arse. He just didn't want to throw them out, was all.

'Remember our Norman the Nutter T-shirts?' I said. I'd forgotten them myself, until just now. It made me laugh, thinking about it.

'Jesus,' he said. We'd got a pair of white T-shirts and Danny'd spent an hour drawing on them, in black marker pen, Norman's aggressive stick-like figure, posing with his foot on the neck of his most hated enemy – Sharon the Moron, a white-haired senile old geriatric who lived down Norman's street. 'What a mad bastard *he* was.'

I sat up in the beanbag. I put the *Beano* I was reading carefully on top of the pile, lining up the edges like before. I sat with my hands holding my ankles.

'Listen, Danny . . .' I said. 'About tonight.' He said nothing. 'Listen, Danny . . .' I really felt I had to say this. 'Tonight . . . We're not really going to *do* it, are we? I mean, actually *do* it . . . You know what I mean . . .'

Dreamily, he said, 'It's funny, but Norman the Nutter was kind of based on him.'

I was shocked, because I'd always had a soft spot for Norman. 'Really?'

'Before I found out what he was really like, you know,' he said. 'Like beating my mum up and stuff. Before I went and lived there. You know when I went and lived with her, up Kilburn?'

'Yeah.'

He shuffled out a cigarette, lying on his back, staring at the upper bunk. He'd bunk beds instead of a single bed because they'd been cheap somewhere. And his grandparents thought Josie was bound to dump another child on them some time. I suppose she would've, if she'd had the chance. The emptiness of the upper bunk was like a little grave now. 'What a load of shit that was,' he said.

'I know.'

'You don't know,' he said. 'I never told you. I never told no one. You don't know what I seen.'

I said nothing. He lit the cigarette, and blew the smoke out around his head.

'You don't know. I never told you. I seen him stab her with the scissors, did I tell you that? No, I never. Great fucking scissor holes in her stomach she got. I seen the blood run down the wall like rain from the back of her head where he had her by the hair and was bashing her head off of it. I seen him break her arm in three places by stamping on it, and keeping stamping on it after it was broken the first two times. I seen him shooting up and making her beg for it for an hour, and kicking her nose in flat against her face before he give it her. Her nose was pulped, flat, red and squishy, man. She wouldn't go up the hospital though, not until he give it her. You don't know what I seen. I was just the kid in the corner crying my fucking eyes out.'

After a bit, he said, with the fag in his mouth, 'I seen things nobody ought to've seen.'

Still holding my ankles, I stared at the carpet between my parted legs.

He said, 'I was just a snotty little boy, watching it all. I couldn't do nothing to stop him.'

No, that wasn't right. He'd got it wrong. I protested: 'You hit him with a lump of wood, man!' Wasn't it part of our shared history, that act, when he hit his mum's boyfriend over the head from behind with a lump of wood, when he was only twelve? I remembered him telling me about it, proud. I was proud of him then. I wanted him to remember that. I hated the picture he was painting in my head, of the

helpless kid, just standing there, crying, unable to do anything, unable to help his own mum, just watching and crying.
Back then he was always the big man to me, a hard man. He
stuck up for me enough, when I was having a rough time over
my dad being gay. He was fierce, Danny.

'For fuck's sake,' he said. 'I was just a kid, that's all. He
didn't even fall down.' He smoked and stared up. He said, 'I
wanted to kill him, and all I had was a lump of wood. I was
just a little kid, and he was a grown-up – I hit him and he
didn't even fall down. He didn't even hit me back. He just
went to my mum, If he doesn't leave now, I'll kill him. So she
made me leave and come back here. And I had to leave her. I
had to leave her, and I knew he was going to beat her up rot-
ten, because I'd hit him with a lump of wood. I'd meant to kill
him, but he didn't even fall fucking down.'

I couldn't think of anything to say. It was just that I'd
always remembered him as the big man. But if you think
about it, way back then, he must've been only a kid after all.

'Danny . . .'

He heaved over heavily on his side towards me, at first
concentrating on rubbing out his fag in the lid of the cigarette
box, then looking up with his big heavy eyes. 'But now I'm
bigger than him,' he said. '*Now* I can stop him. I *am* going to
do him, Si. I can't let him kill my mum. I can't even let him go
on doing what he's doing to her. All right?'

'All right,' I said.

'You don't have to come,' he said. 'It's not your problem.
It's just I'm going, whatever.'

I thought of Danny, doing it alone. 'Supposing he kills
you?' I asked, in a panic.

He shrugged. He didn't give a shit. 'I'd rather be fucking
dead than go on watching, Si. If I can't stop it, I'd rather be
fucking dead.'

We listened to some more music and read comics till it was
getting on for two o'clock. I was yawning and closing my
eyes. Danny flicked off the light, and went into the bathroom

and climbed out of the window, on to the flat roof of the kitchen, down over the side. I followed him. He was carrying a shoulder-bag.

As we came up to the gates of the hill I could see her standing there, leaning under a street light with one foot tucked up behind her, bare arms folded, looking like a tart. She was delighted to see us.

'This is really cool,' she said. 'You know, about six men have been up to me, wanting a fucking blow job or something. One of them wouldn't go away till I told him I'd call the police. I said, What do you think I am – a fucking prostitute or what?'

She was wearing a really short black skirt and tights full of holes and a really tight red top, so you could see her thin stomach, and black high heels. Her belly button was a tiny black hole. Danny kept staring at it.

She said, 'Well, whatcha think, Danny boy?' All up her bare arms were her disgusting cuts and scars, looking black like they were scribbled on to her flesh with biro, and she had on black eyeliner and crimson lipstick, spread thicker than her lips. She looked . . . perfect. She said to Danny, 'Well, darling?'

Danny said, looking away now, confused, 'Well, you look like, you look like, you look great.'

'Well, thank you, young man – you can have a freebie *any* time,' she said to him, smiling and pushing her thin hips out. 'On the house.' He laughed with embarrassment, looking at me. Reaching forward, she ripped the cap off his head.

'Oi!'

He made to get it, but she put it on and danced around, giggling, and going, 'Oh, I think I'll *keep* this.'

'Come on, Eleanor, we've got to go,' he pleaded, trying to grab it, his shoulder-bag swinging about. 'Stop fucking around.'

'Can I keep it?'

'No!'

'Love you for ever, Danny. Love you for ever?' She was jumping up and down on her tiptoes all around him, her curls under the hat bouncing up and down, the black high heels clattering on the pavement.

'No!'

'Ah, come on, Danny – I like it because it smells of you – I want to *think* of you – give you a freebie?'

He stopped trying to get the hat, and stuck his hands in his pockets with a set expression. 'Fucking keep it, all right?'

She finally glanced at me, with a screwed-up smile. 'See what I mean, Si? You're all the same.' And she threw the hat back to him.

'How's your uncle?' I asked. The question just welled up out of nowhere: a sewer in the street suddenly overflowing.

She looked vague. 'Oh, it was all right,' she said, fluffing up her curls. 'He wasn't there.'

We walked to Kilburn. Danny walked by himself, ignoring us, holding his shoulder-bag against his side.

After a mile, Eleanor said her shoes were killing her. She insisted on leaning on my arm, really leaning on it, till my elbow and shoulder really fucking hurt. I tried telling her to take her shoes off, but she wouldn't listen. She kept holding on to my arm, like it was hers, leaning right into me. I wanted to get her off. I just didn't want her touching me, was all. I didn't like the way she wound up Danny. I didn't even know if it was a wind up or if she was really coming on to him. I didn't like the way she moved her hip against me as she walked, the way her childish breast rubbed up and down against my arm. I didn't like how her hair fell on my neck. Every touch of her made me sick, made me think of him, the dark man in the light – the man who pulled her in the door, while she stumbled towards him like she wanted it.

On the boyfriend's estate, half the street lights were out – we could hardly see where we were going. I made Eleanor let go of me. Her shoes banged their way across the crunching ground like hammers hitting nails. The noise they made was screaming 'come and get us!', but it was nearly three o'clock, and even the ten-year-olds had gone to bed. When Danny stopped I walked right into the back of him.

Shortarse's flat was easy to get at – it was ground floor, cut off from the flats each side by head-high concrete walls. A light shone through the glass panel in the door, which was cracked clean through but held together by the wire mesh in the glass. There was no graffiti on his door, or on the concrete wall next to the door, which was weird on a shit estate like that. The kids must've kept well away. The flat was opposite the bin site. What a great view for him when he opened the door in the morning – ten, twelve massive metal cylinders frothing over with the outpourings of the whole estate, lapped by a stinking sea of the careless rubbish which never even made it into the bins in the first place. We stood among the towering bins, our feet sinking into the soft slippery rubbish sea, the smell of stale milk rising.

Danny took a really ridiculously big cartoon-sized carving knife out his shoulder-bag and gave the empty bag to Eleanor. 'Pretend you're looking in this for money or something,' he said. 'After he opens the door.' I was frozen by the knife. I guess I kind of knew, seeing as Danny meant to stab the fucker, he must be going to have a knife. But I thought it'd be a small one – a small, thin one. Not one to make a lot of blood. Sort of discreet – an in-out job – minimum damage. Not a knife for chopping up meat. This wasn't a thin cold knife for murder. It was a fucking great angry knife, for butchering someone. It was a knife long dreamed about by a powerless weeping kid. I tried to see his face in the dark.

He said to Eleanor, his voice cracking, 'What're you doing?'

'All right, hang on,' she said, not keeping her voice down. She stood there at an angle, leaning one hand on the bin, trying to shake off a piece of carton or rubbish or something which had been speared by one of her long pointed heels.

'Well, go on, then,' he said, gripping the knife, gesturing with it.

'Go on *what*?' She was inspecting her heel, foot cocked behind her.

Danny whispered, wound up to explosion point, 'Ring the fucking *bell*.'

'Oh.' She hesitated, looking at me, smoothing down her skirt, adjusting the tight red top. 'Right.' And then she fucking did it. She just went up and did it. And I was so fucking gob-smacked and terrified right out of my fucking skin, I realize, looking back on it, I never expected her to do it. I thought she'd just stand there and make excuses and piss about, and Danny'd wave his knife around in the dark until he felt better, almost like he'd done it, and eventually we'd call our own bluff and we'd all pack up and go home and go to bed and be really relieved. That must've been how I got myself there in the first place, by being so sure we were still just kids playing a game and not adults about to alter the course of our lives. And now she'd gone and rung the bell and started it all going for real and my stomach just dropped like it does when your foot slips off the curb.

'Ssh!' whispered Danny, because I'd groaned as if I'd been punched out.

I thought rapidly, What am I going to do? What am I going to do?

She rang the bell again. It was frighteningly loud in the silent night. The estate was off the road, there were no cars driving by. Nothing could be heard except the bell, ear-splittingly shrill and loud. I thought any minute someone would fling open a window and shout us to shut the fuck up. It didn't happen. The bell again, screeching through the night, calling him, calling him to the door, calling him to his death. But nothing happened. Nothing moved. Nothing at all. The fucker was out.

Eight

I was sick with relief. My legs went like jelly. I thought, Thank
god, thank god – I was so fucking grateful, it was amazing, a
miracle – I looked up to the orange sky. Then, just as quick, it
was blindingly obvious he wasn't there – of course he wasn't
there; how could he've been there? If he'd been there, who
knows what might've happened? It wouldn't've worked out
in real life, him being there. I folded my arms tightly to stop
the trembling. Slowly, trailingly, Eleanor wandered back to
where we were. 'Not in,' she said.

'So,' I said. My voice came out in a stupid squeak, like I was
thirteen again and my voice breaking. 'That's that, then,
right? We better get off.'

'No,' said Danny.

I stared unbelievingly at him in the dark. I folded my arms
harder and harder, but my whole frame kept jerking. 'What?
What? What do you mean? He's not here, right? So what's the
point in hanging around?'

Danny said, running his fingers up and down the smooth
flat side of the knife, 'It's all right. We'll just wait for him. He'll
have to be back sometime, the bastard.' His voice was shaking
too, and he was stroking the knife like trying to calm himself.

'What, here all night?' asked Eleanor. 'It fucking stinks,
man.' She meant literally – the rubbish, not the situation. The
situation was OK by her.

'But, Danny . . .' I couldn't believe he was serious. I really
couldn't believe he didn't feel like me, bowel-shakingly grateful things'd turned out all right. 'Danny . . . You don't have
to . . .'

He wouldn't stop polishing the knife with his fingers. He bent his big black head over it. 'No, it's all right, Si – you go,' he said, between us. 'It's you don't have to stay. It's just me, that's all. I can do this OK. I didn't think I could, by myself, but I can now. Thanks for coming, man, and all that. It really helped. It's OK now. Thanks for coming, man.' He wasn't trying to wind me up, like: make me feel so bad I'd do what he wanted. He wasn't being macho; he was afraid. But he meant what he was saying. We stood in a circle of three in the centre of the bins, me watching Danny stroking his butcher's knife, Eleanor with her arms folded, mascaraed eyes half shut, leaning against a bin, pretty much ignoring what was going on. Danny suddenly made an impatient move, looking around over our heads. 'I'm going to climb up there,' he said.

'What? Where?'

On two sides of the bins was a wooden fence, and behind the back fence were flat garage rooves. He dodged off through the bins, crushing damp cardboard cartons and kicking aside cans filled with foul cocktails of whatever'd been in them and ancient rain water and long clusters of worms; he jumped up to grab the top of the fence, rolled himself up and over it on to the garage roof and flattened himself down – out of sight, I suppose – unless you were looking right at him.

'Well,' said Eleanor, rubbing her arms. 'You're not going, are you? Supposing he suddenly turns up?'

'He won't turn up,' I said.

'You're not going, are you?'

'He won't turn up,' I repeated. It wasn't a statement of belief. It was a prayer.

'Keep me company,' said Eleanor, pulling me by the arm.

I pulled my arm away, filled with a sickness at her touch that was as bad in its way as the sickness of the off-milk smell that rose around us. And yet, wouldn't you know, I stayed, crouching down with her in the abominable dark between the tall high metal wheely-bins flooding over with sodden decay. I sat with my legs bent up to my chest, the stench of the wet sticky rubbish rising up between my legs, the litter of slippery lumps, my arms clinging tight round my knees, my chin pressing on my knees, not sleepy but utterly tired to my soul, not cold but shivering uncontrollably. Eleanor squatted down too close to me. I could see the pale splash of her face and white strips of her mutilated arms. Her leg touched mine and I pulled mine quickly away, so she couldn't feel it trembling, so she couldn't touch me. I concentrated as hard as I could to stop the shivering, but however much I got it under control, my kneecaps just kept jumping. I closed my eyes. I pictured Danny lying still as stone, pressed flat on his stomach on the garage roof above us, waiting, tense, barely breathing, hunter in the tree waiting for the beast, waiting for the object of his lust to kill. In the dense undergrowth beneath I crouched gagging, and I thought, What am I doing? Why am I still here? Why don't I just go? Nobody's going to stop me.

Eleanor was whispering.

I opened my eyes, puzzled. 'What?'

'Are you coming on this cruise?'

'For fuck's sake . . .' I couldn't believe it. I was listening out for feet coming, the slow drum roll of our end.

'Si . . . Si . . . *are* you?'

'Ssh . . .' Only she could squat on top of a pile of shit planning her summer holidays while a man was about to die, and us commit murder, and us completely ruin our lives – our barely started lives, for ever and ever.

But I couldn't get her to shut up. Instead, she cried out in an hysterical whisper, 'You're not coming! You're going to desert me! I'm going to be stuck by myself with *him*!'

Instantly, like flies disturbed, all these sick-making thoughts I couldn't bear to think rose humming round me in a stinking cloud. I hissed, infuriated, the skin contracting over my skull, 'Him? *Him*? Oh, of course you're going to be so lonely with *him*!' What a fucking joke it all was, this so-called holiday. What was I there for – cover? While he, *him*, the dark man in the light – I couldn't even look at it in my head. I couldn't bear to run it by me one more time. 'Just forget it, all right?'

'You said you'd come!'

And then I was more depressed than anything. 'Don't worry, right. We'll all be inside and none of us will be going fucking anywhere.'

'You said . . .'

Hearing him coming, I gripped her slashed wrist as viciously as I could. 'Shut the fuck up, or I'll fucking kill you.' The feet crunched towards us over the broken glass. I was rigid; could hardly breathe. The feet crunched slowly by and off away into the distance. I let out a long trembling breath.

'Doesn't it matter to you?' whined Eleanor, tugging at her wrist. 'Doesn't it bother you one bit?'

'No – no, it doesn't,' I said, letting go of her without warning so that she nearly fell backwards off her heels into the piles of crap. 'It's none of my fucking business.' I wasn't interested. I thought now suddenly that I really, really didn't give a shit. I pressed my cheek against the metal bin, staring at her. I could see her put her hands to her face. Where her flesh was bare it was now bright white – the night had grown lighter, less orange, because somewhere over London the moon was rising.

She took a dramatized breath, and said through her fingers, a prisoner with her face pressed against the bars, 'Because . . . you know . . . if I tell you, you mustn't tell a soul, right? Not no one, not Danny, not your mum, not no one.'

I couldn't get my head round the way she kept on and on: how she could think anything in the world was of the remotest importance apart from the here and now, the terrible now. 'Eleanor, I don't care *what* you fucking do with who – shut the fuck up . . .'

'No, no, listen,' she said. 'He . . . you know . . .'

I was silent, despairing, turning my head away, trying to ignore her, refusing to hear her.

'We . . .' she whispered furtively.

I shuddered. I saw again the lighted doorway at the top of the steps, and his hand on her shoulder, pulling her towards him, and his arms going round her, and her moving towards him, not pulling away from him – not moving away, oh, no. 'I know,' I said.

'I'm not lying,' she said. 'He . . . we . . . you know . . .'

'It's your own business,' I said. 'Don't drag me fucking into it. Leave me out of it. It's up to you.'

She clutched her savaged arms around her head, swaying, crouched on her high heels, the skirt rucked up to her thin hips, big overdone red-lipsticked lips as mad as a baby girl's dressing up. 'Please, Si. Don't tell.'

I sat unmoving, cheek to cold metal. It was weird – there was something else I could smell, powerful even over sour milk. I found myself thinking, What the fuck is it? And then knew with horror I was smelling again the smell of rich green leather and the violet scent of his breath in the car as he bent over me, his mouth so close to mine he could've kissed it. I closed my eyes with a sigh. My heart beat so hard it hurt bad. I didn't want to know any of this, especially not now. 'Look, for fuck's sake, Eleanor, why're you telling me this? It's not my business what you fucking do. Why don't you leave me alone?'

Out of my sight, I heard her moan and roll over crunchily in the rubbish. 'I thought you'd mind. Why doesn't *anyone* fucking mind?'

Why should I care? I opened my eyes and looked. She'd got herself rolled up against the bin, a hard little human ball, filthy with waste; she was desperate for comfort, but I couldn't bring myself to touch her. I just wanted her to go away. Or, more, her to stay, and me to go away.

'I just don't get it,' I said, sadly.

Eleanor whispered, alone and sorrowful, 'I shouldn't've told you – don't tell anyone – please, Si, please, he says he'll kill himself . . .' She wasn't working herself up: the words drifted out of her like wisps of steam, a little continuous trickle of dirty steam. 'He'll kill himself if anyone finds out – I couldn't bear it, if he did. He loves me so. I couldn't live with it. I wish I was dead. Oh, Si, I wish I was dead . . . I wish I was dead . . .'

I stared at her from miles afuckingway, my mind full of images like dreams. It's him, I thought, it's him. Maybe he *makes* her – (do what?) He says, She's strong and I'm on my knees . . . In his leather car, he says she says things she doesn't mean . . . his mouth almost on mine . . . He pulls her from the dark; it's true, maybe she didn't move towards the light, maybe he made her, maybe he *pulled* her in . . .

I said, with uncontrolled aggression, 'Come on, Eleanor, what're you trying to say? He shags you, right?'

'Yes! Yes! I told you, he fucking *loves* me!'

Yet how could I believe anything she said? She was crazy, mad, a nutter; so melodramatic and so murderous. She was trying to upstage Danny – thought he was hogging the heroic glory.

'Please, Si, kiss me.' I looked up in a panic. Her face was too close to mine. 'Believe me, Si – it's *you* I love, only you . . . I don't love Richard, don't worry about . . . it's not the real thing with him . . . it's *you* I love . . .' The moon had risen over the wheely-bins and her face was a pale paper mask with holes cut out for eyes and mouth. She was the night of the living dead. 'Kiss me,' she whispered, 'if you believe me.'

Fearful of touching her, I knelt up and kissed her unwillingly on her zombie mouth, with my hands on my knees. She put her arms around me and her head on my shoulder. We knelt stiffly there among the moonlit bins, crushed milk cartons and sodden newspaper under our damp painful knees. And then the footsteps came. I pushed her back and fell to my hands. I knew it was him. Crunching over the moonlit carpet of glass, he came on, whistling like a winter traveller crunching over a field of frosted snow. I felt much sicker, but my shivering stopped dead.

'He's here,' said Danny, seconds later, swinging down off

the garage roof. 'He's gone in. Nobody's with him.' He was vibrating with excitement, all keyed up, ready to roll. 'Come on, Eleanor, do your stuff.'

She stood up unsteadily. Her mascara was dripping down her face, and lipstick running off her mouth like vampire's blood. She looked more perfect, more desolate, than ever. 'I just knock on the door?'

'Ring the bell! Take your bag – quick – don't forget.'

As her lonely figure walked slowly away from us it struck me in a flash of inspiration we should've agreed on some sign she'd give us if he came to the door with maybe a gun or something – a thing I saw with horror was not only possible, but likely. But she was already at the door. It was too late to call her back. We hadn't thought it out – for fuck's sake, we hadn't thought it out at all, I knew it now, and now it was too late. Everything had begun. It was too fucking late. I couldn't get off the fucking ride.

Danny pulled on my sleeve. 'Come on,' he hissed. We crossed the open ground and stood together behind the wall which separated the boyfriend's ground-floor flat and the flat next door, out of sight. Then Danny lay down, so he could see round the end of the wall. I could hear Eleanor breathing on the other side. I heard the bell ring, short and clear. I thought, this is it, this is it. I tried to clear my mind. I nearly jumped out of my skin when the door opened. He spoke. I could just make out his voice, not words.

'I want to buy some gear,' said Eleanor, naïvely.

His voice was low and unhurried, unafraid.

'I've got money, lots of money,' she said, in answer. Danny glanced up at me, triumphantly – gave me the thumbs up. Eleanor said, 'Here, it's in my bag.'

And Danny leapt to his feet and raced towards the door, howling, 'Right, you bastard!' I followed him as fast as I could, knocking Eleanor sideways against the wall because she hadn't stepped far enough out of the way.

The boyfriend sprang backwards with a frightened yell.

[116]

'This is for my mum!' shouted Danny, stabbing him. Short-arse fell to his knees, threw back his head and screamed. Danny dragged out the knife and blood shot up.

He knelt there clutching at the spurting hole, moaning, 'Don't, Danny, don't!'

'You killed my sister! You're killing my mum!'

'Don't do this, man – don't do this shit!'

And Danny, knife at his side, hesitated.

'I'll never come near her again! I fucking swear!' Kneeling on the tiled floor of his hall, squeezing his shoulder like a red dripping sponge: 'Danny? Mate?'

'I don't believe you,' said Danny, in a distant voice. And, taking a step nearer, he raised the knife.

Shortarse shrieked, 'Fuck it, no!' And to my horror, he was begging me, 'Help me, help me – don't let him do this shit! Don't let him kill me! Help me! Help!' His mouth was stretched into a horrible frightened O, full of sharp teeth; I smelt the blood; it was disgusting; Danny stood with upraised knife, summoning up his courage for the next blow. 'Help me,' cried the hideous O-shaped mouth. And behind me I heard Eleanor give this sigh, like something deep within her had been satisfied.

I flung myself on Danny and grabbed his arm, forcing it to one side.

'What are you *doin'*?' he shouted, furious. 'Fucking let go of me!'

'Stop! *Stop!*'

'Let *go!*'

'He's getting away!' shrieked Eleanor.

'Get off of me!'

'Don't do it, Danny – don't do it!' I had my eyes squeezed shut and was clinging to his back around his neck and arms like a crazy hysterical monkey. And Danny was whirling round and round, trying to shake me off. I suppose it was almost funny, like slapstick. But Danny's trainers kept slipping and sliding on the thin surface of the boyfriend's blood, and he couldn't keep his balance, and between us we fell heavily to the floor and the knife flew out of Danny's hand and skittered across the tiles and into the kitchen and stopped dead with a clatter against the fridge.

The front door crashed against the wall, and Shortarse was gone. I rolled off Danny's neck and we lay staring at each other in amazement, gasping for breath. Eleanor was shaking her head, standing over us, like: totally astonished. Danny was unbelievably furious.

'Have you gone fucking *crazy*?' he yelled at the top of his voice, jumping to his feet. 'Are you fucking *insane*?' His baseball cap'd fallen off.

'Don't do it!' I was shouting, too, up on my knees, as if we'd still to raise our voices above the junkie's desperate screams. 'You're not a murderer! You can't *do* it, man!'

'We're fucking *dead*, all right,' ranted Danny, literally tearing at his hair with both hands. 'Like he hasn't gone to fetch his mates right now and come back to *slaughter* us! Good fucking move, you bastard!' He grabbed his hat despairingly off of the floor. 'Let's *go*!'

Eleanor shrieked, jumping about, flapping her arms. 'Si, you fucking idiot – let's go! Let's go!'

We got out of that place and off that estate as fast as we could: we weren't careful, we just ran, headlong over the broken glass, like we were fleeing from the devil, and I was fucking convinced the devil was going to jump out on us from somewhere, flying out at us from some back alley, black arms waving, bleeding, shrieking, murderous – and yet he was gone. When we reached the main road we didn't stop running, we just carried on and on. Eleanor was dragging along behind, pulling off her shoes. I kept having to turn round – come on! Fucking come on! (I didn't have the breath to shout it, I just begged her with my hands.) I would've gone faster if I could.

In the end, I almost fell over Danny lying on the pavement. I sat down beside him on a low wall with my head between my legs, trying to breathe. My lungs were full of glue and I'd a killer cramp in my right side. Eleanor came limping along, holding her shoes, and fell down next to Danny and laid her cheek on the concrete ground. Danny, curled on his side, was making terrible dragging, creaking, death-rattle sounds, trying to get down air. My heart was pumping so fast I thought maybe I was having a heart attack; I pressed my hand against my chest to stop it breaking through my ribs. It struck me then with a terrible shock that the front of my top was wet. Then I thought, No, don't panic, don't panic, maybe it's not blood, maybe it's off the rubbish, and I looked at the palm of my hand, but couldn't make anything out, and I thought about sniffing at it, to see, but I didn't dare – just wiped it back on my top. Then the three of us sat and lay there in silence, staring back the way we'd come. Nothing, nobody. Not even a car. The devil'd vanished off the face of the earth.

'Maybe he went up the hospital,' said Eleanor, at last. 'You cut him pretty bad.'

'Not fucking bad enough,' said Danny. He was sitting up on the pavement now, lolling and panting.

'He's too scared to come after us,' I said. When I spoke, neither of them even looked at me; Danny actually turned the other way. It was like they thought I'd fucked up so bad they were embarrassed for me. I stared at the back of Danny's furious head. I'd known him so long; he'd been my best friend for ever; I'd ruined all that now; he fucking despised me now, despised me bad. I put my head in my hands and thought, really childishly, almost tearfully, It's not fucking fair! It's not as if I would've got the chance to jump on him if he hadn't struck way off target the first time, then fucked about so long the second time. Part of the reason I jumped on him was I knew he didn't really want to do it, but he needed someone else to stop him because he'd come so far he couldn't stop himself. I'd known him since I was a little kid, for fuck's sake. He didn't want to murder anyone. He wasn't a fucking macho type. He never even bullied anyone at school. He wasn't one of them. He never wore YSL jeans in his life. I'd done him a big fucking favour, was all. 'Look, Danny . . .' I said.

Without turning to look at me, he said, 'Just fuck off, Si. I thought you were my fucking friend. But you're nothing but a fucking coward.'

The ground we sat on was turning steadily towards the sun. There wasn't much night to go. The birds, wherever they were, had started up. We got up and walked on, through the wide empty streets. I walked behind Danny and Eleanor, and they walked along without speaking, alternately brightening and fading as they passed under the street lights in front of me.

When they got to her house, they stopped close together and got talking. As I came up with them they fell quiet, and Eleanor turned very insultingly to look at me. Her hair was sticking up all over the place, and she was holding her high heels in her left hand. The feet of her stockings were ripped to shreds and her top was half-pulled off one shoulder. She looked like a right little slag. I looked right back at her.

'Well, Si,' she said. 'You really fucking let *us* down tonight.' And with that verbal kick in the balls, she disappeared down the side of the house – she'd left the downstairs toilet window open, because they always bolted the door from the inside. Watching her go, I thought dreamily to myself how a house like that was probably packed out with burglars by now, arguing who got there first, fighting over expensive objects on the stairs.

After she went, Danny and I were left standing there, side by side, and for a short while neither of us moved. Then I walked away. I thought maybe Chalk Farm tube would be open, but it wasn't, it wasn't that late, only about four-thirty. But the sun was nearly coming up. The empty road was turning grey, and I stood and watched the traffic lights at the top of Chalk Farm Road changing colour for a single car.

'What're you doing, then?' said Danny, making me jump. I hadn't heard him coming up behind me.

I thought for a bit. 'Nothing,' I said.

'You going home?'

'In a bit.' I didn't want so many years of friendship to end like this, but I knew it was ending just the same. I wouldn't've done different, though. I'd still've stopped him. It was a hard call, though.

'Just fucking look at you,' he said.

'What? What?' I shoved my hands in the pockets of my coat and swung on him aggressively, glaring at him. I thought he meant – look at you, you're such a fucking coward.

But now, facing each other, he simply repeated, 'For fuck's sake, Si – just fucking look at you, is all.'

And, as the day came light, we stood and looked at each other, and we were fucking covered in blood. It was all over our clothes. It was in our hair. There was a big splash of it right over Danny's baseball cap. Our faces were wiped with it. Our shoes were splattered with it. We looked like we'd been washing up in the fucking stuff. 'Jesus Christ,' I said. 'Fucking hell. We look like we fucking murdered someone.'

Danny just gave me a really dirty look and said, 'Nearly fucking murdered someone. *Nearly* fucking murdered someone, Si.'

There we were, right out in the open, the occasional car beginning to go past even – out in the open, in practically broad daylight now, visibly streaked from head to foot in someone else's blood. It didn't seem like a good time to argue the pros and cons of attempted murder as against the real thing. 'Go home, Danny,' I said. 'We can't stand around like this. We're fucking mad, man. The police'll be along any minute. You got to go home.'

Looking down at himself instead of at me, he said, vaguely, 'Yeah . . .' and slowly turned away, facing up the hill to home. I should've gone off as fast as I could, but instead I couldn't help watching him go and inside my head I was thinking to myself, Bye-bye, then. Bye-bye, mate.

He turned right around and walked back. He said, 'Come

on, you can't walk home like that – you'll get done. Come back and clean up.' As I hesitated, he said, 'Fucking come *on* – you get done, I get done.' It was his way of saving face (like no one was backing down here), and my face too, but I knew he was thinking of me, not of him. He was so loyal, Danny – it was his thing. It was what he did best. It was that landed him in this whole murder thing in the first place – look at his mum, betraying him over and over, going back to the scag when she said she wouldn't, going back to that arsehole when she said she'd left him – yet he would have spent his life in prison for her. He had to let me in that night, even though he was sure I'd let him down and fucked his life up good.

We climbed up and in through the bathroom window. It was never properly shut, because it wouldn't quite go. This wasn't Eleanor's house anyway – burglars weren't exactly lining up, rubbing their hands. I turned on the bathroom light and we stared at each other again, pale-faced under the streaks of his blood. On the wall above the toilet where we'd climbed in was a thick slick of whatever was on our shoes. I wetted some bog roll and rubbed at it. I spread out the brown and dirty stain. We must have left a trail from here to Kilburn.

'Come on, leave it, we'll sort it in the morning,' said Danny. He fetched a black plastic bin bag from the kitchen and we undressed in the bathroom to our boxer shorts and dumped everything in it, one after another, tops, jeans, socks, trainers. We washed our faces and our hands and arms with soap – pink frothy bubbles swirling down the drain.

'We'll sort it in the morning,' said Danny. His eyes were nearly closing. He was standing there swaying in his boxer shorts and the baseball cap, which he hadn't taken off.

'Your hat, Danny,' I said. 'There's blood on your hat.'

He took it off and looked at it. 'Fucking hell,' he said, really annoyed. He looked back and forwards from it to the bin bag, like he nearly wasn't going to chuck it in with the rest, but in the end, with a sigh, he did. 'I'll sort it in the morning,' he repeated, like there was nothing else to say.

'Yeah,' I said. I couldn't think what else to do either. All that blood made me fucking retch. In Danny's bedroom I climbed into the top bunk, lay on my face and pulled the duvet over my aching head. I was flat out. I didn't want to think any more about what'd happened. Like Danny, I wanted to sort it in the morning, whatever that meant. But pictures kept forcing their way into my head. I started trembling again, like among the bins. I could see the fucking state of the place as we'd left it. Blood everywhere, man. The knife still lying where it'd ended up against the fridge. Scuff marks of Danny's trainers on the slippery floor where he'd spun round and round trying to shake me off. Our footprints on the floor – Danny's fingerprints on the knife – our clothes in the black bin bag in the bathroom . . . and we were fucking around with fucking alibis! Jesus Christ. Like a faceful of freezing water it hit me then what the boyfriend still being alive could really mean. I ripped the duvet off my head, choking for air. Suppose we got done for attempted murder? Terrible visions of the future began to build themselves inside my head: court rooms, trials, prisons – Oh, god, I thought to myself in rising panic, like a little kid, what's my mum going to say? What's she going to *say*?

Leaning over the edge of the bunk, I hissed, 'D'you think he'll go to the pigs?' I had to know.

I saw him breathing in the dim light, but he said nothing. Then he said, 'Yes.'

I closed my eyes and turned on to my back. Sweat on my forehead; felt hot; pushed the duvet down off my chest. I swear I could see that blood-covered floor, plain as day. Then he said, with his usual helpless honesty, 'No, he can't fucking stand'em, innit.'

'Jesus,' I said.

He said, 'I just don't get it, Si. You were my mate.'

In the top bunk, I pressed my palms against the ceiling, to lift its weight off me – it felt so heavy on my chest. I pushed and pushed till it made a noise like plaster cracking. I tried to think what to say to him, but the only thing I could think about was the hill, and how we'd liked to hang out there that summer. All those fuckers hunting through the urban valleys at our feet.

'You're not like that, is all.'

'I *am* like that,' said Danny instantly. 'You don't understand. I've seen things I should never've seen, man. You never seen things like that. You don't understand. It makes you hard, man. You don't know me, Si – you just don't know me. I'm hard, man.'

'No,' I said, because I had to believe it. I did believe it. 'No.'

He lay so still, and for so long, I thought he must've given up on me and gone to sleep. Then he said, 'Well, you know what *you* are? A fucking arsehole, man.'

'Right.' I smiled to myself in the top bunk. He was a well sweet guy, Danny. The ceiling rolled off of me. I pulled the duvet over my head and fell asleep.

I woke just like that, not swimming up through a warm sea as it usually is for me, but like I'd been hurled on to the beach. Without even thinking, I was up on all fours, the duvet draped over me, looking down. I'll tell you exactly what I saw. I saw the boyfriend's back as he leaned into the bottom bunk. I saw the top of his head, as he bent over Danny. I saw in his moving hand the knife Danny stabbed him with. And I heard this grating sound, and Danny grunt. And at the same time I was falling through the air, my legs and arms stretched out like a cat, and on the way down I noticed Danny lying flat on his back in bed, with the handle of the knife sticking upright out of his white naked chest, and it wasn't until I hit Shortarse and knocked him beneath me to the floor, both of us yelling and screaming with surprise and shock, and the two of us rolling over and over, punching and biting and scratching each other, that I knew to my horror it wasn't a dream. And I knew where I was now, and I had Shortarse by his throat, and I was still yelling, but Shortarse was silent because

[124]

I couldn't let go of his throat. And I heard Jim screaming, 'Call an ambulance, call the police – no, stay out of it, Gabby, just do it, do it!' And he was pulling me away, by the upper arms, and I was sagging and I looked into my hands, and they were cupped full of thick fresh-smelling blood, warm and oily, and the smell of it rising up was appalling, and I fell to my knees. And right in front of me on the floor as I puked my guts up lay Danny's mum's boyfriend, thin and frail, curled up in the middle of the scattered pile of blood-stained *Beano*s like a still-born baby, dipped in blood, completely still. And through it all lay Danny on his bed, flat on his back like one of those pale stone medieval knights on churchyard tombs, only instead of the sword being laid between his feet it was sticking upright from his chest. No longer the hunted, but the hunted down.

Nine

When my mum was my age it was the sixties, and my mum would've given anything to be a sixties cool swinging chick in bell-bottoms and beads. She'd been trying pretty fucking hard to make up for it ever since, with her patchwork gear and her scented candles and a whole lot of draw. But at the time, in that decade of decades, my nan'd made her come home by nine from parties (and no more than one party a month), bed by nine-thirty (can you believe that?) – early to bed, early to rise, etc. Shoulder-length hair and knee-length skirts. Cardigans and socks. I could see why it'd done her head in. It'd be like me being forced to hang with my mates in a fucking double-breasted suit. She never got a whiff of draw, not back then. My nan told her it'd make her think she could fly, and she'd jump out of a window and be killed.

My nan used to say to my mum, What would happen if I lost you? To my nan, crossing the road by yourself was a recipe for getting run over by a bus. Staying in the house alone meant burglars would tie you up and kill you. She lived in a really scary world – a world I personally would've been afraid to live in. And she was as sure as hell something terrible would happen to my mum if she let go of her. You're my only child – supposing I lost you? she would say. As if to say, if she'd had more children, she could've handled losing a few.

My mum, being far too lazy to get off her fat teenage arse and rebel like a proper kid, came home from parties on time, went to teachers' training college in Hull (Jesus!), got married . . . Oops! Bit of a mistake that! Well, at least she'd me to show for it. And the flat.

I wasn't always sure whether her chilled-out attitude to me (Do what you want, but remember – hurt no one, peace, love and all that shit) was because she really believed in it or because she was just getting back at my nan. Or whether it was just sheer fucking laziness. Anyway, it sure did wind my nan up, which could be a laugh. Sometimes when I was a kid, if my mum went off for a weekend with one of her weird boyfriends, my nan would come round to look after me, and then she'd try to sort me out. I remember laughing and laughing at my nan when I was about twelve because she'd got herself into such a state over my dissolute life-style (didn't come in till eleven, no jacket) that words failed her and she started hitting me with the clingfilm. I just couldn't help laughing my head off. Weird world, my gran lived in. Weird city.

Compared to her, my mum was cool. Laid-back about whatever I chose to do. Chilled about whoever I chose to hang with. But . . . coolness kind of ran out when she found I'd been rolling around the bedroom floor with a blood-stained murderer while Danny lay dying in his bed. It must've come as a shock, my nan being right after all, what she said: If you turn your back for one minute, your children *do* die. What a choker, after so many years spent mocking her mother's ludicrous fears.

It didn't help her Danny was hanging on. Not dead yet – critical. Very critical. Fighting. Brave lad. Hope for the best, etc. It didn't help me either. I knew in my heart of hearts Danny was going to die. And I knew it was all my fault. It was like my head was a boom-box blasting over and over: YOUR FAULT YOUR FAULT. Every time I opened my mouth I thought people could hear those words rocketing around my skull. Because it *was* my fault. If I hadn't chickened out . . . if I'd let Danny finish the bastard off . . . The tears rolling out of my eyes were cold and hard like tiny stones. 'It's OK to cry,' said the policeman meaninglessly, like people say to little boys. 'It's nothing to be ashamed about.' I wasn't ashamed of crying; I was ashamed of getting my best friend killed.

Remember years ago when you wrote the weirdest stories and never could think how to end them? And so you wrote: And then I woke up and it was all a dream.

That's what I was waiting for, while the policeman was speaking to me and my mum, who'd appeared, sat, almost whimpering with the shock, holding my hand. I wasn't holding her hand. I was wondering what bed I was going to wake up in – whether I'd wake up in the bunk bed, or whether the dream went even further back than that and I was going to wake up in my own bed. Or maybe the summer'd never started. Maybe I'd dropped off in class, bored out of my skull. It wouldn't be the first time. The real reason I thought it was all a dream was because in real life something like this could never happen. Yes, indeedy: that summer I really thought like that – I thought someone my age could never die.

In my dream I was sat in the kitchen of Danny's grandparents' house. I was wearing Danny's tartan dressing gown, holding it wrapped round me. Underneath all I'd on were blood-stained boxers – wet. I hated that, feeling that murdering fucker's body fluids next to my skin. Danny's grandad was there as well, still in his pyjamas, stripy and stained with tea – so stained, in fact, it looked liked he'd poured a teapot over himself. He'd black wiry hairs on the tops of his feet. The policeman was standing up, holding a notebook, like on TV.

Jim said to the policeman, 'This lad just tried to save my grandson's life. Can't you talk to him tomorrow? I have to go to the hospital to be with my wife and grandson.' He was very calm, so calm you knew he wasn't.

'Just a few things,' said the policeman, 'and I'll be off.'

My mum kept squeezing my hand, again and again, like it was a series of hands she was shaking one after the other.

'What I don't get,' said the policeman, very ploddishly, 'is how come this guy got stabbed first?'

'I left it lying here,' said Jim. He pointed to the corner of the kitchen table. 'That's where I last saw it. That's where the bastard got it from. The bastard.' He wiped his face on his tea-stained pyjama sleeve, like he was sweating. 'He was bleed-ing when he got here. You can see it where he climbed in. He was bleeding already. Blood everywhere. Toilet-seat cover, bathroom rug, the walls, the landing – Jesus god, the carpets . . . What's Gabby going to *say*?' he asked, cupping his hand over his nose and eyes, like the cleaning problem on top of everything else was suddenly just too much, the last straw on top of losing Danny. There was no blood in the kitchen, though, nor on the stairs.

The policeman said to me, 'Did you stab him, then?'

I was shocked. 'No! Jesus!'

My mum gasped. Hadn't I been brought up all peace and love?

'Do you *know* who stabbed him?'

'No!'

'You *see*?' cried my mum, now in tears.

The ambulance'd taken that fucker to hospital in the same ambulance as Danny, like somehow they were equally deserving. Gabriella'd had to travel in the same ambulance as her grandson's killer. It made me sick. Danny was going to die. I knew that murdering bastard'd done him in. I thought in a detached sort of way, Nobody gets away with murdering my best mate. I thought, almost as coldly, Let's face it, it was me killed him really. It was my fault, all right. If I'd let Danny finish him off, none of this would've happened. This wouldn't be happening. It wouldn't be true. It was at that moment I knew I could never wake up. This dream had become my life, and my past life, a dream.

I felt like a dreamer, too, like I was floating in things. I shut my eyes but that was bad – I saw Danny in his bed with the knife sticking up from his chest and a black oily pool leaking out beneath him like under an abandoned car. I opened my eyes, shutting the picture out. If I knew anything, I knew it was important not to think about that right now.

I looked up at the policeman looking down at me and tried to get my brain into gear. I tried to think about what he was asking me. Slowly things started to clear up. I pulled my hand away from my mum's and picked up a teaspoon lying on the table and balanced it between finger and thumb. I kept dropping it. This cop going on and on about who stabbed who first – did that matter? I tried to think. What was that fucker going to say when he woke up? He only went for Danny because he was in fear of his life? 'Listen, Si,' said the dying Danny in my head, rudely interrupting me. 'Don't fuck this one up like you've fucked up everything else. Just because I'm dead, just because you're on your own, don't desert me now. It's up to *you* now – it's *your* responsibility. This is our one chance to get this guy out of my mum's life for ever. Don't fuck it up. Just because I'm dead, doesn't matter. Me being dead is the whole fucking *point*. This way, he's going down for ever.' When Danny's voice said 'going down', I saw not prison but the fiery pit of hell.

'Son?' said the policeman. I realized I was still staring at him.

'We went to see him,' I said.

Danny's voice in my head shouted, 'You moron! What did I say? Shut the fuck up!' But I thought he was wrong on this one. Just because he was the disembodied voice of a dead person in my head didn't mean he'd all the answers. I could see Danny's footprints in the blood. I remembered the kids who'd seen us. I'd bet our fingerprints were everywhere (why hadn't we worn gloves?). I wasn't having that fucker fuck everything up by waking up and saying Danny started it, while Danny died for no reason, and that fucker got off and went back and killed his mum. I wanted to tell the police a good lie, a cunning lie, not a crap, completely transparent Danny-style lie which usually involved just denying everything in the face of the most clear fucking evidence.

'We went to *talk* to him.'

'*Talk* to him?' asked the policeman, taken aback, like: are you mad?

'We went to talk to him last night,' I said. 'Told him to keep away from Danny's mum. He was beating up on her. She lost the baby.'

My mum really wasn't cool any more. Her head nearly came off. She'd only just found out from Jim, like ten minutes before, about the time the boyfriend'd come round the flat and thrown a brick through the window and threatened to kill everyone. She shrieked, 'You went to *talk* to this . . . this . . . *murderer* . . . in the middle of the night . . . when you *knew* what he was like . . . because Danny's mum . . . you risked your *life* . . . because of that little . . .' She just managed to stop herself saying something unforgivably bad about Danny's mum and the baby, like they weren't worth saving, let alone dying for. Instead she jumped up and ran round the kitchen, her red hair streaming behind her, clutching her head like she'd had a brain haemorrhage. 'Are you completely mad? Are you completely *insane*?'

It was awful, but I could feel this laugh struggling to burst out of me, worse and worse as she ran round the kitchen. I put my hand over my face, hoping I looked really sorry about everything. I *was* fucking sorry – I was sorry for me, I was sorry for Danny, I was sorry for her, I was sorry for every-fuckingbody – but however sorry I felt, this laugh kept breaking through my fingers with a bad squirting sound, like farting in public. But I didn't think it was funny. I didn't think it was funny at all.

'Madam – madam – sit down,' said the policeman, getting frightened. He was a lot younger than my mum. 'Don't get so upset!'

'*Upset!*' I thought she was going to have a real go at him, but then she sat down abruptly, like she'd been a kid playing musical chairs and the music'd stopped. I was all choking and shaky. I was wiping tears from my eyes.

Cautiously, the young policeman stepped away from her and said to me, in a rather lowered voice, not to disturb the nutter, 'Now. You went to . . .?'

'We went to his place in Kilburn,' I said, clearing my throat.

[131]

'Like, late on.' I added, because that sounded wrong: 'Because he's never in till late on.'

I stopped and everything was silent. Weird. Everyone was just looking at me. Danny's grandad was really intent on listening. His mouth was slightly open. He'd false teeth, but he hadn't put them in, there was just this round dark hole. I closed my eyes and listened to my voice. I thought it sounded like the voice-over in a film. I kind of tried to imagine what I was saying, like the plot of a film. I could see it happening before my eyes. It seemed like a pretty cool film. The boyfriend picked up the knife. Come on, you fucker! he shouted. What a bastard. It was do or die. Danny grabbed his hand with the knife in and twisted it . . .

'We knocked on the door and told him we wanted him to stay away from Danny's mum. But he really lost it. He *really* lost it. He went for Danny with some fucking great kitchen knife, and Danny shoved him away, just one really big hard push, and we ran off. Really fast. We ran, because we thought he was coming after us. We didn't look back. We were really scared.'

I didn't bother with Eleanor. Partly for a reason – why drag her into it? Even if that fucker remembered her, she might've been a coincidence. Also, my head was still really fucked up over her. I didn't like to think about her, or try to figure her out. So, in revenge, I denied her a part in my film, even a poxy walk-on one.

Danny's grandad, standing, leant forward, supporting himself on the yellow table with his small rough hands. He didn't say anything. He seemed full of emotion.

My mum said to herself, dazed like from a blow to the head, 'It's all my fault . . . I should've known . . . I thought . . .'

The policeman was writing everything down, like what I was telling him was true. He kept saying, 'I see. I see.'

I thought with sudden impatience he was a bit of soft git, really. I always thought the police were supposed to give you a hard time and not believe you. When he finished writing he started going on at me about the dangers of visiting known psychopaths in Kilburn in the dead of night without police protection. He was really serious about it. Like they would've come if we'd called! 'Hey, officer, can you come with us while we go see . . .'

He frowned, poking his cheek with his pencil. He'd acne left over from being a teenager. 'I hope your friend'll be all right.'

'Please god,' said Danny's grandad, startled into crossing himself. 'I'm going to the hospital now.'

The policeman patted me on the shoulder. 'Very brave lad,' he said suddenly.

I was shocked. 'What?'

'Oh, come on,' he said, winking like a mate, going all macho on me. 'Not many lads would jump on some bugger with a knife, just to save their mate.'

It was bizarre, realizing that was the picture he'd of me. Me, the hero, soaring through the air. But it wasn't right. I didn't feel like I'd deliberately jumped on the fucker at all, more like I'd been knocked off the top bunk by a big wave. And he didn't have a knife – the knife was already in Danny. That was the truth of the matter. If I hadn't chickened out in Kilburn, Danny wouldn't be dying now. That was the fucking truth of it. In the end, what'd I risked? Weirdly, the teaspoon I was holding between my fingers suddenly bent nearly in two without me even being aware of putting any pressure on it, like I was Uri Geller or something.

I prayed to god for Danny's life – not that I believed in god, but I thought only he could help me now. And if god'd checked with me that if he granted me this single wish I'd never come crawling to him again, I'd've said, yes, absolutely. This, god, is *it*. Just for Danny to be alive. That's *it*.

My mum woke me in the morning to tell me Danny's grandad'd been on the phone. He was off the critical list. He'd a punctured lung and lost a lot of blood, but that was all.

My mum sat on my bed, her eyes red like her hair, chewing her fingertips, moaning on and on. 'I'm sorry, I'm sorry,' she kept saying. 'I smoke too much dope and I'm always seeing strange men and I was wrapped up in having a baby – I'm sorry, I'm sorry . . .' She was really depressed. It was well unlucky my nan was staying with us – I could hear her voice inside my mum's, and I felt really sorry for Louise because I knew she was feeling like a little girl. If my nan only said the word I think she'd've cut her hair and thrown out the hippy patchwork dresses and gone back to knee-length skirts and socks and cardigans – her equivalent of sackcloth and ashes.

'So what did Jim say? Did the police talk to Danny yet?' I thought urgently, Please, god, if I can only talk to Danny before the police do, then I'll never . . . (god going: Yeah, yeah . . .) What I was worried about now, was Danny'd come up with some load of shite story which would make us both liars. Say we'd never been up to Kilburn or something. Land us both in prison on an attempted murder charge.

'They wouldn't, would they? Not while he's in hospital?' Like I would know. She was wearing a dressing gown with big red poppies on. She folded her arms on her stomach, still big and fat, though empty now, like a fat bloke's beer belly the morning after. The contents of her stomach slept in her room. She shouldn't've had to put up with all this shit, so soon after having a baby.

'Do *you* think I've been a bad mother, Si? Is it all my fault?' she asked, tears coming into her red eyes. She wanted me to save her from her mum's opinion of her. She couldn't save herself. 'Do you think . . . ?'

'No . . . what did Danny's grandad say?'

'He wants to see you . . . No, don't get up, stay in bed and rest . . . I'll bring you up some breakfast. What would you like for breakfast? Have whatever you like. Whatever. I'm so sorry . . .'

'What's the time?' I asked, swinging my feet out of the bed. She looked so miserable, with her 'bad mother' face on, sitting there clutching her empty stomach. I said to her impatiently, 'Don't listen to any of that shit gran comes out with. It's all crap. Remember the pink woolly cardigans you had to wear?'

She wouldn't even smile. 'But you could've *died* . . .'

'Mum? I didn't – OK?'

'But you *could* . . .'

'Mum . . .' I should have been nicer to her about it. My nan must've been giving her a really hard time. But I was in a panic about seeing Danny before the police. I thought I'd've more time to be nicer to her later, when things were sorted. I started getting dressed in a big hurry. 'It's OK, OK?' I pulled stuff out of my drawers. No one seemed to think it was odd, when the police drove us home last night, that I'd just come in Danny's dressing gown. I suppose they thought my clothes were in his room. It was true, I couldn't've gone in there. So my shoes were still at Danny's place. All I had was last winter's trainers, split down the side.

My mum said tearfully, 'Where're you going?'

'Danny's grandad wants to see me,' I said, making for the front door, buttoning up my flies.

She said, following me, 'No, don't go . . .'

I stopped, half-way up the basement steps, looking down: 'Back soon – I got to go see Jim, he said . . .' I figured Jim wanted to see me because Danny was asking for me. 'Don't worry about it.'

My nan came rushing out. 'Where're *you* going?' She was really belligerent, a big fat bouncer. 'You heard your mum – you get back here, young man.' (No really, straight up, she did say 'young man'. It kills me.) She tried to grab my feet and I skipped up a couple more steps. 'You listen to your mum! You're not responsible, you hear? Look what's happened! You'll get yourself killed, mixing with that drug crowd! It's not safe!' Her face was ready to crack and fall off.

I looked down at my mum, barefoot in the area in her red poppy dressing gown and red hair. I was going anyway, but suddenly I was curious what she was going to do. I could see she was in the middle of some terrible internal struggle. At last she burst out, like she couldn't help herself, 'It's OK. He won't be long.'

'*What!*' screamed my nan. I was out of there. Poor old mum. When push came to shove, not all the murderers in the world could force her to give in to my nan, or make her treat me the way her mum'd treated her.

Danny's grandad just stood there after he'd opened the door, glaring at me, fag in hand, head and shoulders poking slightly forwards like a crow. He was wearing an old black suit, short on the leg – it matched his old black hair. I'd never seen him in a suit before. It looked like he was preparing for a funeral, but maybe it was just his way of marking the fact that it was a special, different, stand-out sort of day – the day on which his grandson didn't die. He just looked at me, like he was trying to make up his mind whether to punch me out or not.

'How's Danny?' I asked at last, breaking the aggressive silence, standing on the step.

'They say he'll pull through just fine,' he said, not taking his eyes off me.

'That's . . . great.'

'They've stitched him up nicely, inside and out.' Still he stared at me.

'Oh, that's great – great,' I said. It was great. But I couldn't figure out what he was really trying to say, or what he was so up-tight about.

'You want to see him?'

'Yeah!' Relieved.

He sucked on his lip with false teeth. 'He don't want to see you.'

'Oh.' I just stood there. What was there to say?

'Even though you saved his life and all.'

'No. OK, then.' I thought frantically to myself, But I've *got* to see him.

Suddenly he stepped right back, flinging the door wide open. I hung about on the step. What was he at? He said, 'I think we've got something to sort out, all right?'

I stepped hesitantly and unhappily into the house, like it was a trap.

It was a trap. He took me into the kitchen, and on the table was a big black plastic bin bag of stuff. Before I hardly knew what he was doing, he'd jerked it upside down and dumped everything out on to the table – mine and Danny's tops, jeans, socks, trainers, flopping out one after another, stinking like decomposing bodies (like a cat I found floating in the Regent's canal when I was a kid 'fishing' – fat with water, and hissing with exploding gases when I punctured it with my stick). The last thing to fall out, with a separate thump, was Danny's baseball cap, which gave me a bad shock – it was so much a part of him it was like seeing his face all of a sudden, staring up at me accusingly from the table – *your fault*! My stomach heaved bad.

'You see this?' said Jim. 'What the fuck's it all about? What you and him been up to? What you and Danny done? Look at this – it's fucking covered – you want to tell the cops how you got that much blood on you if you just pushed him and run off? You think I'm fucking stupid or what? You think I wouldn't even look in a black plastic sack in my own bathroom? You fucking mad or what? What you done, Si? What you fucking gone and done?'

I was stood as straight as I could, my back against the doorpost, as far from the table as I could while being in the same room. 'It's not as bad as it looks,' I said. 'A bit of blood . . . it's . . . it just goes a long way, is all!'

'Tell that to the cops,' said Jim, 'why don't you? I'm sure they'll go for it, stupid cunts.' He sat down on the nearest chair. Apart from the awful fucking smell, the atmosphere was far from good. His hands on his knees, he pondered the revolting heap. He said, like to himself, 'How could it, all this blood, if you just pushed him and ran off?'

It was weird how still I felt inside, a sort of floating in my head. For a long time I just stayed standing there. I was trying to figure out what to tell him, and if I told him what we'd tried to do, if he'd tell the police. I thought he was pretty much on Danny's side, but you never know. I thought I had to tell him something. 'He killed Danny's sister,' I said finally.

'Oh,' said the old man, in his sad mourner's suit, clutching his knees with bowed head. 'Oh – I see.'

And then, having started, I told him the lot (except Eleanor). I said how Danny thought it was only time before that fucker killed his mum. How we went up Kilburn with a knife. How I chickened out . . . When I said why Danny didn't want to see me, why if I hadn't stopped him he wouldn't't've got stabbed, I just felt like crying; I fucking had to cry, actually, like a pathetic kid, wiping my nose on my sleeve. 'I'm sorry . . . I'm so fucking sorry, man . . .'

'Never mind about sorry,' said Jim. He was fucked off and frightened too. 'You're mad fucking bastards, the fucking pair of you. He could be dead, you could be dead – what's going to happen when that cunt wakes up – what's he going to say? I tell you what he's going to say, the cunt – he went for Danny because you two tried to murder him. He'll fucking get off and you two'll go down, you stupid fucking bastards. You want to spend the next twenty years of your life shitting in a *bucket*?'

He jumped up and started walking backwards and forwards behind the table in a space barely big enough to turn in, then came round and walked right up to me and yelled in my face, with a blast of old cheese and smoke and light saliva, 'Well, *do* you?'

I shrugged, sniffing. What was I going to say? Ooh, yes, please? What I've always wanted to do.

'Aah, fuck it,' he said, turning away. He sat down, leaning on the table, pushing aside a blood-stained shoe, taking out a fag. He stood up. He said, 'You just stick to what you told that copper last night, all right?'

[138]

I said, panicky, 'What's Danny going to say, though? What if he tells the police something completely different? I have to talk to him.'

'You know something?' he said, lighting the fag off the stove. 'I want this cunt out of her life. Give her a chance. Maybe she'll come off the stuff. Meet someone nice. Get a job.' He said, 'I should've got him killed myself – got him killed proper, like, so's no one'd notice.' He looked sideways at me, to see what I thought of that. I wasn't saying anything. What I thought was, like grandfather like grandson. 'I s'pose you think Danny's got more guts than me,' he said snappily, like we were having an argument about it. 'But I been a hard man in my time as well – you got that?'

'What if Danny tells them something different?' I asked.

He said nothing for a bit, thinking. Then he said, 'We better go talk to him. That cunt's going down for ever.'

I was fucking relieved to hear that, all right. If he didn't, we were all dead, that's for sure.

He said, 'I want to burn this stuff first, you get me?' Now there was a good idea.

A railway line slices through Camden. It runs through a deep cutting behind the tarmacked car park of Danny's block, protected for safety by a high wire fence. The fence is permanently smashed by kids keen for electrocution. Me and Jim, humping between us the stinking bin bag like we were off to bury a body (lucky no one round there would care – oh, would you look at that, another body off to be buried, who is it this time?), shouldered our way through the biggest gap where a section of the fence had half come down completely, and scrambled down the steep falling embankment, trying desperately to keep the bag from ripping open on the dusty grey brambles and scrubby polluted trees, skidding down on the sides of our shoes, raising ridges of filth to serve as steps, down, down into the shit, the bag catching on everything, till we came to the back of a little old brick shed, standing in its own sea of bottles and cans and other rubbish, right down near the bottom, near the track.

I knew where we were, though I hadn't been there for years. Danny and me used to love this spot. We'd hung out here a million times, playing camps while trains rushed by to places we'd never see. We'd lit fires, too, and sometimes heated baked beans to nearly lukewarm. It seemed a hell of a long time – it'd been a kids' thing, was all. Back in the days when you played games. Back when you made up names for gangs which only you and your mate were in and which were just gangs, not murder-fucking-machines. Back then I used to want to live in the wilderness like an explorer and I thought the railway cutting was a wilderness, because it was wild and nobody else was there (except for the several hundred seated people rushing through every ten minutes or so). I never noticed then what a thick layer of metallic-coloured dust covered everything – every leaf and fallen stick furry with it, like they were bits of old junk left up in an attic for years and years and years. Some wilderness, all right – some dusty wilderness.

Danny's grandad was huffing and puffing, collecting old newspapers and sticks to make a fire behind the shed. I gave him a hand, passing him stuff – it was just like me and Danny in the good old days, grubbing around in the shit for crap to burn. He'd several goes lighting it with his lighter. I sat on the rotting ground and watched. 'Fucking thing,' he said, fussing around it like someone's self-important dad trying to light a barbecue the only way he knows how. Eventually he got enough corners started to come together in one reluctant blaze. First thing he chucked on was the socks – what a stench. Then when they got going, on went the tops; then the serious stuff, the shoes and jeans. The trainers stunk and smoked like burning tyres. I was hunched up coughing in the acrid smoke, eyes dripping, while Jim dodged about, encouraging the flames.

The last thing to go was Danny's hat. Somehow that made

me incredibly sad, like we were burning Danny himself, or at least some symbol of how he used to be. I can see that baseball cap right now, sitting on top of its funeral pyre, held in the centre of the flames, something precious and irreplaceable – a sacrifice to the gods gift-wrapped in fire.

Ten

He lay in white like a dead man and thin tubes threaded in and out of him like worms eating him in his grave, snaking into his mouth and chest and arms; they went everywhere; one into a bag of water strapped to his chest; another dangling upwards from his arm into a drip on a stick; he was masked and bandaged round and round.

His nan sat by the bed, holding his hand and praying to herself – or, of course, to god: who else? – an inaudible stream of one-way communication. She was so small sitting by the bed, and the hospital bed so high, that to hold Danny's hand she'd to reach up to it. She hardly noticed us coming in, she was so busy talking to god. I guess she thought god was about the most important person to talk to right then, and we were pretty useless by comparison. Danny's grandad went to stand behind her.

'Did he wake again?' he asked.

'Yes. But he's sleeping now,' whispered Gabriella, then went right back to praying.

If I looked closely, I could see his heavily bandaged chest rise and fall.

Danny groaned.

'Lie still, dear,' said Gabriella instantly, laying her little hand on his leg under the hospital sheet.

He opened his eyes, lifted his head slightly, and looked straight at me, standing at the foot of his bed. Recognition flooded into his face. 'You stupid fucking *cunt*,' he said, ripping the mask from off his face, then dropped his head back on the pillow and sighed with the effort of insulting me.

Gabriella murmured, soothingly, stroking him, 'Hush, Danny, hush. It's not who you think it is. It's your best friend, Si – he saved your life.'

'Oh, sure,' said Danny, rudely. 'Cunt.'

She turned to me earnestly. 'He's delirious still . . .'

'It's all right, Gabriella,' I said. 'Really, it's all right.'

'It's not all right,' said Danny, taking a snatched breath from the mask. 'You're a stupid fucking cunt.'

'He doesn't know who you are . . .'

'Really, it's all right.'

'Fuck *off*, cunt.'

Danny's grandad leant over him and said, 'Danny. Me and your nan're going out.' Danny didn't say anything. His mouth tightened. He didn't like it. 'Right, son?'

Gabriella didn't want to leave. 'He must be delirious, Jim – we should get a nurse.'

'It's OK, OK? They need to be alone,' Jim said, tugging at her little arm. 'Come on, Gabby – we'll go talk to a nurse or something, yeah?'

She kept protesting anxiously as he edged her out of the cubicle: 'But I'm praying for him, Jim – I'm *praying* for him . . .' She wanted god right there by Danny's bed and worried if she left god'd follow her out like an obedient dog.

I sat down in Gabriella's chair. Danny lay with his nose stuck in the air, staring coldly at the ceiling. He was out to make me feel as guilty as sin. OK, then – I could handle that. I sat there feeling guilty as sin. But I got annoyed, eventually. 'Well, I didn't *know* he was going to come after you, did I?' I said loudly.

'Should've let me finish him off,' said Danny, nose in the air, unforgiving. 'Coward.'

'I did jump the fucker, for fuck's sake.'

He kept quiet, but after a while he couldn't help himself. 'What happened, then? You just woke up or what?'

'I just woke up and he was there and I jumped him.' I added, suddenly proud, a kid after a playground fight, 'I was trying to strangle him when your grandad came in. I'd have done him in, else.'

He was unimpressed. 'You wouldn't have done him in, Si. You wouldn't've wanted his death on your pansy girlie little poncy fucking hands.'

'Oh, fuck off,' I said, angrily. 'Just fuck off.'

'Fine, then,' he said. 'I'll just fuck off, then.' But of course he lay there, roped down by his machine and the plastic bags on his chest and on the stick.

I leant back in the chair and waited for a bit. I said, 'Look, chill out, all right? We got to talk.'

'Why?' he said, meaning he didn't want to hear *any* fucking reason why.

'Me and your grandad burnt all our clothes and trainers and things,' I said. 'They were covered in fucking blood.'

He frowned, getting his head round it. 'Trainers?'

'And stuff . . .'

He jerked his face towards me. 'You burnt my *trainers*?' He was well pissed off. He liked those trainers. He'd saved up for them.

'But . . .'

'What the fuck did you burn my trainers for – they're the only fucking shoes I've got!' He stopped. A dreadful suspicion dawned. His eyes grew big. 'My hat . . .'

I could see it so clearly in my head, blazing away on top of the bonfire, like on a funeral pyre. I kept my mouth shut.

'You burnt my fucking *hat*!'

I thought he was going to try and jump me. 'Stop, Danny, stop! You'll pull your tubes out and things!'

He fell back. 'I cannot fucking believe you burnt my hat.' It was a really, really serious blow to him. He was shaking his head, over and over. 'You bastard. You fucking bastard. You fucking stupid bastard.'

'We got to get our stories straight, what we tell the police.'

'First you nearly get me murdered, then you burn my fucking *hat*!'

[144]

'Listen, it's all to do with what we've got to tell the police. We have to tell them the same thing.' I tried giving him the spiel I gave the police, but he just couldn't get over the hat thing. He kept interrupting me.

'If he got cut when I pushed him, even if it was an accident, I could still have had blood on my hat, couldn't I? What difference does it make?'

'Shit, you should've seen it, man,' I said. 'They were covered in blood and stuff, like there'd been a war or something. It was just too much.'

'You could've burnt everything else. You could've burnt my fucking trainers, even. My hat . . .'

'Please, Danny, listen . . .'

'I fucking *loved* that hat,' said Danny, accusingly, completely choked up.

I said slowly, 'So anyway, what I said was, he came fucking charging at you with the knife when all you wanted to do was tell him to back off of your mum.'

'Yeah, like I'd do that,' said Danny, childishly unhelpful.

'Oh, fucking come *on*,' I said. 'D'you fucking want him getting off with anything less than attempted murder just because he can make out you started it?'

'Attempted murder? Is that what they're going to do him for?' he asked quickly.

'Well, what do *you* think?' I said. Sometimes Danny was so another-planetish, he did my head in. 'I mean, the guy comes into your bedroom in the dead of night and sticks a fucking great knife in you. What d'you think they're going to do him for – fucking drunk driving?'

'Attempted murder,' said Danny, awed. 'Cool. What d'you think he'll get for that?'

'Years. Fucking years.'

Danny laughed. 'Fuck.' He was triumphant. Then he looked anxious. 'But what will the fucker say happened?'

'His word against ours – and there're two of us,' I said.

'Three,' said Danny, remembering Eleanor.

'No, I never said her,' I said quickly. 'What's the point of that? Even if he says about her, she could've just been there.'

'Have you seen her?'

'No.' I wasn't going to, either. I think I'd sort of taken a decision that I wasn't up to her really. She was too mad, her and her weird stuff – shagging her uncle? What the fuck was all that about? I'd already pushed her out of my head. Now Danny asked me about her, it was like she was trying to creep back in, little fingers curling round the door. But I shoved her right back out again, into space, out of the hatch, spiralling away into black outer space, arms and legs spread-eagled, calling to me 'Siiiiii!' . . . moving rapidly further and further away. Cut the fucking rope – yeah. 'No.'

'Wait,' said Danny, getting urgent, forgetting for a moment how pissed he was at me. 'Where is that fucker, anyway? Has he talked to them yet? Is he down the station or what?'

I said, 'Fuck no, it's safe, the state of him – he can't be out of hospital, right.'

'Here? He's *here*?' Danny was suddenly freaked. He was staring all round. He was the bravest guy I ever knew, ever since I first knew him, but he was totally freaked out. 'Shit that!'

'Shit!' I said, just as shocked as him, because I hadn't really thought about where that fucker was until right that moment – but it must be here, of course. How must it feel to Danny, pinned down to his bed by hospital equipment while the crazy fucker who wanted to do him in was maybe just in the other room? It didn't feel too good to me, either. 'No – chill – they must have a police guard on him or something. I mean they're not going to risk it, are they?'

We looked scared at each other. In the sudden silence we listened out. Still silence. If there was anyone else in the other curtained cubicles in this small ward, they were asleep or dead. 'No, really . . .' I began.

'Sssh!' said Danny, lifting his hand, lifting up his head. 'D'you hear that?'

At first I didn't hear anything, but then in rising disbelief I heard what he heard – footsteps, hesitant, shuffling, the steps of someone sick or injured, coming down the corridor outside. They'll go past, I thought, but they did not. They came into the ward, slowly, painfully, pausing outside the other cubicles one by one – looking in, moving on, searching, coming closer, closer . . . My hair literally stood on end, I think. Someone was shaking the curtain around us, feeling for a way in. It was only me could do anything. Danny, whiter than white, was tied down. The plastic bag on his chest was bubbling. I stood and lifted up the metal chair. I thought wildly I would shove it in his face as soon as he looked round the curtain and yell like mad for help. A thin hand came through the folds, fumbling at the air like a blind animal sniffing. I thought it was his hand. I stood holding the chair up high. He came into the cubicle.

'Jesus – Mum!' groaned Danny. It was his mum.

'You poor, poor darling,' she said. She wandered forward, totally ignoring me, not even seeming to wonder why I was stood there like a prat with a fucking chair held over my head. She looked the worst I'd ever seen her: smashed nose, both eyes black, her whole face one big bruise, dried blood under her hair. She had a pretty grubby shapeless loose blue dress on, and a dark blue cardigan without buttons she was holding together with one hand, and her pink plastic sandals were too big, so she shuffled, shuffled, and the tops of her feet were yellow and grey with bruises, and you could feel the way her limbs ached and all her body hurt as she sat down ever so carefully on the edge of Danny's bed.

'Mum told me you were here,' she said. She stopped and cleared her throat. 'I came as quick as I could.'

Danny shot a really heavy look at me past her, like to say: You should've let me kill him, shouldn't you, right? Then he looked back at her and smiled the kindest smile.

'How are you, Mum?'

'Oh, never mind me, darling – never mind me . . .' She sat shaking her head and wiping her eyes. 'What about you?

What has he done to you, my darling?'

'Oh, I'm all right,' said Danny, absurdly. Suddenly I realized I was still stood there holding up the chair. I lowered it as quietly as I could to the ground.

'It's all my fault.' She suddenly started howling out loud, shaking her head, shaking it from side to side. 'My fault, my fault . . .'

'No, Mum, don't cry,' said Danny, nearly crying as he would never ever have cried for himself. 'Don't cry, it's not your fault.'

'It is! It is!' Her voice was loud in scary grief. She held his hand and rocked, a weeping nutter. 'I should never've gone back to him, see, not after the first time – look at you, my poor darling, look what he done – and it's my fault, my fault . . . how could he do this to you, how *could* he . . .'

Danny was going frantic, because he didn't want to cry, trying to calm her down. 'I love you, Mum, stop crying, please, please. I'm all right. Mum. Please.'

'All I wanted was his drugs, but all I cared about was you, Danny, honest, all I ever cared about was you . . .' She rocked and rocked, her head thrown back with pain. She wouldn't let go his hand. 'Oh, my god . . . oh, my .god . . .' Her tears poured over her face, a thin flood over her battered skin, washing the snot out of her nose. I heard feet coming briskly. The curtain pulled aside, and a youngish nurse wearing glasses stood looking in.

'You mustn't go upsetting . . .'

Josie raised her voice in an awful animal cry. It amazed me, how she could see what her bastard boyfriend had done to Danny all right, when she'd never seen what he was doing to her. 'I'm so fucking sorry, darling, I love you so much . . . I love you so much and I've ruined your life and it's all my fault and I'll be clean, Danny, and I'll be clean, I swear to fucking god, I *will* be clean . . .'

Not letting go of his hand, she started to slide, twisting sideways, slipping on her stomach over the edge of the bed, down to her knees on the floor at the side of the high hospital bed, still holding on to his hand, her breasts crushed against the side of the bed, clinging on to her son's hand like she was slowly falling off a cliff and begging him to hold on tight, to stop her falling to a terrible death.

Danny didn't know what to do. He kept saying tearfully, 'Please don't, please don't . . .' but she didn't hear him.

'I love you, Danny, you've got to believe, got to, oh, god . . . forgive me . . . Danny . . . please . . .' Her sorrow rose round her – she was drowned; the young bespectacled nurse, transfixed, shocked, silent, stared at the woman kneeling on the floor. Danny's mum pressed her battered face against the side of the bed. 'Forgive me,' she said indistinctly, then, suddenly letting go of his hand, she sunk face down on to the floor and lay there, her cardigan come apart, dress up around her knees, exhausted.

After a minute, giving herself a little shake, the nurse stepped forward and bent over Josie, slipping her hands under her arms. 'Now come on,' she said, quite gently.

Danny's mum, drained of willpower, allowed herself to be helped up on to her feet, pale and bruised, her head hanging down and to one side. The tears were still trickling out of her eyes.

'Come on, now,' said the nurse, half-pushing her. 'He needs his rest, doesn't he?'

Danny throughout this last part had lain avoiding our eyes. As the nurse was leading her out of the cubicle, Josie stopped again and turned towards him.

'I mean it, Danny,' she said. 'I really mean it. I'm done with him.' And then she let the nurse lead her out of the ward.

I stood there and tried to think of what to say.

'Don't say anything,' said Danny.

'I . . .'

'Could you go away? Please.'

'I think I'll go, then,' I said.

'Fine,' said Danny. 'Bye.'

[149]

Eleven

The police never believe junkies. Junkies are just lie-machines to them. It really worked in our favour. They never bothered to question our story, and they didn't believe a word the boyfriend said about us. It made life a lot easier for them, not listening to him, and saved them a lot of paperwork too. At the beginning I'd thought it was going to be like on television, with them trying to trip me up on inconsistencies and stuff, or make out Danny'd told them something different to make me break down and confess on the spot, etc. They did talk to me a few times, but it wasn't that way at all. They knew what they wanted to hear, and so I said it, and so they heard it. And that was all. They had on record what happened the night that crazy fucker came round to Danny's house and how he'd told Danny he'd be back to kill him. And now he'd done that thing – it was all OK in their book. Why should they bother looking for something else? Anyway, with him being a dealer, I think they wanted to get him for whatever reason. They didn't care how.

Sometimes it got a bit embarrassing, having the police believe me when I knew I was lying. Wasn't it the done thing that you told the truth and they *didn't* believe you? Maybe it works both ways. It was weird, the way they weren't giving the boyfriend a chance. It must've been fucking infuriating for him, banging his head against a brick fucking wall.

This cop said to me, in an 'I don't think so' tone of voice, eyebrows raised for humorous effect, 'All right, get this – he says he attacked your friend because he was in fear of his life. He says you two kids went round there heavily armed, armed to the teeth, broke into his house and attempted to murder him before he managed to escape. I have to ask you, right . . . is that the truth?'

'Well . . . no,' I lied carefully. I needn't've bothered to reply. They'd already written down my answer.

'Bit loony-toons, going to talk to a guy like that and expect him not to turn rough?' asked the sergeant, stubbly and sweaty in the heat, scribbling away.

'I guess so,' I said. An incredibly stupid kamikaze part of me wanted to say, Hang on a sec, give the guy a chance – how do you know he's not telling the truth? Instead I turned to look inside my head, at the bruised and broken images of Danny's mum, and the dead child swept out on a river of blood, and the knife sticking silently up from Danny's white chest, and kept my mouth shut. Maybe that was the most moral way. I'd like to think so. It was the easiest.

The only time they shocked me was when they suddenly asked me about Eleanor. 'When you came to the house – or as he claims 'broke into' his house – he'd just opened the door to someone. Do you know who that was?'

I shrugged. 'I didn't really look.'

'Young? Old? Male? Female? Black? White?'

'Some kind of kid pro looking for scag, I think,' I said.

'Very likely,' said the cop. For a scary moment I was convinced he was being sarcastic, but he just wrote it down and didn't mention it again. He didn't even ask if she saw what happened – hung around, ran off or what. It was weird, how Eleanor was so invisible in that scene, how she meant so little to the cops, how in her pitiful common role as junkie whorish little girl she was so well camouflaged against the vast London backdrop of grief, drugs, loneliness and beaten flesh that for the police she disappeared completely from their sight.

She flatly fucking refused to disappear from mine, though. She came hammering on our front door, screeching, 'Si! Si!' for all Camden to hear.

When I opened the door she was dancing in the area, her

[151]

huge man's shirt flapping like a cartoon ghost, legs naked, hair in knots, freaking out. I was pretty freaked out too, by seeing her. She was all I needed.

'What the fuck are you doing here?' I hissed.

'Is Danny *dead*?' (She'd just been round his place and some dickhead neighbour had told her how an axe-wielding maniac had murdered the entire family in their beds.) 'What happened? Was there a fight? Is Danny really dead? Like, really, really dead? Did you *know* he was dead? Why didn't you *tell* me?' She was hysterical, really upset for Danny, but in an incredibly over-excited way, moved to fucking orgasm or whatever by the sweet smell of his death.

'For fuck's sake, Eleanor, calm down – he's all right.' Behind me through the open kitchen door my nan was watching us. She was dunking her biscuit in a cup of tea, but so fascinated was she that she unconsciously kept missing the cup, dipping her biscuit into mid air before sucking at it. I stepped out into the blazing oven, closing the door behind me.

'What d'you mean he's all right – I'm telling you, an axe-maniac . . .'

'He's alive – he's in hospital, but it's OK. That fucker stabbed him in his bed, all right? But it's OK.'

Her eyes went all panicky. She dragged at the knots in her hair. 'It was *him*? He came right into his bedroom and stabbed him in his *bed*? Is he going to try and kill us all? One by one? Why didn't you let Danny *do* it, Si? Jesus, this is scary. God, it's like one of those teenage snuff movies . . .'

I ran up the steps into the hot street. I started walking fast up the road but she bobbed along at my side like a balloon tied to my wrist.

'Did he sneak into his bedroom?' she asked, eyes wide and shining. 'Was Danny really scared? How much did he hurt him? How much blood did he lose? Was it with a knife or an axe?'

'Listen, just listen,' I said, desperately. 'Please. Calm down.'

[152]

'Is he going to come after us, Si? Will he kill me? Will he come into my bedroom in the night and stick it in me?'

I stopped dead, pulled her towards me by the elbows, and held her really tight to stop her jumping about. 'Shut the fuck up, Eleanor. You don't need to get so fucking wound up. It wasn't you got stabbed, is it? He doesn't even know who you fucking *are*.'

'But I was there,' cried Eleanor, tugging and tugging in my hands. 'He saw me! What if he comes after *me*?'

'Ssh! Ssh!' I glanced at passing people and pulled her even closer, her face in mine, like I was some sort of fucking gangster or drug-dealer type. I said under my voice, 'Listen to me. He doesn't know who you are. It don't matter you were there. Me and Danny told the police we didn't even know who you are. We didn't even fucking mention you.'

Eleanor ripped her arms out of my hands. She stood on the hot pavement stamping her feet, flapping her arms in their long unbuttoned sleeves. 'Well, fuck you very much!' she screeched into my face. 'Fuck *you*!'

'You what . . .?'

'You can't just treat me like I don't fucking exist!' She was working herself up into some big crazy toddler tantrum scene. 'You can't treat me like I don't *exist*!'

'For Christ's sake, Eleanor . . .' It came to me with horror she was going to break up again, like when she saw the madman under the trees, that she was yo-yoing on an ever-stretching close-to-snapping elastic string between this reality and a world on the other side – a fantasy world or maybe some other simultaneous reality even weirder than the one I was living in. 'I *know* you fucking exist!'

'I don't exist!' she cried, really frightened, like she'd just found this out about herself.

I shouted across the invisible widening gap, 'Of course you fucking exist! I know you do! Stop fucking about!'

'Who's that bitch keeps staring at us?' She narrowed her eyes, ready to pull a gun on someone. 'What's with her?

Who's she looking at? Why's she ignoring me?'

Wandering innocently down the road, her hand raised to me in hesitant greeting while drinking at the same time from a can of coke, was Louise, back from the shops with Sophie slung heavily round her neck.

'Who's the killer bitch?'

'Jesus! It's my mum, for fuck's sake!'

'Oh, your *mum*!' She shot off madly down the road and, before I could catch up with her, rushed up to Louise, shouting nearly at the top of her voice, 'Hi, I'm Eleanor. Remember me?'

'Oh, hello, Eleanor,' said my mum, startled into missing her mouth and spilling coke down her front. 'How are you?'

'He didn't want me to come say hello to you,' said Eleanor, folding her arms with a backwards jerk of her head. 'He's embarrassed about having a girlfriend. In fact he's not sure I even exist. But all boys are like that, aren't they?'

I could only stand there behind her making sweeping hand signals at my mum like I was flagging down a plane.

'Are they?' asked Louise, thoughtfully draining the can of coke. 'Yeah? I suppose they can be a bit vague.'

'He's just shy. And I bet a million he hasn't told you about the cruise,' she said. Fuck! I flinched with the sharpness and unexpectedness of the blow.

'Cruise?' repeated Louise, wonderingly.

'I knew it,' said Eleanor, wagging her finger, a right little bitch. 'I *knew* it. He thinks I'm invisible, you see. We're off on a cruise in September. That's in, like, a couple of weeks. But he still thinks the yacht doesn't even exist. He thinks none of it exists. It's strange, I tell you.'

'Cruise?' repeated Louise.

'Hey, Eleanor, come on – we gotta go,' I said. I put my arm around her rigid shoulders. 'Let's go, OK?' Slowly she gave way towards me, still nodding with dark meaning at my mum.

'What cruise?' asked Louise. She stood, like, dazed, in the

middle of the pavement, with the baby crashed out against her chest, watching us struggle clumsily away.

'Jesus, I need a drink,' said Eleanor, suddenly leaning her full weight against me, so I could feel the hard warmth of her on my arm. 'I need a fucking drink.'

'You want a can?' I asked, feeling in my empty pocket for change.

'No, a *drink*, dickhead – here.' She pointed into the pub we were passing. 'All right?'

'I'm skint.'

'I'll buy – Jesus!' Like I was nothing but trouble.

We went in and sat down. It was about six in the evening, but it wasn't packed. We sat at a small round table with iron legs. I hadn't been in this one before. It was dark – small frosted glass windows and a big mahogany bar fresh out of the rain forests. Some guys sat in round the back playing dominoes, and two blokes were leaning against the bar drinking pints. Eleanor gave me a twenty pound note (flashy); I went up to the bar and ordered a pint of lager and a gin and tonic. 'Who's the G and T for, darling – you?' asked one of the blokes. His hair was too short and his sleeves rolled up and he'd a load of tattoos – mermaids and dear fucking mothers, stuff. YSL crowd got old.

'You eighteen?' asked the Australian barman.

'Yeah.'

He gave the twenty the once over and stuck it in the till.

'She's not, though,' said the short-haired bloke, staring at Eleanor. 'Good luck to you. '

Sliding in beside Eleanor, I tried telling her what happened in Danny's bedroom, and what I'd told the cops and everything. She kept interrupting, very hyper about it, 'I can't believe that bastard did that,' she said. 'Sneaking in like that in the middle of the night. Sticking it in him when he was asleep – such a sick thing to do.' She was jogging about in her seat, like quivering, almost panting. 'Blood everywhere. No

[155]

one knowing. How can anyone do that? Sticking it in him while he's asleep. It's so terrible. What a way to wake up.'

When she spoke about it in her jabbering way I felt quite vomity again, almost to the point of having to head for the bog. Jesus, what must it feel like, waking to feel a thin metal strip parting the meaty fibres of your chest, knowing in the next second you'll be dead and the world gone black for ever.

'Shut up about it, Eleanor.'

'It's bad, though.'

'I was there, wasn't I? I saw it. Tried to stop it.'

'Poor old Si,' she said suddenly. 'Poor old Si.' She knocked her bare leg against my mine. I was wearing shorts.

'I'm all right,' I said. 'Really.'

She fished her lemon out of her empty glass and sucked it dry, then sent me up to get another drink. The two blokes were playing the quiz machine and arguing about why neither of them had any answers. 'Fuck's sake, don't you *watch* any television?' asked one of them, exasperated.

'You mustn't think it's your fault,' said Eleanor, when I sat down again.

'What?'

'Danny – I know you didn't let him kill that bastard and all, but you mustn't feel too guilty about it.'

I took a mouthful of my first pint, which I'd left unfinished. It'd got warm already. Should've got another one. I tried to think whether she was being nice or trying to wind me up. 'I can't help feeling a bit shit about it,' I said, experimentally.

'Shit happens,' said Eleanor, agitatedly. After downing half her drink in one, she said, 'Of course, you should've let him do it. I mean, seriously, Si, that was a really bad time to bottle. Did you *know* you were going to bottle? Or did it just happen?'

'Jesus,' I said, drinking in a hurry. 'Leave it out, Eleanor.'

'No, really,' she said. 'D'you think Danny'll ever forgive you?'

'What'd'you tell my mum about the cruise for?' I asked, pretty aggressively.

Her eyes opened. She was sucking her lemon again, like a kid with a lolly. 'Come again?'

'You heard.'

'Someone's got to tell her, don't they? Can't just run off leaving her a note.'

I looked her straight in her cute pale eyes. 'I can't come,' I said.

She looked straight back at me, very direct, sucking the lemon. 'Why?' She knew. She was just asking for form's sake.

I thought, Fuck's sake, Eleanor, what d'you want me to say – I can't lie there doing nothing in my bunk bed while your repulsive uncle sticks his fucking dick in you? I don't understand what's going on here? If you don't want it, why do you let it happen? Maybe you like it? Is it happening at all? Is it in your other world?

I said, 'You know why.'

'Because you're a fucking coward,' she said, tipping her head right back to drain the last dribble from her glass. 'Go get another drink.'

I stood up, then sat down again. 'No, fucking wait,' I said. 'Hang on a fucking minute. You know fucking well what the problem is.'

'You tell me,' she said, spinning her glass on the table till it fell rattling on its side.

'All right, then,' I said. 'All right, then – I'll fucking tell you what the problem is. It's Richard. Richard, all right? Fucking Richard.'

She put her head on one side, setting the glass upright with a bang. 'Fucking Richard?' she said. 'I thought that was *my* problem.'

I stood up and walked out of the pub.

I hit a wall of heat and light – bounced off it wincing and hurried down the pavement, shaking an ice-cream wrapper from my shoe. Eleanor caught me up by Camden tube, hustling through the crowd, shoving apologetic tourists ruthlessly out of her way.

[157]

'Si! Si!' She wrapped herself around me from behind, arms pinning my arms, one leg round my bare legs. Sweat sprung from me like a river source from every point where her flesh touched mine. 'Si, don't leave me!' she shouted, above the uproar of the cars which boiled at standstill in the stinking road.

'God's sake, Eleanor,' I said. 'Get off of me!'

'Don't leave me!'

'Get *off*!'

'Don't go – don't go . . .' She slid down to both feet, but hung on to my top. 'Why don't you come round to my place? Just come round – it's OK, my parents aren't there . . . please, Si, please, Si . . .' She was like tugging at me, leaning at an angle away, big shirt billowing like a sail – you could see it was wet under her arms – and giving it her sweetest smile. 'Come on . . . silly . . . love you, Si . . .'

I moved towards her and she squealed, little brown fingers burrowing like muscled worms into the inner crease of my elbow, 'I *love* you, Si . . . Come on.'

Along Chalk Farm Road we struggled upstream, thrashing our way through the talkative crowds.

Her house was empty, silent; the green-carpeted hall hummed with distant traffic and a dying fly.

'Do you want anything?' she asked.

'No.'

'Come on, then.' And she skipped up the stairs. Following, I could see up her legs from below. She was wearing under her enormous shirt the very short skirt she'd worn a few days ago, limping over to Kilburn to do someone in, in high black heels. She'd on trainers now, no socks.

We came to a landing with doors off of it, all closed, but she ran up another flight of stairs, exactly the same. 'Come on,' she said, without looking back. 'Come on.'

When I reached the top she was gone. The doors on this floor were all ajar. I pushed open the nearest, into a dark room with the curtains drawn. A suit lay flat on its back on the four-poster bed, jacket wide open and unbuttoned. Eleanor called anxiously from across the landing, 'You're in the wrong room.'

Beyond the opposite door, she crouched in a huge white armchair with the sun striking through the tops of trees behind her, unlacing her trainers. The leaves outside were crumbling, baked old summer-green. I gazed around. I'd kind of thought it'd be one of those nutter rooms, painted black with purple streaks or something. But it wasn't like that at all: it was white, empty – rather dirty, like places look when people move away, taking all their stuff. There were no posters on the walls, no books on the shelves.

'Sit down,' said Eleanor.

I sat on the edge of the bed, and, not knowing what to say, turned back the corner of her pale pink duvet to uncover a teddy bear I could see the ears of – a teddy bear's tortured corpse, more like: she must've been eating it for years.

'Oh, god,' said Eleanor, wriggling.

'What's its name?' I picked it up. One leg was chewed off to its knee, by sharp little teeth.

'My Bear.' We both half-laughed. But it was kind of sad, looking around. I thought it looked like a kid's room with all the stuff thrown out, packed in cardboard boxes somewhere and never replaced with anything older. All gone, except for My Bear.

She said, 'I don't like having stuff around. If people buy me stuff, I get rid of it. It gets in my way.' The room was ten times as large as mine.

'You got any music?' I couldn't see a stereo. The white armchair was miles off. I wanted her to come nearer to me. She seemed to've calmed down a lot, like she'd forgotten about Danny and murder and blood and death. I kind of wanted to talk about it to her, but I was glad she'd shut up about it.

'I've a CD thing, but it's in my sister's room.' She added, 'Don't you think music's boring?'

'It's all right.'

She yawned, jaw cracking. 'It does my head in.' Throwing her trainers, undone, across the room, she asked mock-shyly, tucking her hair behind her ears, 'So – d'you want me to sing for you, then?'

'What?'

'I could sing if I wanted to. Richard says I could sing if I wanted to. I could be in one of those groups and be incredibly rich if I wanted to. I could be famous by myself, actually – like . . . you know. I'd write my own songs. Richard really encourages me to sing.'

'Go on, then.' I lay down on her bed, on one elbow and hip.

Suddenly standing up on the chair, feet sinking in the cushion, she lifted her arms up wide, bouncing, bending at her slim brown knees, the man's shirt spreading out around her, head flung back, mouth open wide. The sun poured through the window behind her; the air of the pale empty room around her was glittery with hanging dust. 'TA-DA!' she yelled, and dropped on her arse again, looking brightly at me, like: Where's the applause?

I said, 'Danny's mum came to see him in hospital. She was really upset.'

She answered, 'Didn't you know I wanted to be a singer?'

'You never said.' Still on my side, I pulled my feet up on the bed behind me. 'I want to get another band together soon. Maybe you could sing in it.'

'I don't mean like that.' Knees up, distracted by her toe-nails. 'A famous singer. Like Richard says.'

I said, annoyed, to Mutilated Bear, 'I thought music did your head in.'

She came running across the floor and fell on the bed beside me. 'Your band'll be *great*,' she cried. 'You don't want me. I can't sing straight. I'm going to be a model, anyway.' She took my foot on her lap and tugged furiously at the knot. 'Jesus, how d'you do this?'

Rolling on to my back, my head on her pink pillow, letting

my foot lie heavy in her lap, I said, '"I'm so beautiful, no one'll ever forget me, I'll be rich and famous."'

'You are,' she said, in delight. 'You *are*.'

'No – *you* said that – back when I first met you . . .' In our summer of love.

'But you are,' she said, shaking her curls. 'You are, Si. You're beautiful. Your skin is like this yellowy brown and I *love* your mouth – it's so sweet, the shape of it . . .' And she stretched out her hand from where she was sat so that the very tip of her finger brushed my upper lip. I closed my eyes. 'And your eyes,' she said, touching my eyelids like I was dead. 'Your lovely eyes.' I felt my body gently rise and fall with the mattress as she changed her position on the bed. I opened my eyes – she knelt, gazing down, hands on her knees, licking her teeth. I turned on my side; she flopped; we were face to face.

'Tell me about Danny again,' she said. 'Tell me what Short-arse did.'

It was too late, I had to hold her, my arms tight around her, the too-big white loose shirt foaming up between us, getting in the way of my mouth, her kid's bendy body slippery in my aching grasp. She pushed her hands against me, pulling her head back: 'Tell me.'

'I told you.'

'Tell me again.'

The white shirt was in my face, and I was trying to get it away. She sat up and stripped the shirt off completely, like what I'd been doing was trying to get it off her, and leant her naked back against the wall, legs in her short black prosti-tute's skirt crossed at the calves, palms turned up flat beside her on the pink duvet cover, looking down rather critically at her arms – her scars'd faded to mild violet scratches. Without any top on she was thinner than I'd thought she was; her small tits threw sweet crescent shadows; her stomach seemed to sink like a sail under my breath as I leant forward to kiss her belly button. She fingered my hair and sighed.

'Was there really a lot of blood?'

'Sssh,' I whispered. 'Don't think about it.'

'Was it everywhere? Was Danny conscious? Did he see the knife sticking out of him?'

One hand on her leg, half under her skirt, feeling the blood running under the moist skin, I answered, not looking at her, 'Eleanor, please don't. Please.'

'I just want to know. I care about you. Where was the knife sticking out of? His stomach? Were you really, really scared? Did you think you'd killed him?'

She lifted her arse off the bed and pushed her hips forward, so my unmoving hand moved up her thigh, and fingers touched the soft material of her pants. With both sets of fingers, she rolled her skirt back neatly. Her kiddy pants were patterned with little red ladybirds. I shut my eyes against them, willing them to fly away. From the heat, she smelt so strong of salt.

She slapped my head: 'Listen to me!'

But someone far away in the house was yelling rather pathetically, 'Eleanor . . . Eleanor . . . '

'God,' she said. 'That's all we need.'

I slid down on to my knees, pressing my elbows into the bed and my face into my hands.

'He's only pissed,' she said, stroking my hair where she'd hit me. 'Don't worry about it.'

I groaned: 'Richard?'

She laughed. 'Richard? Are you mad? It's my dad, for fuck's sake. Come on, let's go in the other room.'

She pulled on the shirt in an unbuttoned rush, and dragged me by the hand, her skirt still screwed up around her hips, across the landing and through the opposite door.

'Eleanor! Eleanor!' cried the deserted man.

I closed the door behind us, quiet as I could, and turned towards her in the darkened room.

'Sssh! Sssh!' she was going. She picked the suit up off the four poster and draped it tidily over a small striped padded chair. 'Come here . . .' Throwing herself into the centre of the double bed, with a fit of the giggles. I ran and jumped on beside her – she gave a girly shriek and wriggled away. 'Catch me first!' Our fight sent waves across the bed, storming over the dark green cover, and shook the dark green canopy above us. I seized her from behind, my slippy hands crushing her half-formed breasts, and she suddenly tucked into me, her little arse hard and warm against my prick – we lay in sweating silence for a while, among the dark wooden furniture of the room. I wondered if the windows were open behind the closed curtains – I could hear the traffic, but the air I breathed seemed burnt to death. Her curly head was pushed up under my chin, her shoulders against my chest; but her feet came half-way down my calves, brown toes pointed like a dancer's. I realized again how small and thin she was, and in my head this voice whispered lovingly to her, Dear little girl . . . dear little girl . . . but not aloud, because how sexy would that've been? Like talking to a baby.

She struggled to leave me; I let her go. Running up the bed on her knees, she unhooked the dark green curtains from the posts and drew them along the sides of the bed, locking us in a soft material box. 'Now,' she said, pulling back the cover to show the white pillows, and laid her head down on one, smiling. 'Tell me again.'

I crouched on the bed, thrown by her smile. 'What?'

'Where did he stick the knife in?'

'Why . . .'

'I wasn't there! Tell me! I can't imagine it!'

'In his chest, Eleanor – in his fucking *chest*, all right?'

She sighed. 'Yes.'

Unexpectedly, I saw Danny lying there in my head and nearly burst out fucking crying again and dropped for protection to my face. The pillowcase was cool: I buried my face in the stiff white cotton, and smelled the smell of him – his violet breath. For a second I didn't know what it was – only the memory of his face, so close to mine in his leather car, surged into view. My hand closed on something under the pillow. I tugged it out – a folded green T-shirt. Sitting up, I thrust my face into it, sniffing like an eager dog. Violet. I could smell the fucker's breath freshener. I wrenched the curtain nearest me aside, like I was looking for air, and, sat right there at the side of the bed, one arm casually draped over the arm of the chair, legs elegantly crossed and jacket suggestively unbuttoned, sat watching and waiting – his fucking suit, where she'd so thoughtfully laid it, in the small stripy chair.

'Si – what're you doing? Aren't we having fun? I'm so turned on . . .'

'It's his bed,' I said. 'It's his fucking bed. I don't fucking believe you, Eleanor. You're fucking *sick*.' I couldn't fucking believe she'd brought me in here, she would've taken me into his bed, between his used cum-covered sheets. What was it she said between the wheely bins? It's not the real thing with him – it's you I love . . . Yeah, right – so much she had to fuck me in *his* bed, like she couldn't imagine doing it anywhere else – like she needed the feel of his sheets to do it – like she needed (unfuckingforgivable, Eleanor) . . . needed his fucking *smell* to turn her on.

'I love you, Si,' she said, crawling over the soft bed towards me. 'I really do. You can fuck me now, if you want . . .' And touched my neck, so all my hairs stood up.

I rushed to the window and threw open the curtains. The sash was wide, but nothing moved. The tall grey backs of other rich bastards' houses fenced us. I rested my forehead on the frame, and breathed in the lung-singeing air.

'I love you, Si! Do you love me?'

From the depths of my heart, I cried, 'Do you *want* him, Eleanor?'

She didn't answer.

I looked angrily behind me, but she was hidden behind the green curtains of the bed. I stared back out, at the shining windows opposite. Down below, old ivy crawled over the high dividing walls. Going back to her side of the bed, I lifted the drape. She was sat there fiddling aimlessly with the sheets, eyes lowered. I stood there, bed curtain in my hand.

'Did blood come out of Danny?' she asked softly.

I stared disbelievingly at her. 'You *are* sick in the head,' I said. I knew it, too.

She raised her cute little face, and pale green tears of protest filled her eyes. 'You don't understand,' she whispered. 'I need to know if it was the same for Danny, what happened.'

'What? What happened? What're you *talking* about, Eleanor?'

'The night he came through the window in the dead of night and into the bunk-bed and just stuck it in me.' Her quiet voice suddenly began to rise in rage. 'There was blood *everywhere*, Si.' She yelled out, uncontrollably, 'The blood burst out of me! You should've saved me but you never came!'

I groaned, horrified: 'You're mad! It was Danny, not you! You never were in any bunk-bed!'

'D'you think I'm lying?' she shouted. 'I shared a room with Debbie! I've got the scar where it happened! Here! Here!' And for the second time she ripped open her shirt and bared her heart to me like it was visible through her bones.

'There isn't . . .'

'Oh, god . . .' She stared down at her chest, in fright. 'Look at it! *Look at it!*'

'Eleanor . . .'

'Look at it! Put your hand on it! It's broken open! It feels . . . oh, Christ . . . it's full of blood . . .'

Still holding the curtain aside, I kept my eyes fixed on her face, but I was too scared to look down at her chest; I thought if I looked, I'd see it too: a dark red squelching hole, glistening and squatting in the shadow of her breasts.

'Please,' I said, trying to keep calm, 'please, Eleanor, you've got to stop this.'

'No! Why won't you listen? Why won't you ever *help*? Why won't you stop it happening?'

'I don't know what's happening . . .'

'You don't want to hear . . . You think I'm mad . . .'

'Just *tell* me!' But I didn't want to hear, and I thought she was insane.

At last it poured from her like the blood from her terrible wound: 'I was only five! I was in the bunk, in the lower bunk, and Debbie was in the cot, I couldn't say anything, I didn't want to wake her, she was only a new baby, you don't under-stand, and he stuck it in me, it makes me throw up, every time he does it, ever since then he goes on and on . . . It's not fair, Si! I never said anything, but I think he does it to her! I think he does it to *her*!' And we stared at each other in mutual horror at knowing together such an untellable thing. I couldn't speak or move towards her. 'You see,' she said, turning her head away. 'You'll never save me. It's just like with Danny. You don't love me. You'll leave me to die.'

In the silence between us, feet climbed the stairs, and we could hear a man's slow deep breathing. The door opened and he came in. He was pinkly naked to the waist in jeans. 'What're you doing in here?' He was skinny, with a ginger pony-tail, but bald on top, holding a can and a cigarette. He smiled at Eleanor, asking again, a bit aggressive, 'What you doing in here? I was looking all over.'

'Hi, Dad,' she said, very cold, openly buttoning up her shirt. 'This is Si.'

'Right, then.' He seemed insulted, for some reason. 'I'm going.'

He started to go; then, maybe forgetting why he was going, swung back, swapping the can to his left hand with the fag, holding out his right hand, consciously friendly. 'You must be Si,' he said. 'I'm Walt.' The touch of his hand shocked me, it was so freezing cold from holding the lager, and my skin so burningly hot.

'Hi,' I said, my voice shaking.

He pushed Richard's suit off the chair on to the floor and sat down, dumping his feet on the bed. 'You all right, love?'

he said to Eleanor. She yawned, and he said to me, 'She's an artist, isn't she?'

'Yeah,' I said.

'That's from my side,' he said, trailing the can to the floor.

'He's a session drummer,' said Eleanor to me, showing her teeth.

'I write my own songs,' he answered, stroking his pony-tail.

Eleanor laughed.

'No, no, I'm a . . . real drummer,' he insisted, looking for the right words. 'But I write my own songs.'

'I play guitar,' I said. 'I like writing songs.'

'I do that.' He nodded seriously at me. 'I write my own songs. Any talent there –' he pointed at Eleanor, a touch aggressive again – 'it's from *my* side, right?'

'Which explains a lot,' she said, reaching the lowest button.

'That's right.' He crushed up the empty can and threw it under the bed. 'I'm off.' He stood up with determination, then hesitated, winking at me. 'Talented, yeah? Cute little girl – it's from *my* side, right?' He looked down at his pink freckled chest, scratched his right nipple, flicked his pony-tail like a happy horse, and went out.

Eleanor fell back down, closed her eyes and yawned. Looking down on her small delicate body, laid so carelessly stretched out, the insides of her arms criss-crossed in violet, I saw in a flash Richard's soft plump hand creep up between her baby legs, and her small brown body convulsed in a locked bathroom over the bog, puking pale green bile to match her pretty eyes.

'Eleanor,' I said.

'What a dickhead, right?'

'Listen . . .'

She sighed irritably. 'Do stop going on, Si. Sometimes you really get on my nerves. Do you want a fuck or don't you?'

Twelve

I tried going up Primrose Hill again. I thought I'd find some
space up there, some distance, up out of the valleys of the
streets. Get some air, watch the sun go down with the hippy
crowd like I used to, the stars swim out, smoke a little draw,
listen to a bit of music, try and touch base. It was so near the
end of the summer, but nobody noticed. The day I went up
we got caught in a little storm, raindrops big as saucers, distant thunder – everyone just loved it, holding out their hands
for the rain. I wanted to join in, but I knew it wasn't for me.

I loved that crowd, man – I loved them all. It was just I
couldn't stand to be around them any more, them and their
summer of love. Getting poetically stoned, playing sixties
favourites – they were all so fucking innocent and naïve; they
couldn't know, they couldn't understand.

Instead I hung about at home waiting for August to end,
and played with Sophie – or rather, looked at her as she slept,
and went and sat out the back with my Walkman on when
she was awake. Our concrete yard was my own little desert:
plants hot to touch in the silvery rumbling haze.

There was some good stuff. My mum got it off Danny's
grandad – like, for the first time in her life, his mum decided
to get a life. She said she'd stand up in court and tell how that
fucker used her for a punchbag, day in, day out. She said
she'd give evidence against him on the drugs front and everything. Danny's grandad had it from the police that Shortarse
(on remand) went ape-shit when he heard this: wanted to
know if the cops were going to charge Josie with possession
and prostitution and theft and burglary and fucking fucking

dead animals or whatever – everything she'd ever done. 'I'm not covering up for her no more,' he cried, 'the dirty, thieving, mental junkie. I loved her, I really loved her, right?' Funny thing love.

Another thing Danny's mum was doing, apparently she was talking about doing the twelve steps, starting over again. I didn't much believe it. I knew Danny'd had so many fake stop-gap promises off of her, so many beautiful loveable lies (it's the *last* time, darling), lies he wanted to believe, that he'd try really hard to believe (I'm clean now, Danny darling), really *try* to believe long, long after in his soul he'd lost faith in everything she said. I wished I knew how he felt about this one – whether he could bring himself to listen to her one more time, to wonder one more time if it might be true, or if he'd just said, when she'd told him, Yeah, Mum, yeah, Mum, yeah, Mum – sure. He loved her so much, but no one was more cynical about her than him.

I'd love to've known what he thought, but every time I went to go up the hospital to see him, I didn't go. I knew he wouldn't want to see me. He'd've asked to see me if he wanted to. I knew he could never forgive me for nearly getting him killed, just like Eleanor said. I was his best friend – *was*. It was a really hard thing, getting my head around the end of all that. I couldn't face it, going to see him in the hospital and him just turning his dark head away. So I didn't go. I just hung about at home.

I wasn't safe from Eleanor, of course. She came round the flat every day. First time, my mum let her in; she just appeared in my room, wearing those red leggings, where I was sat trying to find a song on my guitar. She asked, 'Why d'you go so quick the other day?'

'I thought you wanted me to,' I said.

'Not really,' she said, taking my guitar off of me, breaking a string.

My mum really liked her: she thought she was cute. She said to me, 'She's really pretty, isn't she? And so lively.'

'Lively? She's completely mad,' I said, with feeling.

My mum laughed. She told me she thought Eleanor seemed lonely.

Partly Eleanor came round to flash off to me about how great her and Danny were getting along, with her going up the hospital to see him every morning, and how well he was doing (no thanks to me, of course). She never said anything about him wanting to see me. But mostly she hassled me about this Mediterranean shit. She told my mum I hadn't mentioned this chance-of-a-lifetime offer to her because I was so sweet, I didn't think it was fair to go swanning off on this mega-amazing cruise while she was stuck with Sophie 'so he didn't like to ask, because, you know, he knew you'd want him to go . . .'

'Really, Si?' My mum was so fucking impressed by how sweet I was, she just rolled over under Eleanor's little brown thumb. (Eleanor knew how to hit the buttons all right, manipulative little bitch.) 'You can't pass up an opportunity like that!' (Just because of li'le ol' me.)

'Really marvellous,' said Eleanor. 'My uncle says we can swim with the dolphins. Doesn't he, Si?'

'But Mum . . . it's like in September . . . I'll miss school . . .'

Louise looked at me and laughed mockingly. 'Oh, no, shit, *really*?'

'But how will you manage?'

'You're so sweet, Si!'

'Isn't he *sweet*?'

'Really sweet!'

I think Louise quite liked the idea of me being well away from Camden and druggies and mad murdering bastards (both friends and enemies), and what further than a yacht, trapped far from land on the surface of the deep deep sea? She didn't realize that all she was doing, she was shoving me off into the deep deep shit, with nothing at all to keep me afloat. I didn't know what to say to her. I just didn't know where to start.

And Eleanor wouldn't let up. She went on every day about that fucking cruise until my head nearly broke in two. And she was so fucking insane, she never seemed to have the same feelings about it two minutes in a row.

For instance, she said, 'I'm so glad you'll be there. We'll have a great holiday. It'll be really brilliant fun, won't it, being on a yacht?'

I pleaded with her: 'Listen, Eleanor, this is crazy – how the fuck can I come on this yacht with you and pretend everything's OK when I know what I know?'

She looked offended. 'Know what? What do you know?'

'You and Richard . . .'

'Oh – that!' She laughed, unbelievingly. 'What's fucking got into you? What does it matter? Everything's cool. Honest, it's all bullshit.'

But then, the next minute, she yelled out of the blue, 'If he tries anything on, we'll just tip him overboard, the dirty old man.'

'Jesus, Eleanor . . .'

'Do you think the sharks will eat him? Will we be able to watch as the sharks eat him? Will he scream while they rip his legs off? Wouldn't that be *great*?'

We were in my bedroom. She was crouching at my feet, hands on my knees, grinning like a nutter. I stared into her cute, pretty little face, her pale green eyes and sun-pinked cheeks. '*Did* he rape you, Eleanor? Since you were so little? Does he?'

'Well, of course he did – what do *you* think? I love only you, Si – it's not my fucking fault!'

'This is insane. If you don't want what's happening, you should tell your parents,' I said, in desperation.

She wept horrified tears. 'Are you fucking mad? It'd *kill* my mum. She'd die of grief!' Then she sobbed and clung whispering to my knees. 'Don't say anything, Si – please, please don't do it – he'll kill himself – you know he will – I couldn't bear it if he died – it's *my* secret – you promised me – my mum'll kill

[171]

me – I'll tell them you're lying . . .' She argued, 'I just want you to get in his way, all right? Jesus, it's no big deal. What d'you think I'm asking you to do? We don't have to kill him. I've decided. It's cool. My mum'd be too upset. All you have to do is *be* there. It's not that big a deal. Jesus!' Then, burying her face in my lap: 'Don't say anything, Si – oh, please, please don't – my mum'll kill me. He really loves me. Help me! Help me!'

And then she jumped up and skipped about like a fucking five year old, actually clapping her hands, bursting out, 'Oh, come on, Si. Think of it. A yacht. It's the Mediterranean. It'll be fun, really fun. Stop being such a pain. Do stop going on about it. Who cares about him? It's *you* I love. Just let's forget it and have fun. I never get any fucking fun.'

Forget it? I'd these terrible pictures in my head, and I just kept over and over wanting to ask, Do you really think he really might . . . you know . . . with Debbie? Finally I did ask her, but she slammed out of the house before I'd finished asking. My mum thought we'd had a row. She said, 'She really likes you, you know. You're not being horrible to her, are you? Don't be horrible to her. She really likes you.'

I didn't see Eleanor again for a whole day. I was glad, but I was lonely without her, what with having lost Danny and avoiding the Primrose Hill crowd. She turned up again the day after, surprise, surprise. She said, 'You didn't help Danny, and he nearly died. That's why he won't talk to you.'

I said, 'Why don't you take Danny on the fucking cruise, then? I'm sure he'll be more fucking help.'

She stared at me, like I was mad. 'What? Danny?' She paused. 'He'll probably still be in hospital.' When she said that I got a feeling of guilt so strong it made me feel empty, like quite sick, inside. 'So you see,' she said, 'it *has* to be you.'

I wasn't going to go. But I kept getting this picture of her standing in her bright blue strip of a bikini on that white fast-moving deck, swaying small and unprotected in the warm wind, and Richard standing at the wheel, taking pleasure in watching her standing there, desperate and alone, all but naked in her bikini. I didn't know what to do. If only none of it was true.

She said, 'If you don't believe me, if you don't look after me, I'll cut my wrists properly. Then you'll be sorry.' She said, without looking at me, 'Come to the Mediterranean, Si. I'll have sex with you any time you want.' She thought she could bribe me with herself, and blackmail me with her blood.

Richard rang my mother up and told her when we were going. I asked her what she thought of him. 'OK,' she said, staring out into the garden with a cup of tea in her hand, thinking about something else, something she thought mattered more – Sophie, I suppose.

It wasn't like I was even sure Eleanor was telling the truth. What about that picture of her on the yacht – her as a little girl sitting on Richard's lap? She looked so happy and content, but if she was telling it right he was fucking her by then – no, no, she was well pleased, you could tell, sitting on his lap, she wasn't frightened of him. How could it possibly be true? What room could there be for a man in a five-year-old's bunk-bed? Even now she was so young. A five year old is only a big baby, for fuck's sake.

She was crazy, so hung up on sex, and so hung up on murder, too – not just a murder of her own – any old murder. She'd been so fucking keen for Danny's mum's boyfriend to get his blood-soaked come-uppance. I guess it's much easier to kill the devil you don't know than kill the devil you do. There's not a single piece of you owes them anything, or a stupid babyish loving little part of you that remembers the one nice thing they ever did, like hold you tight in their arms on a beautiful white yacht. Not one of your many voices cries, I couldn't *bear* it if he died.

As for me, I realize now I'd just wanted to slaughter Andy. Poor old Andy. He was still coming round – to see Sophie, he claimed, but I think it was just in case he might lose his custody rights over the remote control. He said the room he was renting in Finsbury Park was a real shit hole with no telly. Sometimes I sat and watched a film in the front room with him. Sometimes I even thought again about telling him what was going on – when I forgot for a moment how angry I felt.

What bugged me most, Eleanor acted like I'd this duty to protect her. Maybe I did – I felt I did – but she wanted me to do it her way, whatever that was, and I couldn't get my head round it. I couldn't even see where she was coming from, let alone where she was going. She didn't know herself, but wherever she was headed I was getting dragged along just like I had with Danny, right up to that last moment in the hall. I knew I had to stop just being dragged along. I had to stop and think about what was the right thing to do. Really think what was the right thing to do, not just have some knee-jerk reaction, not just tag along to yell 'no' at the last moment, the very moment when it finally matters and everything becomes seriously real.

I thought, OK then, I can go on this fucking holiday and just make sure she's never alone. OK then. But after that? What am I going to do? I walk around with my mouth shut, and as far as he's concerned, everything's safe. (Since she was five? Since she was *five*? It wasn't fucking possible.)

I thought, OK then. I'll tell her parents myself. I thought, No, she really doesn't want me to do that, that's betraying her like I betrayed Danny. She says, My mum'll go seriously mad – my mum'll kill me. Who am I to say she won't?

But sometimes it seemed that Eleanor was dying in front of my eyes anyway. It was like she was splitting up into crazy fragments – the cold-blooded psycho who wanted to watch sharks eat her uncle while he screamed for help; the giggly, silly five year old who lived for fun; the weeping child who was really, really scared; the mad girl demanding to be fucked. I thought that in all the frenzied mess something that was Eleanor's essential soul was slowly slipping away, like some shy guest quietly leaving an intolerable party.

'No Eleanor today?'

[174]

'Thank god,' I said. I was sat in the kitchen with my mum, holding Sophie while she did the washing up. She started to wake; her eyelids fluttered and fingers and toes extended and her mouth stretched open; then she pressed her nose against my collar bone and fell asleep again, snoring lightly.

Louise frowned. 'Why do you see Eleanor if you don't like her? Do you really not like her?' She came and sat down, and took the sleeping baby away from me.

I tried to think whether I liked Eleanor or not. It seemed kind of irrelevant, somehow. 'It's not I don't *like* her,' I said. 'It's just that she's . . . difficult.'

'What do you mean – difficult?'

'Weird.'

Louise looked at me seriously. 'You know, you shouldn't agree to go on this holiday if you don't really like her,' she said.

That was fucking *it*. The idea that I was stringing Eleanor along just so I could go on the cruise from fucking hell. It was so fucking ironic it made me sick. It would have been fucking funny if I wasn't so fucking insulted. I jumped up like a nutter and yelled, 'Do you think I *want* to go on this fucking holiday?' I was incredibly angry. I hadn't even realized how angry I was. I hammered on the table like a locked door. 'Fuck! Shit! Fuck! Shit!' So of course I scared Sophie awake and she started crying, and whatever I might have said next was meaningless and pointless beside the unmentionable horror of waking a sleeping fucking baby, and I slammed myself into my bedroom screaming 'Kill! Fuck! Kill!' a thousand times. In the silence after I heard the doorbell go.

Face down on the bed, the sun boiling my left elbow, Louise came in and said, 'So – you don't really want to go on this holiday, is that it?'

I laughed.

She came over all embarrassed. 'Andy wants to know if you want to do something – go to the Trocadero or something. He knows you haven't been going out much.'

Jesus. I knew immediately what'd happened, right: Andy'd just come round to watch telly, and my mum'd told him how I'd got girl trouble, and he'd offered to do the man to fucking man thing. I should've told him to fuck off, but the thought of hearing what Andy had to say about how to deal with women sounded too good to miss. Anything for a laugh. Anything for a fucking good laugh. 'Hey, if he's paying,' I said. But I bet a million quid she'd given him the money.

He looked pretty damn nervous: he knew he was still in the dog house so far as I was concerned. But when I said I was coming he cheered up as quick as a stupid dog does when you give it a pat. He wasn't that bothered about upsetting people, but he hated people being mad at him. 'Yeah? Great!' he said. 'You want to do Quasar?' He loved that.

'Whatever,' I said.

'Yeah, really? Great!'

On the northern line to Leicester Square, he stood up even though there were seats to spare and drivelled on and on about Sophie. 'I'm really into this baby stuff, you know: like passing on the genes and stuff, like the whole procreation thing. And what's so great about it, right, I thought it'd be really hard, man, but it's just so cool, I mean, it's so fucking easy, man . . .' (guess who got to go home most nights) '. . . and she's so beautiful, man – like, you always think babies are going to be ugly, right? But don't you think she looks like me, man? She's got my mouth, yeah? . . . Si? Yeah?' In the end I went and sat down in one of the spare seats and left him hanging there from the overhead strap, gibbering mindlessly to himself like a monkey dangling from a tree.

Andy was such a kid. In Leicester Square I'd to drag him past all the dancing androids and sad blokes feeling their way along invisible walls, or he'd've hung around all day with the snap-happy tourists who rush up and crowd around street acts like the way starlings rush down on thrown-away food. And once we got into the Trocadero the only thing he wanted

to do was Quasar. I didn't mind – I'd pretty much done everything there a million times. The first time I'd gone in Alien
Wars it was really exciting for me, but the last time I'd gone
the little kids in there'd used my legs for a shield against the
monster, and I realized I was getting too old. There was a
group just ready to do the Quasar thing, so we put on the gear
and in we went. Andy rushed about like a nutter, firing off at
anything that moved. 'Hit the base! Hit the base!' he shouted
at me, all excited. There was a time me and Danny used to
come quite often. Danny was never much good at it – he was
always shooting up the wrong base, or not noticing some
sneaky kid blasting him from behind. He really tried, though,
rushing about through the dark silver corridors, chasing after
everyone whether they were on the other team or not. One
day he decided he was sick of always getting rubbish scores
and came up with this great plan: he trapped the littlest kid
on the enemy team in a corner and threatened to beat the shit
out of him unless he stood completely still while he fired at
him non-stop for fucking ages. The kid's elder brother turned
up eventually, but not before Danny'd chalked up a really
fantastic score. When the points got added up at the end he
got the top scorer's T-shirt, and he was really chuffed. I
started laughing now, just thinking about it. I'd got myself
into a quiet space, where no one could see me – I wasn't really
in the mood for rushing about. I peeped out and saw Andy a
few feet in front of me. He was breathing hard, probably just
done slaughtering a few twelve year olds. He didn't know I
was behind him. On impulse, I fired off a whole load of
rounds at him without him realizing where it was coming
from. In fact I plugged him so many times I could have
brought down an army. It wasn't very good team spirit, but
as the virtual bullets rattled off of him I felt increasingly
cheerful and relaxed. He figured out where they were coming
from at last and I had to run like fuck for him not to know it
was me. He was really gutted at the end when he turned out
to have the lowest score – couldn't understand it. 'I usually do

really well at this,' he said, about three times.

After that he insisted on buying me a beer, so I knew my mum'd slipped him a fair few quid. Almost as soon as we sat down, in the thin metal café on chairs overlooking the escalators, he said, 'So, what's all this about this girl?'

I was still feeling pleased about the Quasar and it took a moment to realize what he was talking about. Then I said, 'Oh, it's nothing.' I thought now I didn't really want to hear the fruits of Andy's experience with 'girls'.

'It's always better to talk about things than bottle them up,' said Andy – something out of my mum's magazines, which he liked to read on the bog. He tucked his hair behind his ears and looked up at me from under his eyebrows so that his high forehead wrinkled upwards. 'I won't say anything if you just want to talk.'

We sat there in silence, me sipping my beer, and him gazing at me with soulful eyes.

Eventually, with a 'patient' (impatient) sigh, he said, 'Look, your mum says you're freaking out about this holiday with this girl.'

'It's nothing to worry about,' I said.

'Do you like her?'

'She's all right.' She was, really. (Since she was *five*? No, not true.)

He poured the rest of his beer clumsily into his glass. 'Look, you can like girls, right? It don't mean you have to jump when they say jump.' Distracted, he watched his beer's inevitable rise like boiling milk, and sighed as it frothed over the top. 'Like, girls can be pretty damn demanding sometimes.' He dug an old stringy bit of tissue out of his pocket and dabbed at the table meaninglessly. 'Like, actually, the more pressure they put you under to do something, I think the better you are not doing it.' He added to himself, after silently checking over what he'd just said, his eyes raised to the distant roof. 'Yeah. I'm right, you know.'

I thought – yeah, you would say that. If someone wants you

to stay, like me and Louise, run away, run away. I said, 'This girl, Eleanor, she's kind of scared to go on this holiday . . .'

Andy, leaning across the little round table, got his sleeve in the pooled beer without noticing. 'Has she told you what's scaring her?'

I said, 'I should go, you know. I feel – responsible, kind of.'

'You can tell me, Si. I really do care about you. You know I'll help all I can . . .'

I longed so much to say, Listen to me – her uncle's been fucking her since she was *five*; fuck knows what's going on with her sister; she wants me to protect her and how can I do that? How? What do I do?

But what was the point? Tell him something like that and I wouldn't've seen him for the dust. 'It's OK.'

'Look, Si.' He got very serious, like he was about to reveal to me the meaning of life which only he knew. 'If something shit's going on, she's got to tell her mum. No, actually, you tell her she should tell her dad. You make sure she tells him. It's his job to sort it out.' What an amusing thing to hear, Andy on the responsibilities of fatherhood. He picked up his beer and tried to drink out of it before he realized it was all gone. 'Shit – you want another one?' Thinking was such thirsty work for him. When he came back with more beer, he said, 'Like, everything doesn't have to be your responsibility, Si. Everything that happens, you can't control it. You have to see that. You can't always be the one to save the world.' He looked me straight in the eyes – he meant every word. Then, feeling he'd done his bit, he settled back in his thin metal chair and took a big gulp from his glass and looked around at the people coming and going, up and down the escalator, all the people come to spend a lot of money for a little bit of fun; he sat and watched them, and lost interest in whatever we'd been talking about, in favour of watching a million people he'd never seen before and would never see again.

As for me, I sat staring straight at him, thinking how extra-ordinary it was he could sit there and talk about deserting the people you like if it turns out to be too much hassle, and not realize what it sounded like to me, who he'd deserted, who'd deserted my mum, because it was too much fucking hassle. He thought it was so easy to chuck away his responsibilities like litter– he never looked back to see who was picking them up for him, like us looking after Sophie. He asked, Where was Eleanor's father? He said, Let him look after her. That made me think, Yeah, where was my own father? I didn't even know what he looked like, apart from some incredibly embarrassing photos of the wedding. He left me when I was born, to grow up however I wanted. Where was Sophie's father? Sitting here talking about running away. He'd left before she was born. What about Danny's sister's father? He'd done more than desert her – he'd punched her out of life before she'd even made it to her first day. Would my father ever protect me? Would Andy even notice if Sophie was in trouble? I didn't fucking think so, right. Eleanor's parents might live in the same house as Eleanor, but she didn't have any faith in them – maybe they knew her as little as my dear old dad knew me. And if they weren't picking up their responsibilities, someone had to do it, and do the right thing. Someone had to be around who didn't run for it at the first sign of hassle. Someone? Who was I kidding? There was only me. As much as I looked around, as much as I would have loved to take Andy's lazy, fucking-who-cares sort of advice, I could see only me, standing alone in the deserted landscape.

'Si . . . Si . . .' said Andy.

I blinked.

'Staring at me sort of funny,' he said, uncomfortably. He shuffled his half-empty glass. 'Hey, did I help?'

Thirteen

Yeah, in a way Andy helped. I realized it wasn't so much he didn't give a shit, it was just it never struck him to make a difference. He was happy that way, letting things drift, letting everyone else get on with it. Maybe that was the right way to go about life – maybe that way you did the least damage. But after talking to him I knew for sure I couldn't be that way. It did my head in, doing nothing. I couldn't get her invisible wound out of my head, a wet red squidgy hole big enough to shove my fist in. I thought it would kill her in the end – drain out her soft insides. I couldn't stop thinking about Danny in the lower bunk.

Eleanor's fun cruise was due for launch in days. August ended in a blast of fumes. Right up to the last minute I was trusting to global warming that the Mediterranean would dry up (dear god, one last favour . . .). Surprise, it didn't happen. My mum bought me bright orange swimming shorts (my god *had* deserted me); I was alone.

It was a Sunday: feeling the urge to hurry, I took the bus, or maybe I took the bus because it was much slower than walking, going slowly, slowly up Chalk Farm Road, forcing its way slowly through the thick tide of trendies flooding Camden Lock. I looked down on them from the top deck and had a feeling I'd to look closely at everything, to fix it permanently in my mind, all the fashionable people, like I was seeing everything now for the last time, like I was going somewhere very different, very far away, somewhere from where there was no return. I felt kind of calm and relaxed. The top of the bus was empty and filled with September sun, drifting over the people's noisy heads like a sun-filled yacht skimming the surface of London's polluted sea, a yacht sailing calmly on over deep dangerous seas where sharks as well as dolphins swim.

I got off at the bottom of Adelaide Road, and crossed over and walked up the side road to Eleanor's house. I felt so weird, like: calm and together. I was thinking, I'll talk to her, make her see sense, that she has to tell her parents. ('Hi Mum! Hi Dad! Guess what..?') I just wanted to get it over with. No, I just wanted *her* to get it over with.

Actually, walking up to Eleanor's house, what I remember most about what I was thinking was that the sun on my skin was unbearably hot, like it was coming down on me through a greenhouse. I rang the bell.

Eleanor's dad opened the door in a sad heavy-metal T-shirt. 'Eleanor!' he yelled. She appeared at the top of the stairs. She was barefoot, wearing green leggings, but with the white man's shirt. He smiled. 'Good luck, mate.' He went into the kitchen, closing the door, leaving me standing in the green-carpeted hall. When I looked up again, she'd disappeared.

I climbed the stairs slowly. I pushed open the door to her room.

Richard was looking straight at me. He was sat in the white armchair with his back to the sun, and on his lap lounged Eleanor, her small face tilted sideways like a child's. Threads of his black hair glittered in the early September light. He nodded and smiled; Eleanor smiled too. She was lolling against him, her head on his shoulder. He was wearing his suit, the jacket unbuttoned. He took one hand off the arm of the chair and parted her white shirt to place his hand flat on the flesh of her stomach. I closed the door behind me, and stood with my back to it, silenced.

'Well, then, Si,' said Richard, light-heartedly, at last. 'We weren't expecting you.' He was a happy man. Why shouldn't he've been? It was Eleanor's bedroom he was sitting in, with his knees apart and her in his lap.

[182]

I looked into Eleanor's face – she was watching me care-fully from under her eyelashes. I looked back at him. The paleness of his skin made his eyes so green, greener than Eleanor's. Suddenly, he enfolded Eleanor in a protective embrace. She cuddled up to him with a sigh. The armchair they were sat in was so soft – they sank in it together.

I said, 'I can't come on this cruise.'

Eleanor grunted, like someone'd stepped on her toe, and twisted a little in his lap. But he bent his head forward so his lips touched her curls, and closed his eyes.

'Eleanor . . .' I said, painfully.

'Just fuck off, Si – go home.' She shoved her nose into the lapel of his beautiful suit. She despised me, all right, from the depths of her hellish soul.

He cradled her sideways with one hand under her arse like a baby girl. He said to her, 'It's just you and me, sweetie-pops.'

There was no air in the room. I leant my sweating back against the door. I thought, All right, then, I'll go home, like she wants. I thought, Some things are better left unsaid. I didn't want to stay standing there. I'd never thought they'd both be here, like this, together, cuddling. They'd made me an observer. I felt dirty inside. Anyway, you don't know what's going to happen once you start telling people to stop. I told Danny to stop, and he nearly died. I didn't want to let her down. I didn't want her to die, but I didn't want to let her down. My stomach sat inwardly puking in the hole reserved for my heart. In her bed next to the wall I could see poor old My Bear's ears poking out.

Richard rediscovered me standing there. 'What now?' he asked, faintly annoyed.

'I know about you,' I said.

He seemed amused. 'And? . . .'

I started blushing (for fuck's sake!), staring at my trainers. I could see one lace a bit loose. I murmured under my breath, fixated on my shoes like a true kid, 'I just know – that's all.'

After a pause, he asked Eleanor, carefully stroking her hair, 'What's he on about, Ellie?'

She said, 'I don't know,' shaking his hand impatiently off her head. He leaned back in the chair, looking at her, eyebrows raised. 'How should I know?' she repeated. 'He just follows me about, is all. I don't know what he wants.' She got down off his lap and sat picking at the carpet at his feet, pulling up bits of white wool like meadow flowers.

He pushed her gently with his polished foot.

'I didn't say *anything*,' she protested, shuffling on her arse petulantly out of his range. 'All he does is follow me about. He never leaves me alone.'

'Didn't you promise, Ellie?' he asked, pulling her head up softly by her hair. 'No lies? I said, You bring him along, you don't go telling your lies? Didn't you promise?' Gazing up at him from under dampening eyelashes, she shrugged, half-chastised but half-insolent too. He tightened his grip on her hair.

She squeaked, the skin of her face dragged painfully back, 'I haven't told him any lies – I never did!'

'Let go of her!' I cried, in fright, running forward.

'Fuck's sake . . .' Letting go her hair, he said to me sharply, 'No need for fucking heroics, you moron. Haven't you figured it out? She's got serious problems. She cuts herself. That's why she wears my shirts. You should've left her alone. She's a *liar*!'

'She's not!'

He mock-laughed out loud: 'Ha!' and added bitterly, 'Look, Ellie – someone dumb enough to trust you. Tell him you're a liar.'

She smirked up at me, dimpling, and said in her sweet baby five-year-old's voice, 'I'm a leetle li-yar.'

I was revolted by her. I couldn't help myself – I spat it out like retching: 'It's the truth! You *do* it to her!'

He sprang from the chair, grabbed my shoulders and ran me backwards across the room, bang into the closed door,

[184]

smacking his palm across my face, and said under his breath, 'It's a filthy fucking *lie*. You take that back.' His wet breath showered my skin, and clouded the air in violet stench. I wanted to puke in his disgusting face. He hissed, 'It's *you* want to fuck her – I know all about you, see? But she doesn't want you to fuck her, you little fuck. Get out before I throw you out the fucking window.' He drew back his fist and I twisted my head aside.

She was acting really childishly scared, hopping about in the background, tugging her curls. 'Please, I didn't do it,' she kept shrieking tearfully. 'I didn't do it. Stop it. Please stop it.'

'Why do you *do* this, Ellie? Over and over?' He punched the door furiously beside my head. 'You'll kill me, Ellie, with your dirty lies!'

'No, no, no, *no*!' She came with a little-girl rush across the room, throwing her arms around him from behind, pressing her cheek closely against his broad back. 'I never said nothing! I didn't mean to lie again! No, no, no, no! Don't die, unky! I couldn't bear it!'

'You should've thought of that before, if you didn't want me to die,' he said, more gently, lowering his head so his black hair brushed my face like silk as he propped himself wearily against the door, her hanging around his soft body from behind.

'Don't die, unky! Don't die!'

Slowly straightening, he turned towards her awkwardly within the tight human circle of her thin grasping arms.

I opened the door and ran. I heard him shout, and Eleanor shriek. I nearly fell down the stairs, slipping on the top step of the next flight, regaining my balance, running on down – Eleanor flying after me, screaming, 'No, Si! No! Wait! Wait!'

I heard Richard, behind her, half-way down, saying to her through his teeth, 'Get out of my way.'

I banged open the door to the kitchen. Eleanor's mother was surprised, leaning sideways with her elbow on the counter, which was littered with orange chrysanthemums, her black curly hair floating down to her arse, wearing a tight green dress. Debbie looked up from the table when I burst in. She'd been drawing a white yacht on a bright blue sea. I walked up to Eleanor's mother and said, 'You have to ask Richard what he does to Eleanor.'

'Hello, darling,' said Eleanor's mother, looking through me. 'Are you all right?'

'Hi, Mary,' said Richard, panting slightly. He stopped still, just inside the kitchen, shoving the tips of his fingers awkwardly under the tight material of his pockets, flexing them a little. 'Fine.' He said, 'I'm on my way out.'

'What – now?' she asked.

I cried impatiently, 'Wait a minute . . .' but she'd turned to the flowers, picking them up one by one and stripping off their lower leaves, letting the dark dying green fall to the floor.

Eleanor, who'd run in after him, came to stand right behind me, tugging down on my T-shirt. 'Come on, Si,' she kept whispering, her breath like an insect. 'Please, Si, just leave it, forget it, come on, it doesn't matter . . .'

I looked down at her desperate little fingers clutching the sides of my shirt from behind. I thought, she's right – leave it – who am I to act like I can save anyone?

Debbie dashed at Richard, grabbing hold of his jacket. 'Take *me*, take *me* on your yacht, Uncle Richard!' she shouted.

Eleanor moaned, pulling down on my shirt till I felt the seam under my armpit begin to give. Falling to his knees, Richard put his arms around the girl's waist and said, 'You want to come on my yacht, sweetie-pops? If you're very, *very* good – maybe you can.' And while he squeezed her tight he smiled past me at Eleanor and said, 'You tell him the truth, Ellie. You tell Si.'

'It's a secret – ssh!' whispered Eleanor in my ear.

'Tell what?' asked Walt, walking into the kitchen and straight over to the fridge.

'Don't ask,' said Richard, still smiling.

I said loudly, 'Ask Richard what he does to Eleanor.'

'Pardon me for fucking asking,' Walt muttered, tossing his ginger pony-tail, pulling out a beer.

Mary said, 'For god's sake, Walter.' She turned and reached down a huge crystal vase off a high shelf.

Debbie said in a small, uncertain voice, 'Let go . . .' Richard was holding her very tightly. Her sweet little body wriggled in his grasp. He wasn't paying any attention to her. He was watching Eleanor. Debbie pushed him sharply in the chest, her glasses nearly popping off her nose.

'Let her *go*!' hissed Eleanor, in her psycho voice, stepping out from behind me.

Shocked, he let Debbie go. She dashed for the door and disappeared. Eleanor's mother, standing with the glass vase folded to her chest, exclaimed, surprised, 'Don't talk to Richard like that!'

Richard, his arms wide open like Christ, sighed: 'Ellie . . . darling . . .' (I pictured unexpectedly he was like a fat fucking Shortarse, kneeling disbelievingly there, his face upturned.) She stared him down with psycho eyes. He slowly lowered his gaze.

I said to Eleanor's mother, 'There's something you need to know.'

'No,' said Richard, looking sharply up. 'Listen to Eleanor.'

Mary went to the sink and started filling the heavy vase with a long deafening gush of water.

'Do I need to know?' asked Walt, being sarcastic.

'Yes, you do,' I said, panicky and relieved at being suddenly heard. But he was concentrating on opening his beer. Richard got to his feet. Eleanor came grabbing on to me again from behind. I said, 'Richard's been having sex with Eleanor.' Eleanor screamed, ripping apart my shirt.

In the silence, the vase cascaded over. Eleanor's mother turned off the tap and stayed facing the sink. I could hear the water trickling down the drain. She picked up a handful of the chrysanthemums and started slotting them, one by one, into the vase. Eleanor's dad took a very long swig of beer. He looked at me over the open can. I couldn't look straight at anyone; I felt like I was back in that rubbish sea under the bins, smelling disintegration and the fear.

'Of all the . . .' Richard started. He stopped dead, took out his dark-rimmed glasses and put them on. I thought of him fucking her in his scented bed, leaning over her in bed, with all his white flesh hanging down, then sticking his fat prick fiercely in. Maybe he was thinking about it too. He laughed out loud. 'Oh, god, Ellie, not again . . . For . . . *Tell* him, Ellie. Tell him it's a sick . . .' Of course, of course – who else but Eleanor can save you now? Hasn't she saved you for ten long years? Isn't she the strong one, and you – on your knees to her? He took the glasses off again, running his hand over his face, taking a step towards her. She jumped with a scared cry back out of his reach – a five year old again, as he loved her best, tremble-mouthed, prettily pathetic, inarticulate.

Eleanor's mum turned round from the sink. She wiped her hands on the front of her tight green dress. 'Yes, Eleanor,' she said very slowly and deliberately. 'Go on. Say it's a lie.'

Eleanor shook and shook, without being able to help it. She wanted to say something but she was shaking too much to get the words out. Really, it seemed like she might physically fall over. Richard took a step closer to her. '*Tell* them, Ellie!'

Eleanor jumped a mile and burst into hysterical tears. 'Don't! Don't!' she babbled, in a high, silly voice. 'Don't hurt me, unky!'

'Oh, for god's sake . . .' he said, impatiently. To me he said, low and intense, 'You fucking moron. You're just encouraging her. Do you want to send her completely mad?'

'She's at it again,' said Mary to Eleanor's dad, calmly. He gazed at her blankly.

Richard said to Eleanor, sweetly, persuasively, lovingly, 'Come on, sweetie.' He put out his hand to touch her. Eleanor screamed.

'Get away from her,' I cried, spreading my startled arms in front of her.

[188]

He stared at me in utter disbelief. 'You . . . you . . .' He shouted, 'Get out of my *way*!' He shoved me in the chest. I stumbled back against Eleanor, who immediately lost it completely and started screaming in short, repetitive bursts, over and over again.

Eleanor's dad, roused from his stupor, came over to her and made to put his arms round her, saying, 'Ssh, ssh . . .' but she pushed him away and shrieked at me, 'You fucker! You fucker! You fucker!'

Mary said to me without much emotion, 'Si, why have you told this dreadful lie? Tell him it's a lie, Eleanor – tell him – *now*.'

Eleanor crouched down to the floor and put her hands over her ears. I squatted down beside her, putting my hand on her back, but she elbowed me away.

'It's not a lie,' I said stupidly, looking up at her mother.

'She's lying,' said Mary, cold and quiet. 'Everyone knows she's a liar.' She started putting flowers into the vase again. She said, 'I think you ought to leave now, Si. It's not useful to come barging into other people's affairs like this. Nobody appreciates it, and you're bound to get it all wrong. '

I looked at Eleanor's dad.

'Don't look at me for sympathy, mate,' he said. 'She's the boss lady. I never get to . . .'

'Off you go, Si,' said Richard. He took a step towards Eleanor, but when she cringed he froze, raising his hands, like: Look, I'm not going to touch you. He said to me, 'I'm sorry about all this, Si. It really is better if you leave.'

'Yes, leave us alone now, Si,' said Eleanor's mother. 'Leave us to pick up the pieces. Think a bit harder before you go rushing in next time. It's not easy for us, Eleanor being the way she is. She won't want to see you again. You know where the door is.'

I stood up, hesitating, gazing down at Eleanor. She looked so pitiful and small I thought I really did love her, sort of, though I'd never said. She'd said it to me, but I never really believed her.

'Go *now*,' insisted her mother.

And I left her. Helpless, guilty, sick and silent, I walked away from her towards the door.

Behind me, I heard her say wistfully, 'I *do* love you, unky Richard.'

'Of course you do, darling,' said her mother's voice, brightly. 'And Richard loves you, too.'

'Of course I do,' he said. 'I dote on you.'

'What a loving family,' remarked Walt sarcastically, against the splutter of an opening can.

Eleanor, added, a little shyly, 'It's just you prodding inside me makes me sick . . . I do throw up, you know, a lot –' she paused, and added, self-consciously, by way of explanation, 'like, not at the time, of course – that'd be gross.'

I turned slowly, cautiously around. Mary had gone over to the kitchen table, and was sitting with her head in her hands, her beautiful long hair falling straight down her arms. Walt leaned against the tall white fridge, eyes on the floor, like he was embarrassed. Eleanor stared at the floor between her parted legs.

Only I of all of them was watching Richard, with a sort of sick fascination. His long lashes were drooping against his cheeks. His whole body was trembling. He said painfully, 'Ellie. Ellie. Why are you doing this?' She glanced up at him with a tiny little smile, but then looked down again, and said nothing, plaiting her fingers together in her lap.

'Ellie . . .' But she didn't look up again. He stood gazing at her with terrible grief, like he wished she'd stay frozen that way for ever and ever, the look of her fixed for ever in his mind, then quietly left the room, passing me in the doorway, head lowered, turning sideways so as not to touch me, and left the house, pulling the front door gently to behind him.

Walt stayed with his cheek pressed against the fridge. Eleanor frowned at him, got up and went over to her mother and started stroking her hair. 'Mum . . .' Her mother reached up and ruthlessly pushed Eleanor's hand away. Eleanor stood with her hand hovering in the air, uncertain whether she was allowed to touch her again. She checked round the room. Her dad seemed hardly there. I was still standing just inside the doorway. Our eyes met. She was almost going to say something, but Debbie startled her, rushing into the kitchen.

Debbie was excited, frightened. 'What's the matter? What's the matter?' she kept asking. 'Why aren't you talking? Where's Uncle Richard gone? Is he mad at us?' She stared around but no one spoke or moved. Eleanor and me watched her as she hurried first to her dad, then to her mum. 'Why aren't you talking? Why are you staring at me? Where's Uncle Richard gone?' She ran over to her sister and tugged at the front of her top. 'Why won't you talk to me, Ellie? What's the matter with Uncle Richard? I saw him from my bedroom window – Ellie, why was he crying?'

'Oh, god!' cried out Eleanor's mother, a howl muffled by her hands.

Debbie repeated, 'Why? Why?' pulling and pulling at Eleanor's top, jerking her forward step by step.

Eleanor seemed confused. But she said to herself, remembering, slowly and clearly, 'No.' And repeated, in rising horror, '*No*.' And immediately, pushing Debbie aside, she threw herself on her mother, arms round her neck, crying, 'Help him! Mum! Mum! He's gone to kill himself! Mum! Help him! Stop him!'

Mary leapt up and grabbed hold of Eleanor's upper arms, shaking her about like a doll, shouting into her face, 'You stupid slut! How could you do it? You've killed him with your lies, you stupid *slut*!'

Eleanor, her head snapping backwards and forwards on her neck, screamed, 'Stop him!'

Mary swept her furiously aside and shrieked at Eleanor's dad, 'Walter! Stop him!' But Walt just stayed there, staring dully at her. Debbie, in tears, was holding her dad by the hand, and he was mechanically stroking the back of her hand

[191]

with his thumb. 'Stop him!' begged Mary again, clutching her stomach like diarrhoea and stamping her foot. He didn't move.

Eleanor's mother said to herself, 'We should call the police . . . No . . . No . . .' She pushed her hand through her long black hair, looked round, saw me standing there frozen, in one swift bitter movement seized the glass vase and hurled it. It hit me so hard on the side of my head I crashed against the wall, and a sea of freezing water full of chrysanthemums cascaded over me, down my front and back, while the vase smashed to pieces on the floor. 'Get out!' she screeched. 'Get out of my house! Get *out*!'

Fourteen

Me, Si, so into peace and that summer of love; me, Si, whose aim in life was not to hate anyone; me, Si, growing my hair all summer so I could get a pony-tail and be a regular laid-back, music-loving, dope-smoking, longhair – me, Si, the only murderer. Funny how things turn out. Si the saint – the only one left with blood on his hands.

Because he'd gone off to kill himself, hadn't he? Of course he had. Wouldn't you if you were him? Si, the murderer.

Eleanor's mum knew it. She knew I was a murderer. I'd hardly got home, sitting in my bedroom changing my torn, soaking shirt, when the phone rang. I heard Andy pick it up. He said, 'Really? No shit! You sure you got the right number? No shit! . . . Say, it doesn't *sound* like something he'd do . . . Give us a sec and I'll ask . . .' And he came to my door, receiver in one hand, phone trailing its wire in the other, lounging in my doorway, giggling. 'Got a lady on the line here, Si, says you murdered her brother . . . bit upset . . . ring any bells?' It was cracking him up, the stupid old bastard. He thought he'd some nutter on the phone.

Sat on the bed on that crappy faded Superman duvet, I leaned so far forward my forehead touched my knees and rested there. All my energy seemed to've soaked away; I thought to raise my head, to ever move again, would be too fucking tiring for all the world. I wondered blankly if Richard was already dead (still warm but dead – sitting in his flash car with the grey paste of blown-out brains spread thinly over the green leather). Then I tried not to think about it, because just the having of that thought made me so much more tired on top of what I already was that I might die suddenly myself.

I heard Andy say, 'Look, sorry, something's up, I've gotta go . . .' and I felt him come sit on the bed beside me, and put his warm arm around me, suddenly anxious. 'What's going on, Si?' he asked. 'What's the problem, man? Everything *is* OK, isn't it?'

I didn't answer, just sat with my head on my knees. He asked, scared, 'Fuck's sake, Si – what's happened – has there been an accident or something?'

In my head, Richard walked quickly down the hall and out of the house, closing the door behind him. 'Sort of,' I said.

'Oh. Right.' His arm around me tightened for a moment, then he took it away to wipe his face with his hand, both hands, and then wipe his hands on his long greasy brown hair. 'Sort of . . . Right. OK, then. Yeah? Look, let's not panic, OK? . . . It's probably not as bad as it seems . . .' I turned my head on my knees so I could see him. He was bending forward, his long face drooping with the effort of paying attention. 'I'm sure everything's not as bad as it looks, man,' he said, with his serious brown eyes. 'Really.' I could've almost let myself be comforted by that, except I knew he knew fuck all. 'OK, Si? Are you OK?'

'No,' I said. 'Andy – I'm fucking *not* OK.'

He wrinkled up his forehead. 'But we can sort it out, right?'

I said, 'Listen, Andy – it's all shit. Eleanor's uncle, who was going to take us on that cruise? You know? He's killed himself, because I told her parents what Eleanor told me. He fucks her, OK? Eleanor's really upset about me telling. They don't believe it anyway.'

Andy was staring at me. 'No shit,' he said. He pulled a strand of hair into his mouth and started eating it mechanically. 'Right.' He kept staring at me. 'Jesus. The bastard.'

The phone rang again, on the little table at the side of the bed where he'd left it. Andy switched his stare to the phone, but made no move.

I picked it up. I had this weird idea it might be Eleanor. It was Eleanor's mum. She sounded like she was being burnt alive. 'He's dead! He's dead! He must be dead! I know he's dead! Murdering fucker! Murdering *fucker*!' I put down the phone. It rang again. My mum came into the room, holding Sophie.

She stood looking from me to Andy to the phone on the table. The phone rang and rang. 'Pick it up, then,' she said to Andy, like: what-the-fuck's-the-matter-with-you?

'Yeah . . .' said Andy, meaningfully.

'What? Pick it *up*!'

'Look . . .' said Andy, sliding his eyes towards me. 'Kind of . . .'

'For Christ's sake!' She pushed the baby into Andy's arms and snatched up the persistent phone, listened for a disbelieving minute before she slammed it down again and yelled at Andy, 'And what the fuck was that about?'

Clutching Sophie, he said hastily, 'Ssh, sweetheart, you'll wake the baby.'

'Mum . . .' I said.

'*Who's* dead?' She still thought it was to do with Andy, not with me. Kind of touching, really. 'What've you done this time, you useless fucking fuck-up bastard?'

'Hey!' He was getting a bit offended. 'What makes you think I . . .'

The phone rang. 'For Jesus Christ's sake! You're pathetic!' She grabbed it. '*What?*' Then her face calmed down, she glanced at me, held the receiver close to her ear and said, 'Oh, hello, Eleanor. Do you want Si?' She closed her eyes to listen, so Eleanor must've been speaking pretty quiet. 'OK,' said Louise. 'That's OK. OK.' After a bit, she said, 'I don't know, he never said anything to me about anything like that . . . yes, I'll tell him . . . yes, of course I will . . . yeah . . . OK . . . OK . . .' She put the receiver back on the phone and stood silently for a while. Then she said to me, 'Eleanor says it was all a stupid lie.'

'Oh, right,' I said.

[195]

'She says you told her mum her uncle was having sex with her but it was a lie she told you for a joke.'

'Oh, right,' I said. 'Right.'

'She thinks he'll kill himself. Over a stupid joke? Pretty extreme, I thought.'

'Right.'

'Fucking right it's extreme,' said Andy, with feeling.

'Was that her mum on the phone?' asked Louise. 'Is it him she thinks is dead?'

'Yeah,' I said. 'Yeah.'

'He did do it, right? Like what she said was a joke – it did happen, right?'

'I think,' I said. 'Yeah. Really. I really think he did.'

Louise sat down on my other side, holding her eyes. 'I hope he's dead, the dirty fucking bastard. What a fucking lowlife. That poor little Eleanor. Jesus . . . *men* . . .'

'And her,' said Andy. 'That woman. What a cunt, right?'

Louise sighed. Ringing again. Louise picked it up. She lowered it. 'It's Eleanor for you,' she said, looking me closely in the face. 'Do you want to speak to her?'

I took the phone with care.

'Hi?'

It was so fucking sad, you know. She said, 'I love him, Si. I just love him, right? And he loves me. If he kills himself it will be all your fucking fault and I will never ever forgive you.'

I put my head back on my knees, because it weighed too much for my tiredness to hold it up, still with the receiver to my ear. I heard myself say, 'Eleanor, how *can* you love him?' Stupid thing to ask, I suppose. I really wanted to know. How could you love anyone who did such terrible things to you? It was just so fucking weird.

'How could you say those awful things about him? I *never* want to speak to you again.' Then she said in a painful but unEleanor-like way, 'You have driven an innocent man to his death.'

'Fuck's sake, Eleanor,' I said. 'Fuck's sake.'

'You have driven . . .'

I threw the receiver into my mother's lap and leant back against my bedroom wall. Louise listened and hung up.

Andy said, 'So that's why you were so uptight about her. Poor little kid. Her dad must be a real arsehole, not realizing what was going down. How could he not know? Do you think they knew? Jesus. I hope I never not notice anything like that.'

Louise said, 'Thank god you told them.' She was in tears. 'I hope he's dead, the bastard. *Dead*.'

It was weird, her saying that – she'd always insisted on everything being so peace and love and candles and live and let live. I got out from between them. 'You just don't get it, Mum – I didn't want anyone to fucking die. That was the whole fucking point.' I went to look out the open window. I could smell all the flowers, warm and heavy, very rich, shrubs bulky in their pots. Nothing had changed, nothing had started visibly to rot, but you could smell the end coming.

She asked, 'You think it's your fault if he's dead?'

Did I? There are such thin lines everywhere, between doing the right thing and doing the wrong thing. It's so fucking impossibly hard to walk on the right side of the line, when no one even tells you where it is, or you're only carrying some outdated map from stupid childhood. And the line between life and death is so thin too. When I was a little kid, I thought it was a big thick line. I thought it was really difficult to die. But now I know you only have to walk a little crooked and you can wander over the line without hardly noticing. It's like life and death are no distance apart at all. One day you're walking along in the sun, just relaxing, paying no attention to where you're going, and the next thing is . . . fuck! you've gone and stepped over the line, just by not paying attention enough to where you're walking. Like Danny's mum's boyfriend nearly did, and Danny himself, and even me. And the kid I kicked off his bike, nearly falling into the road. You can so easily end up on the side of death, like Danny's sister, born into it, or Richard, threatening to leap over the line on purpose.

'He said he'd kill himself, if Eleanor told,' I said.

'Oh, yeah,' said Andy. 'Like fuck.'

I said very quick, looking round, 'You think he won't?'

'Of course he won't,' said Andy, getting comfortable on the bed, stretching his long legs out a bit. He liked to feel part of things these days. 'Trust me.'

'No, listen, Si,' he said, as I turned back impatiently to the flowers. 'He's done a runner, right? Don't fucking worry about it. That's what bastards like him do, when things get too heavy for them. Cut loose when the going gets tough. They just can't hack the responsibility. Trust me, Si. Trust me, man.'

After a couple of days the police found his car on the Cornish cliffs – his green, leather-smelling car standing empty on the flat green grass, far, far above the grey salt-smelling sea, circled by gulls. Its doors were locked – through the closed windows the police could see his grey suit jacket folded on the seat, his keys on top. We knew all this because Eleanor's mum phoned us up, screaming the news down the phone, literally screaming like someone was ripping out her insides while she stood clinging desperately to the phone, screaming out the news of his death.

'He's done a runner, hasn't he?' said Andy. It was that obvious to him, he acted like he'd personally solved the case. 'He'll probably turn up soon.'

Eleanor's mum phoned up so often, my mum paid to get our number changed.

One really weird thing: it was in the papers. Not the Richard I knew, leaking cold water, jumping me in my panicky dreams, but somebody different – the public Richard, rich bastard Richard, awash with dosh. It was all crap, though – stories about the company he owned with his sister. (His tragic sister, she's still so upset . . . Money missing? She won't

[198]

say anything. Where's this body, then? That's missing, all right.) I read all the stories, but nothing was true, because nobody said a word about Eleanor. Poor old Eleanor, always invisible, always getting written out. No wonder she thought she didn't exist. It's like you can live but never be born. At this rate, her gravestone will be blank.

I wanted to talk to Danny. I didn't ring him, though. I waited for him to ring me. Maybe it was because my number was changed that he didn't ring. I only found out he'd got out of hospital because I bumped into Viv down the shops. Maybe he didn't ring because my number was different – but then, he knew where I lived. It wasn't that far away. School'd started again, but I kept finding I was too sick to go. Flu and stuff. Things. Good reasons, really.

My dad wrote to me. My mum put him up to it, because she'd got this great idea that hearing from someone I'd never met and who didn't give a fuck about me might cheer me up enough to get me back to school. I suppose that's what she was thinking. He'd always sent her money, but I'd never thought of him as a father – just as my mother's business arrangement. I never really thought of myself as having a father, and now here was this Canadian letter. The weird thing was, it was in a neater version of my own handwriting. At first I couldn't figure out who it was from.

'Dear Si,' he wrote, 'I hear you're a hero. PS this sort of thing is all in the genes!' And so on, a long letter. He sent his boyfriend's love as well, which was strange (but all right, though, I'm not an arsehole about that sort of thing), and offered me to visit him. One day I might. He sent a picture of himself. Looking at it, I was sure I must remember him, it seemed so certain I knew his face. He looked quite young. He'd short brown hair and pale brown skin. His eyelashes were black and his eyes very wide open. I thought, I've seen you before, somewhere. Yet he'd left before I was even born. My mum laughed, 'Come on! What do you think?' I looked at his eyes, his hair. It was the strangest thing, seeing for the first time roughly how I was going to look in the future. It was like I'd woken up and looked in the mirror and found I'd aged by twenty years since falling asleep – a *Star Trek* thing, pretty fucking weird. It fitted in with everything I'd been thinking about how close we are to death all the time. But reading his letter was kind of nice. All that hero crap didn't have to be true – I just liked hearing it from this familiar stranger, as if an older version of myself had contacted me out of the future to tell me everything was going to be OK.

My mum said, looking at his picture in amazement, 'It's incredible how much you look like your dad. I never realized. Some things you do remind me of him.'

I asked, surprised and interested by the idea that everything I had wasn't originally mine, 'Like what? What things I do? You never said.'

'Just seeing him again reminded me,' she said.

'Like what?'

'Oh, I don't know,' she said vaguely. 'Things.'

'Go on – say.'

'Oh, god – picking your nails, things like that,' sighed Louise, passing the picture back to me. 'Funny, isn't it, what you remember?' Innit just.

Eleanor wrote to me. My second letter in a fortnight, after a lifetime of postal silence. She wrote:

Dear Si, I'm never going to speak to you again. I can't believe what you did to me, after you promised not to say anything. You make me sick. You are evil. My mum is going mad because she loves Richard more than any of us. I am living a nightmare. My mum says I have gone mad. It is true. His body has disappeared. It is all mangled in the sea. The sharks have chewed it up slowly. Didn't they tell you he jumped off a cliff? There are sharks in the sea, you know that. Why didn't he just drive off? He could of sunk in the car and not got eaten. I love him just as truly and purely as my mum does. It is terrible to think of him being eaten. What you said is sick and it is all lies. My mum says it is sick and it is all lies. It is true.

She loves Richard more than any of us. How could you do that to me? I trusted you. I thought you were my friend, but you are evil. My dad wants to talk to me. I won't let him. Some of us can keep our mouths shut. Some of us can't. Maybe I can't. Maybe I'll tell the police how you and Danny tried to murder his mum's boyfriend. Then you'll go to prison for a long time, because you are a murderer. I'm writing to you because it would make me sick to see you or even speak to you on the phone. Just to let you know, if they find his body I will definitely go to the police. I know what you're thinking. Some people can't keep a secret. I know that's what you're thinking. Now you know what it is like. Something bad happens. Someone has a secret for you, and then they tell everyone and nothing will ever, ever be OK again. Are you scared now, Si? Are you scared to think your secret might be out? Now you know what it's like, living with a dirty secret. I bet you haven't told your mum your dirty secret. She'd be so fucking upset, wouldn't she? She'd never believe you were her pure little boy again. So you daren't tell her. Well, that's OK because here I am, your friend. I'll tell your mum for you. Isn't that nice of me? You've got a bad secret. Don't forget it. Watching over you as always, Love, Eleanor.

I was sat on my bed when I opened the letter and read it. I would have burnt it then and there, but I'd no matches and nowhere to burn it, so I put it under my mattress like stupid people do in films in the way that makes you think, Oh, Christ, you stupid bastard, that's the first place they're going to look, get it *out* of there. In the end, I took it out from under the mattress and put it in my pocket.

I went along to my mum's room. Andy was there, hanging over Sophie's cot. He was singing something completely tuneless, a nursery rhyme or Beatles song or something. She was fast asleep. It was raining out, and the noise of the rain made the room seem warmer. He said to me, 'All right, Si?'

'Not great,' I said.

'I love her when she's asleep,' he said. 'It's so fucking great being a dad. I think it really makes you grow up.' He was really trying to be one of us, screwing up his serious eyes. 'It's like . . . really real, it's like – passing yourself on, like . . .

immortality, sort of.' Even he, with all his aimless drifting, turned out to be looking for some sort of solidity, some personal immortality, a tree like Sophie on which to carve his mortal name. I looked him over as he stood singing to her. I didn't think he'd ever do her any harm. In a moment of tolerance, I even thought, Well, maybe he's not such a bad old bastard. He's a lazy fucker, but he's not such a bad old bastard – at least he probably won't do her any harm. Maybe that's the main thing. Maybe the best you can hope for is just that: that the people around you will fuck you up as little as possible, and do you as little damage as they can.

'Isn't it great,' he said, 'when she's asleep? Just peacefully asleep.' The rain battered away.

I wondered if Richard's body had surfaced yet, rolling up from the depths with a gushing and sloshing noise as the dead man plopped up and turned over in the grey polluted sea, flesh palely swollen, ready to burst if poked, nibbled by fish, perhaps, but in the end, despite all Eleanor's desires, untouched by sharks. No sharks in the Channel, Eleanor – no sharks. The wrong sea for him to die in after all. Her letter was in my pocket. I wanted to show it to Danny before I burnt it. It was only right to let him know what new danger I'd put him in. Richard had no children, but he had his own immortality, I suppose – the shock waves from his destructive power, his mighty splash into the freezing sea, spreading in rings around us all.

It was getting towards evening when I finally knocked on Danny's door, and his grandma Gabriella opened it, very chirpy, well pleased to see me. She acted happy-amazed, like I was her long-lost friend. I'd forgot I was Danny's guardian angel, the one who saved him from the evil devil. She wanted me to come on in, have something to eat, feed me some serious gratitude.

I asked, 'Is Danny there?'

'No, but come – come inside and eat – why didn't you

come before? You shouldn't stay away, you're too modest, keeping away like that . . . You're a saint, your friends need you, you mustn't stay away from us so long again. We've missed you so much.'

'Sure, Gabriella – sure.' Her world was so different from mine – all the same players, same things happening, and so fucking different. 'Do you know where he is, then?'

'Oh, Si, how would I know? The usual places, he doesn't tell me. Come in and wait, he'll be here – he'll be so glad you came. Come in and wait.'

The evening was cool, even shivery, smelt of afternoon rain. It was nearly October. I had my jacket on. To warm up I walked fast down Adelaide Road. A gang of kids ran past me, swung round on one collective foot, looked me up and down, grabbed me by the arm, called me a wanker, threatened me for all my cash. I only had twenty pence, but they were just doing it for form's sake really, they didn't care, I didn't care, it was only twenty pence – they ran off again. I'd fifteen quid on me when I came out, but it was in my shoe and anyway I'd spent it a couple of hours ago – done something stupid, got Danny this thing in an American shop in Camden Town, a baseball cap actually, sort of cool: I had it folded in my inside pocket. Eleanor's letter was folded in my back jeans pocket. Not so cool. I went to stand at the foot of Primrose Hill. Looking up, the sun had fallen behind the hill – down here was shadows but up there the enormous sky hanging over the hill was still pale cold yellow. I couldn't think whether to climb up or not; Danny'd said he wasn't going to climb the hill again until his mum's boyfriend was dead, and Danny always stuck to what he said. And as for me, I'd kind of given up on the hill – it hadn't seemed the right place for me, not since then. It was easier down here, more real anyway, hanging about in the shadows, getting fucked over by total strangers.

I climbed the hill slowly. I'd kind of forgotten how steep it was. It looked greener, now the autumn rain had come, ended the brown summer. The grass squashed where I trod, and the little stones didn't roll under my feet but sank down into the softened ground. The air smelt different, cleaner and wetter; it moved and shook the trees, and star-shaped leaves came gliding down.

Up at the top it was pretty deserted. But two of the old crowd were still there, talking on their feet, hands in pockets, shivering in unbuttoned jackets – Viv and big Al, last of the old crowd, still hanging on. But their summer of love was well over.

'Jesus, Si – long time no see, mate,' said Al, tucking his hands under his armpits. 'You all right? You coming back to school or what?'

'I'm all right,' I said. 'What you doing?'

'Just going actually – fucking cold up here now,' said Viv, rubbing his nose. '*Fucking* cold.' He wouldn't button his jacket, though. He was too cool. 'Just came up for a look, is all. We had a laugh this summer, didn't we, Si?'

'A real laugh,' said Al. 'Good all right. What you doing, Si?'

I looked around at the empty hill, its trees shaken by the visible autumn above a city without seasons. Nobody else was there. 'Kind of looking for someone,' I said.

'What, Danny? Over there.' Al pointed towards the trees. 'Just sitting, crazy bastard.'

'Fucking freezing,' said Viv. 'He's freezing his arse off. Gotta go, man. See you later.'

'See you then, Si,' said big Al. 'Going for chips. See ya later, OK?'

Off they went, running down the hill, leaving me behind.

I walked among the dripping trees, splashing through leaves, until I came to the other side and found him there – his back towards me, sitting completely still on the side of the hill, gazing obsessively down to the polluted city, watching the long process of London flushing from lavender to orange, warming up as the sky cooled down, lighting up as the true light faded. I went to sit beside him. He was a lot thinner since being in hospital – his arms and legs'd got skinny-looking, his eyes larger, and big nose sticking out more, the hands around his knees sharp with bones. He didn't take his eyes off of the view.

But he said to me, 'All right, mate?'

I pulled my jacket tight around my neck, trying to keep out the gathering cold. I looked at his bony hands. 'You all right, then? Like after hospital and shit?'

He glanced at me and as quickly away again. He shrugged. 'Yeah, I'm all right. I'm good. I'm all fixed up.'

'That's good. That's great.'

We just sat. The longer I sat the more uncomfortably wet my arse got off the damp grass. I kept looking round at him. He was fixed on the valleys below. Me and Danny could sit for ages not talking – it was one of the ways I knew we were friends. But that was then. Now I didn't know whether this was a good silence or a bad silence.

I said, 'I didn't think you'd be up the hill, man, but I came anyway.'

He shifted around, rubbing his knees.

'You said you wouldn't come up the hill again, not till he was dead,' I said. I wasn't trying to say anything, I just wanted to know what was in his head.

'Yeah,' he said. He sniffed, and wiped his big nose with the back of his sleeve. 'Y'know,' he said, locking his fingers together back-to-front, glancing back towards the trees, 'my mum's as fat as a pig these days. She's doing that twelve-step thing.'

That was pretty fucking amazing news. I was really knocked out for him. 'That's *great*, man – shit.'

'She was kind of mad, my mum – but she's getting OK,' he said. 'She's like been doing it for a month now. She's going to stick it out all right. It's run by nuns.'

'Nuns! What, nuns like in god?'

'It's weird, but it's OK. It's working out, man. I just want you to know. That's why I came up here. I wasn't going to, before, right. But that's why.'

'Like, you weren't going to come up before, not till he was dead.'

'Yeah – but it's working out, man. Everything's cool. He's dead to us, innit. Just the trial to get through, is all.'

I didn't want to spoil it for him, but there you go. I fished Eleanor's letter out of my back pocket and handed it over. 'You better read that, mate,' I said.

He read it slowly, his whole face crunched up in the bad light, then folded it up as small as it would go and squeezed it into the little pocket just under the waistband of his jeans. He stared straight ahead of him, keeping his face without expression, breathing a little faster, was all, shivering slightly in the autumn chill. 'What's all that about, Si?' he asked. 'Who was it died, man?'

'Thought you might've known – haven't you seen her? That was her uncle Richard, drowned himself.'

'*Is* it? The yacht guy?' He couldn't believe his fucking ears. 'He's *dead*? When?'

'It was in all the papers. Over a month ago.' Not that he ever read them. 'Haven't you seen her?'

'I went round once, but her mum said she was sick . . . the *record* guy? The guy who was going to take you on a cruise? The guy she didn't like much? Why's she so pissed off at you about it?' He shook his head in amazement. 'She fucking mad, or what? What's the big secret anyway?'

'It's kind of bad. She told me . . . listen, Dan . . . that guy'd been having sex with her for years.' I paused a brief second for his reaction, but he didn't move, staring steadily down the hill. 'So I told her parents, right? Because she wouldn't. He said he'd kill himself. She's really fucking angry, man. Her mum don't believe her either. I can see why she didn't want to tell them now. It's total shit. She's, like, going to go to the police about us if it turns out he's really dead.'

Danny still didn't say anything. He brought his knees up

tight against his face and tied his arms around his knees, in the dying light.

'I'm sorry, man,' I said.

Danny said into his knees, 'How can people do this shit? What's going on inside their heads? I don't understand. I just don't fucking understand. How can they do this to us? To little kids and things.'

'They must be mad, I guess,' I said. That's what I really thought, too – you got to be mad, innit, to do that?

'No,' he said. 'I just don't get it. Like my mum's boyfriend was brought up in shit. He was a total bastard. Fucking scum of the earth. Killed my little sister. But this guy was *rich*.' He sat up and looked at me, pressing his hands hard down on the dark wet grass. He said in furious exasperation, 'He owned a fucking yacht, for fuck's sake, Si. He didn't need it. What the fuck was he doing? What the *fuck* was he doing? What was going on inside his *head*?'

I said, 'You should've seen him, Danny – you should've seen him with her . . . it was like he thought it was OK. It was fucking disgusting, horrible.'

'But he was *rich*,' said Danny. He couldn't get his head round it. 'He could've had anything he wanted. What did he want to do that for? All that dosh, and all he wanted to do was . . . Jesus Christ. That's fucking crazy, man. That's fucking sad.'

'I'm sorry, Danny, about her saying she'll go to the police and everything. I didn't think what she'd be like if he went and did it, man.'

In the dark grey dusk he leaned over and shook me by the shoulder, holding it, pushing it back and forwards, a real solid gesture of friendship. 'Fuck's sake man – what're you sorry for? It's good you told. Best thing you ever done. I'm proud of you, man. It's all right. You did right. You have to do the right thing, man. You can't just not do it. I don't care what she tells the cops. We'll be all right. Maybe he won't turn up – he hasn't yet, right?'

'No.' But again in my head his rolling corpse, so bloated it burst the buttons on its shirt, heaved up gross and grey through the swelling water. A soaked leaf landed on the back of my neck, sending a bad shiver down me. 'Maybe he won't turn up – his body, I mean – he might've faked it, just – gone and done a runner.'

He nodded hard, keen for it to be true. 'He just done a runner, man. They always find the body. I mean, it's a month now, innit? If he was there, he'd be there. He's gone, all right.'

'Just my mum and Andy think he faked it, right.'

'Is it. That's it, then – Jesus, Si – you can't get sorry about it, anyway, whatever happens. You done the right thing.'

I pulled at the unbuttoned sleeves of my jacket, trying to force them down over the chilled backs of my hands. 'But she didn't want him dead,' I said. 'She really didn't.'

'She wanted to throw him to the sharks, though,' Danny said. 'I remember her saying. She wanted you to go on that cruise and help her push him off the boat, didn't she? I didn't know what she was fucking on about at the time, man. I just thought she was a bit mad. The way she cut herself up as well and all.' He thought about her then, and sighed in the dusk. 'She was a bit mad, wasn't she, Si? Sometimes she reminded me of my mum.'

We huddled separately in the chill damp dark grey evening, the city blazing at our feet. After a while I said, 'I think she *has* gone mad, Danny. I mean, really. Look at that letter. I think she's really flipped this time. We were up here once and she thought an axe murderer was after us.' When I said that I looked behind me. The trees were all dark now. I felt again for a passing moment her infectious fear. 'S'pposing she tells them anyway?'

'Don't forget *she* was there,' said Danny. 'She'd have to say she was there too.'

'She's mad enough,' I said.

Danny made a noise in his nose like he agreed with that all right. 'Does her mum really not believe her?' he asked. 'She must be a right bitch.' Then he said, like proudly, 'It's weird isn't it? My mum on scag and being a pro and all for years and years, but she'd never let anyone do anything bad like that to me and get away with it. She'd let him do anyfuckingthing to her, but she wouldn't let him do anything bad to me.' I thought she'd let the fucker do quite a bit to Danny actually, like completely fuck up his childhood, for instance, but I didn't say anything. It was typical of him, of his mad bastard's heart, to decide his mum had been the best mum of them all, in the end. I suddenly had this weird clear thought that the world in Danny's head was sort of more like a Wild West movie than the world in mine, with saintly mothers and sisters and him and me cast as masked avengers – he should've been born in the Wild West or something, it would've suited him better. He was the stuff heroes are made of – he was too brave and straight down the line for this crappy old world.

'Why didn't you come and see me, man?' he asked suddenly.

I went, shocked, 'Oh, come *on*, mate – you know.'

Danny sat tapping his knees with thin fingers, like he was considering what he knew, then said almost aggressively, 'Well, anyway – it's sorted now, innit?'

'You think?'

'You gotta do the right thing.'

I stood up and moved about, feeling quite stupidly pleased and also trying to get my blood going round in my legs. It really was fucking cold up there. A bitter night was rising. I said, reminding him, 'It's kind of rough about Eleanor, though, man – like it's not sorted if she starts mouthing off and stuff.'

'You should go and see her,' said Danny.

'What?' I was amazed. 'Like *talk* to her?'

He stood up himself, stretching till his cold-stiffened fleshless joints clicked loudly into place up on the silent hill. 'No, listen, right,' he said. 'I don't mean about what went down in

Kilburn and stuff – that's just shit she's coming out with, right? I mean, she needs someone she can talk to, for real. It's hard, man, being on your own with all that shit going down and nobody believing you.' He looked over at me, like: to make a point.

'She wouldn't want to talk to me, man,' I said, with real certainty. 'Not now. No way. Why don't you go?'

'It was you she told,' he said. 'Not me.'

'It was me told on her,' I said.

'What else could you do, man? Jesus! What d'you think she wanted you to do? I don't know. Why d'you think she told you? Maybe she wanted you to do it.' He threw up his hands. 'Go and fucking *talk* to her, is all I'm saying.'

'Let's go, Danny,' I said. 'It's fucking freezing up here.'

'Seriously, Si – seriously. She's your girlfriend, man – you gotta look after her. You're good at all that shit. If you don't, who will? It's your responsibility, man.'

My skin was shrinking with the cold. To shut him up, I said, 'Sure, man. OK. Sure. I will, all right? I'll go.' I ran for a second on the spot, beating my feet off of the ground. 'Let's go, Danny,' I said. 'It's fucking freezing up here. Summer's over, all right?'

But still he hesitated, turning back, looking down at the distant miles of London, getting brighter and brighter as the night closed in. 'You know what I'm remembering, Si?'

I shrugged.

'You and me, mate. How it was at the beginning of this summer. You and me, mate – sitting on Primrose Hill. I mean this –' and with a sweep of his arm he took in the vast, dangerous city – 'this is all *right*, you know . . .'

'Oh, Jesus, I nearly forgot . . .' I reached into the inside pocket of my jacket. 'I brought this for you.'

He took the baseball hat and turned it over in his big now thin hands. It wasn't much like the one me and his grandad had burnt on the embankment. When I bought it I thought it was cool, but now as he fingered it, trying to check it out in the bad light, I knew it was crap, not what he'd've got for himself at all.

'It doesn't matter, man,' I said, walking off. 'Come on, for fuck's sake, Dan – I'm freezing my balls off here.'

'Hang on,' said Danny. 'I gotta test it.'

Pulling himself up, straight, he stuck it on his head and stood silently for a while just gazing at the view. Then he tugged the peak down sharply over his eyes, like it was coming home.